MW00629666

THE AGE OF WATER LILIES

the *Age* of Water Lilies

Theresa Kishkan

BRINDLE
&GLASS

Library and Archives Canada Cataloguing in Publication
Kishkan, Theresa, 1955–
The age of water lilies / Theresa Kishkan.

ISBN 978-1-897142-42-4

I. Title.

PS8571.I75A74 2009   C813'.54   C2009-902913-8

Editor: Lynne Van Luven
Cover image: Doug Hohenstein
Proofreader: Heather Sangster, Strong Finish
Map: Pete Kohut
Author photo: Keith Shaw

 Canadian Patrimoine
Heritage canadien
 BRITISH COLUMBIA
ARTS COUNCIL
 Canada Council Conseil des Arts
for the Arts du Canada

Brindle & Glass is pleased to acknowledge the financial support for its publish-
ing program from the Government of Canada through the Book Publishing Industry
Development Program (BPIDP), Canada Council for the Arts, and the province of British
Columbia through the British Columbia Arts Council and the Book Publishing Tax Credit.

 **Mixed Sources**
Cert no. SW-COC-001271
© 1996 FSC
FSC

Brindle & Glass Publishing
www.brindleandglass.com

1 2 3 4 5 12 11 10 09

PRINTED AND BOUND IN CANADA

For my parents, the Fairfield years

To remember Walhachin is to set a place
at the table for the absent . . .
　　　　—Stephen Hume

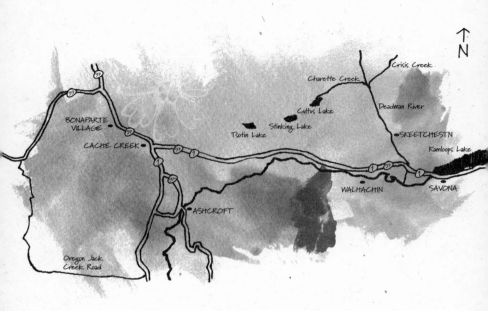

PART ONE
Grace

ONE
April 1962

Begin with rain, the soft water splashing down from broad new leaves and needles onto the pavement, the call of crows unearthly over the graves. Primroses show yellow blooms, daisies dust the ground like snow, daffodils emerge in the wide clearances of grass, while the voices of children ring out from the breakwater where a seal has washed ashore, half its belly eaten. A girl is on her stomach, oblivious to rain, her ear against the earth, listening.

Begin with that girl, age seven, riding a bike along the verdant narrow lanes of the Ross Bay Cemetery, past the blind angels, the obelisks, past the exotic trees planted on the slope of land overlooking the Strait of Juan de Fuca, the lights of Port Angeles twinkling in the distance as dusk settles on the neighbourhood. A girl who has played under the floor joists of Stewart Monumental Works in sand ground down from slabs of granite and marble shaped into tombstones, hoardings used for cement, to anchor the stones of memory. She has breathed in the dust of both the dead and their markers in air stung with salt, broken by gulls. This girl has gone to sit in a kitchen near the corner of May Street and Memorial Crescent where an elderly lady poured tea into cups of thin china mottled with roses and offered biscuits from a tin crowned with dour Queen Victoria. There were also squares of oatcake filled with sweet dates.

"If you lie on the ground by the Spencers, you can hear the buried stream," the girl told the woman. "You can hear it in the park by our house too, gurgling under the far corner, almost where your fence is. But it's loudest by Mr. Spencer's obelisk. Did you know his family still runs his store downtown? It's where we go to shop for clothes for going back to school. There, and sometimes Tang's Pagoda."

"A good store," agreed the woman, who had shopped at Spencer's Store for nearly fifty years. She liked to enter the cool premises, to move between the tables stacked with sturdy sweaters that sailors might wear, and then up one step to where the Ladies' Apparel hung neatly on railings with curtained fitting rooms kept swept and waiting. It was an entirely serviceable store. "And why do you like to listen to water?"

"It seems wrong somehow for a creek to travel underground. You can see where one comes out at the sea if you stand on the breakwater. Why would anyone bury a stream?"

The woman smiled. "My dear, more is buried in a cemetery than you could imagine. Think of its secrets. I often do. Notes tucked into burial suits, two stones placed at a woman's feet, unspoken names on the lips of the people who have just died. And the living think of the dead as their anchors, keeping them close and steady. One day I will tell you about one of the graves, speaking of secrets. But you will be older, I think, and might not be so interested. And perhaps I should not talk to you about such things so I will pass you this plate and you may help yourself to another matrimonial square."

The girl could not imagine a day when she would be uninterested in the cemetery and its secrets. It was her favourite place to play. There, and the shelter under the monumental works office, where tall posts supported the back part of the building—it was built on a hill—where bins of sand waited for children to bury themselves like the dead. The girl and her brothers played there, the fine sand, pink and grey and bone white, lingering afterwards in their socks and shoes, the cuffs of their trousers where they were rolled up to last over a growth spurt. Brushing the children's clothing off on the veranda before allowing them into the house, their mother would sigh and make them remove their shoes. She shook the sand into beds of peonies and azaleas planted against the foundation. The girl remembered the weight of sand on her chest when her brothers buried her the last time, new creamy sand, fresh and clean, untouched yet by cats. In the yard of the monumental works, the men laboured on a stone and called hello as the children darted under the joists.

In the pink house with its gracious windows looking out to the cemetery, the girl gazed around her as she drank her tea, milky and lukewarm. There were paintings everywhere, and drawings framed by thin wood. Some of the drawings showed a girl, some showed rows of trees and a big sky stretched over top. One was a village with stone walls, soft colour washed over ink. Somehow there was sunlight in it. One showed two horses in stomach-high grass, a shed off to one side.

"Were the horses yours?" the girl asked.

The woman, who was Miss Oakden, looked for a long time at that drawing. "No," she said finally. "No, they belonged to someone else. They were special horses. The one with his head down is the one I rode. His name was Agate and he really was that colour, like caramel. The other one was Flight and she could run. Oh, my, she could run! The Indians had races on the flats by the river, and Flight would put all the other horses to shame, even the quick Indian ponies."

The girl, who was Tessa, wondered about that for a moment. And then, "Which Indians do you mean?" The only Indians she could think of were the ones on television, with war paint and bonnets made of feathers. There were some out at Tsawout, near where her family sometimes went for picnics at Island View Beach. Tessa had watched a girl and her mother dig clams where the public beach ended and the Reserve began. But she had never seen horses there.

"It was such a long time ago, Tessa. Another world, really. One day I will tell you. But now I think I want to have a rest. Take some squares home to your brothers, my dear. Here, I will wrap them up for you."

A small girl dozes on a blanket under an apple tree in an orchard of flowering trees, her body warm in the layers of dress and pinafore, stockings, bloomers, undervest. She is almost asleep and doesn't hear her name for the first few calls. *Flora, Flora.* The voice comes closer. *Flora, come and see what I've found.* And she is awake, rubbing her eyes, rising, calling, *Where are you, George?* And, unseen, he is directing her to find her way through a gap in the hedge, a small passage that only a child as young as five could fit through, and into the pasture, the one sloping down to the water meadows by the river.

She runs in the direction of her brother's voice. She sees him coming across the pasture, something over his shoulders. *Is it, is it . . . ?* She doesn't know what it is. She runs closer. *Flora, look what I found in the swamp. Do you remember old Dobbin?* And she sees he is carrying a rocking horse on his back, the head looking over his shoulders. Mud falls from the burden, long weeds drip from its body. For a moment she doesn't know what to think. *Why would . . . ?* But then she recognizes the horse. It is a moment heavy with memory and recognition.

Dobbin. How could she have forgotten Dobbin?

He had been her favourite plaything, a horse to ride by the nursery window where she watched the hunt gathering on the cobbles of the front drive, her father seeing her in the window and waving his crop, handsome in his scarlet coat and bowler, the hounds taut on their leads as the Master waited for the moment when they could be released to take the hunt far over the fields in pursuit of the fox. She would make Dobbin gallop as she watched and waved. When she was three, she asked her brother to move Dobbin out to the wide stone terrace, so she could ride him in air pungent with horses. Her mother would not allow her down off the half-moon of stone, fearful of what might happen in the excitement of dogs and mounts. A few of the horses danced sideways as their riders drank a stirrup-cup of mulled wine before heading out onto the field.

Dobbin had been forgotten overnight on the terrace. The next morning, he was nowhere to be found. Later, when Flora's father, Henry Oakden, tried to work out what might have happened, the cook remembered that gypsies had come with a cart to sharpen knives and it was assumed they had taken the horse, though when their camp was approached, the patriarch questioned, any knowledge of a child's plaything was denied. Henry and his groom were invited to look inside the caravans themselves, if they liked.

And Flora had forgotten about her rocking horse. Two years later, she was the owner of a fat grey Welsh pony, her own riding habit, pretty boots. And she had been dozing in the orchard after a picnic lunch, her mother having left her in the safety of grass to deadhead the roses while the nanny took the basket back to the house. Now this: Dobbin returning over the pasture, a gift of sorts from her older adored brother, who was saying that he didn't suppose the rocking horse could be cleaned of its long residence in the slough but that he would give it to their gardener, Higgins, to see what might be done.

Flora, Flora. She could still hear her brother calling but realized she was not at Watermeadows at all. She was lying on ground among the apple trees at Walhachin. You could not yet call it a mature orchard, although the settlers were optimistic about the future. Rows of thin trees, a few blossoms opening to the sun, some of the rows in between the trees planted with potatoes and onions, some with tobacco. Grass and sage grew also, and plants with burrs or sticky pods or prickles. Nothing was lush or verdant. Flora had been warned to watch at all times for rattlesnakes although they were found more commonly among the rocks leading down to the river.

Flora rose from the warm ground and oriented herself to the voice, smoothing her dress, checking for twigs in her hair. Sometimes it seemed to her that George had such expectations of her that she was nervous she could never meet them. She had imagined that there would be more freedom in this new country, spacious and open to match its skies, the wide expanses of earth undulating in the heat, hills shimmering in the distance like mirages. And for some, perhaps there was freedom, or moments of it. She admired the women hanging out sheets on sunny mornings, their bare arms, ruddy and freckled, rising to the lines. Sometimes she'd see them drinking tea on a laundry stoop afterwards, in damp aprons, tendrils of hair escaping from pins. Or walking with children and dogs, bare-headed, laughing, their feet stockingless in sandals. George and Flora had driven to a farm near Ashcroft to take possession of a box of young birds from Norah Careless, who raised chickens and geese and beautiful vegetables and greeted them wearing sturdy trousers and a work shirt such as the labourers wore. There was nothing deferential about her manner. In fact, she corrected almost everything George said until finally he paid her quickly and put the box of young pullets in the boot of the car. He expostulated noisily half the way home.

"A woman like that, well, it's no wonder she hasn't a husband," sputtered George.

Flora refrained from commenting that he, in turn, did not have a wife.

She did not like to disagree with George. Or disappoint him. It took so little. Surely he hadn't always been like this? She remembered him as a patient and helpful brother when she was young. When he was away at school, she'd send him a little story within a letter, and he'd write back, full of praise, with gentle corrections of her spelling. On his holidays he'd teach her things, help her with projects, include her in outings with his tutors. Now it seemed he was determined that Flora should observe high standards of behaviour and dress. At the sign of a lapse, he would brood in silence until she had seen the error of her ways. Which might have been as slight as not wearing gloves to the hotel for tea. He did not like her to argue with him, although their own parents had had tremendous differences of opinion. The senior Oakdens had led separate lives to some extent, had separate bedrooms, dressing rooms; her father did his botanizing and her mother did needlework when she was not in a dark room with a cool cloth over her eyes. But Flora's father listened to her mother's ideas about everything, women's suffrage included; although he argued with her vigorously, it was without anger. Both parents came from families long planted in rural Wiltshire, each tracing a line back to the *Domesday Book*. Each was accustomed to people paying attention when he or she spoke. Neither had bothered much with Flora, apart from arranging her debut into society in 1909 and encouraging one or two desultory attempts at courtship by young men who were sniffing for fortune but who did not seem in the least interested in Flora herself.

There were times Flora wished for someone, a friend, in order to share a particularly potent moment. For instance, at a meeting, Mr. Footner, the man who built most of the houses at Walhachin, had argued heatedly in favour of women having the vote. Flora had been so surprised to hear men refuse to acknowledge that their wives, the women who bore and raised their children and ran their homes, might actually be able to make a wise decision about leadership. These were women who organized dances for the community, raised money, taught piano, and were generally as capable as could be imagined at every task before them. One man shouted, "What next? If they have the vote, there is no saying what they will ask for next!"

Although she lowered her eyes and said nothing, Flora thought the man deserved a swift retort of the kind she knew she ought to have had at the ready. But if she had difficulty expressing an opinion to George, surely it would be that much harder to reply to a stranger. Still, in her imagination, she was accumulating a list of responses. She was dreaming of a way to be the kind of woman she admired though she had not come up with a way to abandon her gloves just yet. She wished for someone to ask how a vote might be so dangerous a thing for a woman to have that it would incite men to anger and shouts.

Flora hurried towards her brother's voice, finding him with their two horses saddled and bridled. "I am taking Fred out to the flume," he told her, "and I won't be back for dinner. Mary has put up a lunch for me, and I'll eat when I can."

Mary was the woman who did for them, an Indian from Skeetchestn, the Deadman River village. She hummed as she went about her work, something George did not like but made no objection to, fearing that the woman might decide to leave their service. She really was an efficient worker, polishing the woodwork with lavender wax and keeping the windows clear as the sky. Her biscuits were light, she skimmed the milk and made lovely butter, and she was not averse to cleaning the chicken house. Most households that could afford help had Chinamen; the native women were not thought suitable for inside work. Mary was good, perhaps an exception, though they still might yet come to grief, Flora was told by one matron of the community who sniffed as though she expected to be proven right. Flora had answered airily, "If we come to grief, I am certain it will not be the fault of Mary." The matron's face had turned livid. Flora found it easier somehow, standing up for Mary, who was so hard-working and reliable.

Flora watched George ride away, mounted on Titan, his gelding, and leading the grey mare for Fred. She wished herself back asleep under the trees, a child again. Or else mounted on the mare, sleeves rolled up to help George with the work ahead. The flume required constant attention. It carried water for the orchards and fields from a creek on the north side of the river, something like twenty miles away, through a system of troughs and trestles made of wood milled in Savona. The weight of water constantly undermined the structure, so the boards warped from water and hot sun; George was not alone in thinking that far too much water was being wasted before it ever reached the trees. One of the labourers, a taciturn fellow called Fred Dunne, shared his frustration. Fred had been involved in the initial construction of the flume before George had arrived from England, but her brother was inclined to listen when Fred suggested ideas for improving the system. They would ride out along the miles of wooden troughs, checking for leaks, for debris, and might not come back to the community until well after dark. Upon his return, George would expect a bath to be ready, clean towels warming on the fender. These were things a servant would do at home at Watermeadows, but this small household ran only with the assistance of Mary, who would be long gone by the time George wanted his bath. So Flora watched the skyline for the sight of the horses and had the bathtub filling as her brother removed his boots and tossed his saddlebag to the floor of the kitchen.

After his bath, George appeared on the veranda, lighting the oil lamp on the table before him; he drank a small whisky while moths made soft noise around the lamp, a whirr of wings, a click as they touched the glass of the globe, a quiet hiss as they disintegrated in the heat. Flora sat with him while he spoke of the flume, pointing north towards the tracing of its structure on the hill. She wondered what the whisky tasted like but was refused a drink of her own.

"Whisky is a man's drink, Flora. Come now! I can't have my sister drink such a thing. But I will fix you a Pimm's Cup! How would that be?"

He went into the house, turning on the carbide light in the kitchen, and for a few minutes Flora heard the tinkling of spoons and glass. George returned with a tall glass smelling of cucumber. A Pimm's Cup was a drink she liked at a sporting event—the one time she was taken to Ascot she remembered that was the drink everyone savoured as they waited for the races to begin. The concoction never failed to impress, the dance of the fizzy lemon making it taste of the nursery. Her mother had scolded her for trying to fish out the slices of fruit, though it seemed wasteful to leave them.

After his second whisky, George became quite exercised by his day at the flume. "By God, Flora, it was a false economy to use second-rate lumber to build that thing. I don't know what they were thinking of. It will take some work to get it functioning reliably. And there must be some way to pump water up from the river. It's right below us, for Heaven's sake! Why on earth we must bring it from such a distance when a river runs through our community . . . Well, I am going to consult a man in Vancouver about pumps at the next opportunity."

One of the other labourers, now working at the rail siding, actually knew something about irrigation since he'd been employed over at the Coldstream Ranch, but he had not been consulted during the planning of the settlement's system. George was determined to seek this man out as well and ask him to help.

Flora could smell soap as George waved his arm in the dim lamplight. She heard rustling in the field just beyond their house and hoped it wasn't a snake—sometimes you could hear their bodies in the dry grass, and the insistent harsh rattle when they were startled—or a coyote lurking for their hens or the one splendid Muscovy duck their neighbour kept and that waddled between the properties, aching for water.

"What will it mean for this year's crop, this trouble with the flume?" Flora asked. George said none was really expected, the Jonathans and Wagoners might produce something, but that the real harvests would be in two or three years' time when the Rome Beauties and Wealthys came to maturity. Some orchardists had interplanted potatoes between their trees, some onions, and when Flora first arrived the previous fall, she'd been shown enormous earth-covered potatoes and had seen the onions drying on the ground, their papery skins fragrant and golden, their green tops withered. They had very good flavour, she was told, and would travel down to Vancouver by train in bushel baskets. A drying shed was being built for tobacco too, which proved congenial to the soil and weather.

Flora had been eager to leave Watermeadows, the family home near Winsley, in Wiltshire. Not that she had been unhappy there, for how could unhappiness find a toehold in a life so utterly calm and pleasant? The estate was more than two hundred acres; an eighteenth-century house of mellow golden Bath stone stood on a slope above the river with gardens and pastures leading down to the water; a ha-ha separated the two so that it seemed that placid Jersey cows grazed in rhododendron groves, a student of Capability Brown having arranged this effect. Right down by the river were meadows that flooded each spring, giving the property its name, rich with water avens and ragged robin, flag irises providing cover for snipe and water rails. The land upon which the estate was built had been inhabited for many thousands of years; flints and arrowheads showed up frequently when a gardener turned the soil. A small spring in a secluded limestone escarpment was a place used over the centuries by those wanting to bathe in its warm restorative waters, not as hot as the spring at Turleigh but very pleasant all the same. Flora's father had spoken of creating a large warm pool around the spring, then introducing the *Victoria regia* water lily and perhaps some other tropical water lilies as well. But nothing had come of that plan and the area remained wild with ransomes and bluebells and red campion, a perfect place to come for picnics.

Some days, Flora stood in the middle of the house at Walhachin, in the hall as the rooms radiated around her, clean and polished, and remembered the house as she'd first seen it, new, smelling of freshly sawn wood. George had arrived first but had done little to make a home. That had been left for Flora: she opened the tea chests of china and linen and curtains and hung chintz from the dowelling over each window, filled needle-worked covers with goose-feather cushions, arranged pretty jugs on windowsills and the mantelpiece, some of them with dried grasses and the vivid yellow plant she was told was rabbitbrush. She hoped her arrangements would pass muster, that the linens would smell as sweet as those from the cupboards at Watermeadows, that her table settings would be proof that she had learned her lessons well and that the fish service could be reliably found next to the cutlery for meat and salad, that the small bone-handled fruit knives were gleaming and ready for the apples that she served with cheese at the end of their meal. Coffee from the tall silver pot with the monogram and the eagle on the lid, segments of ivory alternating with sections of ebony on the graceful handle, a little creamer to match. And silver tongs to grip each lump of sugar, a pretty long-tined fork to skewer the thin slices of lemon when indeed lemons could be found.

Some days she regretted that the house had been filled with what she had imagined they were leaving behind. She remembered the rooms as she'd first known them, airy and bright, the plaster freshly painted, and the floors bare of any covering, just the bees' wax protecting the wood. There were possibilities in the long shapes of sunlight on the floorboards, in the smell of fir and window-screening. She'd had a momentary sense of herself as newly born, anticipating a future unlike any she might have expected, in a house without any history at all.

Happiness and purpose: Flora puzzled over the accommodation of these in her daily life. As much as she loved her mother, she did not want to pass most of her days at rest in a dark room. She did not want to sit in a chair by a window consulting with a servant about the day's meals. She did not look forward to having her hair dressed for a cotillion or being fitted for a dress she would wear once or twice and then forget. Coming to Canada with George had seemed such an adventure, and it certainly was, though not necessarily in the ways Flora had expected. She supposed that George was under pressure to succeed and that made him seem stern and proper, no longer the boy who jumped into the river below Watermeadows without a stitch of clothing. He had never taken notice of his sister's more casual habits until the two of them were living alone at Walhachin. She valued his company and wanted to keep the household harmonious. But sometimes, walking alone up Brassey Creek, she would let her hair down and tuck up her skirts to feel the sun on her legs. And on those walks, she certainly did not wear gloves.

Flora sat in a wicker chair on the veranda and looked out towards the river. She could see far into the distance, the brilliant sunlight rippling up from the road like water. Grasshoppers rubbed their legs together, a steady monotonous clicking. Someone was coming. Little clouds of dust rose from the road as Mary, it was Mary, rode towards the house on her quiet mare. The horse was carrying something else too; as Mary approached, Flora could see it was a child, a baby of about a year, fastened into a carrying frame of wood. Mary put her horse into the small paddock adjacent to the house where a cottonwood provided shade.

"My baby isn't too well, and I thought I'd better bring her with me. She'll sleep mostly." Mary placed the sleeping child, still in its carrier, on the floor of the veranda, under the cooling blades of the fan.

Flora poured her a glass of lemonade, chips of ice clinking as they fell into the tumbler. George wouldn't like it, Flora thought—a servant bringing a child to her place of employment. But she was interested to see this woman with her child. Mary was already tying on an apron, her hands filled with rags to begin to clean. Flora could not have imagined a child sleeping on the floor of Watermeadows while one of the housemaids swept the carpets or dusted the furniture.

"Shall we move the baby to one of the bedrooms, Mary?"

Mary shook her head and answered that the baby would be fine where she was and would sleep for the next hour or two at least.

There was so little for Flora to do in the house. Mary kept it clean. Apart from a soft-boiled egg in the morning with some toast and marmalade, there was not much food to prepare other than tea and biscuits. George Oakden usually liked to eat his evening meal in the hotel where Eleanor Flowerdew presided over a proper dining room and members of the colony gathered, those staying in the hotel while waiting for their own homes to be finished and those who chose to partake of the full service at a reasonable price. The occasional sandwiches would be cut and wrapped in greaseproof paper and a flask filled with tea for treks across the river to the flume for repairs.

Sometimes Flora found the days endless. A basket filled with needlework was always handy, but you could only stitch for so long. She was working on some pillows as a gift for her father, a pattern of the Egyptian blue lotus, Nymphaea caerulea, which was cultivated in a special glass house at home in Wiltshire, along with its white cousin. Some days, she loved choosing the right silk from her workbasket, finding a stitch to express the petals, the cupped sepals, the dramatic anthers covered in pollen, an element she worked in the tiniest French knots. Other days, it was a chore to pick up the linen and try to dream her way into the blossoms, the dense texture of a leaf. On those days she would put on stout shoes and walk into the sun-parched hills in search of cacti or the sight of coyotes at play in the draws.

Mary's child was waking. Flora went to the veranda to take her out of her carrier, a clever device made of basketry; the baby was fastened in with thongs of soft buckskin. A smell of urine rose with the child as Flora lifted her out. She was not wearing a diaper but had been padded with what looked like the fluff from cattails gone to seed. Little bits of the fluff clung to her buttocks. Flora held her over the side of the veranda with one arm and brushed the baby's skin with her free hand. Mary came to the door and quietly took the child from her.

"No need for you to do that, Missus." She deftly finished the job and then felt the baby's forehead. "Not well, this one."

Flora urged her to do what she needed to with the child, that there was no need to polish the woodwork or iron yet another set of pillowslips. She suggested a bath in the large zinc basin they used for gathering potatoes and offered to draw water for it, bring towels. Mary nodded and Flora brought the pan from the scullery, placed it on a folded towel on the veranda after Mary had indicated that this was where she would bathe her baby, then filled a jug with tepid water.

The baby grew quite animated in the water, chirping like a sparrow and smacking her plump hands down on the surface. Flora brought a tablet of her own lavender soap and a large towel still smelling like the outdoors; it must have been one that Mary had laundered recently.

"May I hold her, Mary?" she asked as the mother lifted the baby from the pan, wrapping her in the towel. Mary handed her the sweet-smelling bundle. The baby's face was very solemn as she looked into Flora's eyes. She had several small teeth, not a mouthful yet, and wisps of very black hair damp from the bath. Full cheeks. And her shoulders were the warmest brown, so soft that Flora could not resist pressing her mouth to each one in turn.

"She is so lovely, Mary. What is her name?"

Grace, she was told; the baby's name was Grace. Mary's other children had come through a time of fevers, and Grace was the last one to become ill. The children had been cared for by a relative while Mary came to do her work at Walhachin—she cleaned for another two families as well as for George and Flora—but that relative had come down with the illness too. So now Mary's husband, Agrippa, was minding the younger children but couldn't manage Grace as well.

"Did you have the doctor come, Mary?" asked Flora.

Mary smiled and shook her head no. The nearest doctor to her home at Skeetchestn on the Deadman River was at Savona but wouldn't travel to an Indian Reserve to treat a family that would not be able to pay him. She explained that her mother and her grandmother had prepared teas of mint and the bark of the willow tree, that yarrow and juniper had been burned to cleanse the air of the small cabin the family shared, that tonics of nettle and rosehips were given to the children. And now just Grace had the lingering heat but was otherwise recovering.

Flora realized, listening to Mary, how little she knew of the woman who came several days a week to wash her clothing, clean the house, darn George's socks, and lug buckets of water to the area where the kitchen garden flourished. Flora had come to Walhachin with only the most rudimentary notion of Indians. Any literature she had read presented them as savages, half-clothed, with pigment smeared on their faces in a particularly horrible way. But here they were fieldworkers, servants, some of them working on the railway. There were stories, of course, of their lack of hygiene, their irregular marriages, their heathen beliefs. But Flora could not say she had observed any of this. Mary was scrupulously clean and wore both a wedding band and small crucifix. Occasionally she had seen Mary touching something in the parlour, a piece of china or an embroidered cloth, with a stillness that unsettled her; she had felt so completely the woman's otherness. But for the most part Mary was simply a woman who did for them. Now, seeing her with Grace, Flora sensed something like power—a deep maternal core, perhaps, or the clear confidence of a woman who knows who she is and what she is doing. That two jobs would need to be done simultaneously, caring for a sick child and cleaning the house of her employer, was nothing to Mary. Or so Flora imagined as she held Grace, breathing in the sweet baby smell of her, feeling the dense reality of weight in her arms.

"Let me keep her for a time, Mary. I'd like to get to know her. And may I make her a nappy with an old towel?"

Grace was more than happy to be pinned into a soft cloth and carried on a walk around the garden, one of Flora's straw hats on her head to shade her face. The child made soft noises as the woman told her about the roses—"Slips of plants from my father's garden in Wiltshire, that's a long train and boat ride away, Grace"—and shifted her from hip to hip for comfort's sake. It felt so wonderful to hold a child, a warmth that spread out from her arms to every part of her body, including her heart. Flora hadn't had much contact with children and had been raised mostly by a nanny, then governess; maternity had never been discussed; her one encounter with a child had been on a visit to her cousin in Devon at the age of fourteen when she had helped her cousin bathe her infant daughter. Flora had seen how she neatly pinned a nappy around the baby's posterior after towelling her off. Yet she felt a kind of familiarity with Grace, as though she had known her in some way for the length of her small life. She wanted to learn things about the child—what she liked to eat, whether she had a favourite plaything; she wanted to know what Grace might become. She whispered to her of Dobbin, the day he had come home over the field on her brother's back, and shared her own sense of the mystery of Dobbin's absence, her wish that he had become real for a time and had galloped away to join the wild ponies of the moors. Grace made small agreeable sounds and drooled.

After a while, Mary came out with a tray of tea things and put it on an iron table in the shade of a young cottonwood tree. At Flora's insistence (because Mary would not normally sit with the lady of the house), the two women drank a cup of tea while Grace gnawed on a biscuit. Then the child turned to her mother and began to nuzzle her chest. Flora was startled to see Mary undo a few buttons to release a brown breast for Grace to suck. And yet the mother and child were so at ease with the process that she could not feel startled for long. It was peaceful to sit with Mary and her baby while bees droned in the garden and far away men shouted to teams of horses ploughing the bench above the river. Grace finished drinking from her mother's body and fell into a deep sleep. Mary took the child to place her in her carrier on the veranda and return to her tasks. Flora remained in her chair, musing about the miracle of a child being nourished by a mother's breast, and gazed about her at the garden. How else would a child feed, she asked herself, wondering why she had never thought about it before now, having seen young foals nuzzle for their mother's milk, and the lambs suckling in the fields. Even the tiny offspring of the barn cats lined up against their mother's belly and sucked themselves into a drowsy slumber.

Supposedly I am the gentlewoman, she thought, and Mary is the Indian servant. But which of us is the more accomplished? The one with a full position in the world? Mary is a mother who can nurse her child while caring for my house and doing my laundry. I can boil an egg and do fancy needlework. Mary has even been to school whereas I had such sporadic education. The world needs Mary and her kind, I fear, far more than it needs me.

She dozed off under the shade of her sunhat, hearing Mary in the kitchen as though from a great distance. A fly buzzed near her ear, a lullaby of sorts.

George was determined to grow flowers, and his small collection of roses was doing quite well. Keeping the plants watered was the thing. In his luggage, he had carried a vasculum with rooted slips of favourites from the family garden—a Gloire de Dijon and an old-fashioned pink rambler that he was training along the fence—and their father had sent seed from his delphiniums; the crowns of leaves were well along and would soon send up spires of deep blue and, Flora hoped, one the colour of summer skies. She remembered drifts of them at home in the Long Border, with pink phlox and baby's breath. George was also digging a deep hole for a small pool to attempt to grow their father's water lilies, or one at least. Some of them were so large that they covered the entire surfaces of ponds at Watermeadows. Flora remembered being taken to see a glass house that covered tanks in which grew the fragrant white water lilies from the tropics, the *Victoria regia* her father had thought might be coaxed into growing at the spring with leaves the size of dining-room tables, and blue lotuses from Egypt. It was very warm in the glass house. When Flora looked closely, she saw small brown beetles sleeping within the blooms themselves. Flora and her father had been urged to sit on wicker chairs covered with a print of water lilies, yellow ones, and tea was brought by a man in full livery.

The outing to the glass house had inspired her father to build his own, an elegant construction of domed glass and iron, and order his first root of N. *caerulea*.

And now Mary was standing by her chair, asking if she might leave early, the work had been done, biscuits were baked and under the pink tea towel. There was one other house to clean still and then it was a long ride with Grace to consider.

"Of course, Mary, and there's no reason to come in two days if the baby is still poorly."

But she understood from the look Mary gave her that there was all the reason in the world: the small sum the woman earned. Otherwise she would not be in the townsite at all but in her own cabin on the Deadman River with her children and Agrippa.

And then she had an idea. "Mary, would you like to leave Grace with me while you go to the Wallaces? It would be a shame to wake her now that she's so comfortable" —Flora and Mary both looked at the carrier where the baby slept— "and I would be so pleased to have a visitor."

Mary agreed. Without any more fuss, she left for the second house she was expected to clean.

Grace slept for another hour and woke up as the sun was moving around to the veranda. The heat was sudden and intense so Flora gathered her up and took her inside. The old towel she had used for a nappy was wet, so she found another one, washing Grace first with a soft flannel. She sprinkled a little of her lavender talc on the baby's buttocks before pinning her into the towel. The child's skin was like velvet, rich brown, the colour of hazelnuts. She knew little about babies but remembered that they liked to be rocked. She settled into the rocking chair and cuddled Grace, singing "Greensleeves" in her best choir voice. Grace laughed and snuggled in. It felt so completely right, holding this child, the way a lap contained the weight of a baby and gave a purpose for the bench the thighs formed. "For I have loved you all my life, delighting in your company," sang Flora, while the baby touched her face and snorted. She was still very warm, with little beads of perspiration on her shoulders and chest. "Greensleeves was all my joy, / Greensleeves was my delight, / Greensleeves was my heart of gold, / and who but my lady Greensleeves?" Grace chuckled and stretched her toes. That reminded Flora of "This little piggie" and a host of other rhymes. The baby watched her face and waited for the next one and then another.

When Mary returned, she found them both in the rocker, asleep, a damp patch growing across Flora's lap where the nappy had soaked through. Flora helped her collect her things, held the horse while Grace was secured in the carrying arrangement, then watched them disappear over the bridge, the dust of the road collecting them inside it. She rinsed out the towels, the scent of urine growing fainter and fainter until there was none at all. She hung the cloth on the line and wondered how to spend the rest of the day.

THREE
1913

The community had been founded in 1908 when the Pennie Ranch and other surrounding properties had been purchased by the British Columbia Development Association with the intention of developing both a townsite and orchards; the BCDA hoped that well-heeled English families would buy acreages and farm them in a leisurely way. By 1910, the flume had been built, a hotel erected, thirteen bungalows designed by Bert Footner with their overhangs and stone fireplaces stood in their bare tidy lots with more under construction. Potatoes and tomatoes flourished in the ploughed fields.

Flora's was a nice house, not simply four rooms like most of the Walhachin bungalows. It was two storeys in fact; an additional two rooms had been constructed at a cost of one hundred and twenty-five dollars per room. But still, it had taken some getting used to after Watermeadows. That house had been in their family for six generations although the original structure had been added to, wings to accommodate large families, expectations. Once, the Oakden family had been very wealthy, though now economies must be made. Henry, the oldest son, had taken a Classics degree and taught part-time at a school in Bath where he also involved himself with an antiquities society. He would inherit Watermeadows when their father died, though no one expected this for decades. George's decision to emigrate was a result of his being the second son. A man who visited their father to acquire graft wood from a very old apple tree told him that the British Columbia Development Association had an office in London and was advertising the sale of acreage in a very promising area of Canada. He showed the brochure to Henry senior, who thought it might be a good prospect for his younger son. George knew something about orchards and their care, and his future in England was rather uncertain, due to his coming down from Oxford with a very poor showing.

George's decision had been met with some relief on the part of their father. He himself had read theology at Oxford but had never needed a living of his own. Still, he had the expectation that his sons would find meaningful work and knew that only the eldest Oakden son, named for him, would succeed him at Watermeadows.

The arrangements, nearly a year in the making, were complicated, but eventually George was the owner of a plot of land and a house. It was a destination to which containers of bedding, clothing, kitchenware, rugs from the attic at Watermeadows could be shipped. ("I am willing to let you have this Aubusson. And some Wilton for the stairs." "Thank you so much, Mother." "Once you know the rooms themselves, what pieces will fit well within them and how the windows are sized, we will send window drapes and side tables.") People were not entirely willing to trust the Canadian shops, and business for the carters was brisk as shipments of furniture and everything under the sun arrived at Pennies or Ashcroft and deliveries went out to the townsite. After George's arrival in Walhachin, but before Flora joined him, an acquaintance of their family, the Marquis of Anglesey, invested heavily in the community, establishing his own estate on the north side of the Thompson River and assuming ownership of the hotel. The senior Oakdens were comforted by the thought that suitable society existed in the colony their son was settling in, for surely there would now be polo.

Sleeping in the bed that had come by such intricate arrangements to a room that overlooked the Thompson River, its changing grey-green waters, and the hills surrounding it, Flora dreamed of Grace that night, the child's mouth on her own virgin nipple. She sang a song she remembered from her nanny, "Lavender Blue dilly dilly, Lavender Green," while the baby chuckled and urged Flora's breast to let down its milk.

There is a child, she wrote to her mother, *the colour of hazelnuts, and I spent part of the day earlier this week caring for her.* Then she realized her mother would have no idea of what this meant and would only imagine gypsies or savages, so she began the letter again. She thanked her mother for sending the Panama hat and told her she had draped a pretty scarf over it and that it looked particularly fetching with her blue lawn dress. She needed a corset—could her mother send to Dickson and Jones for that? And while she thought of it, could she also order a few Shetland hoods for the coming winter? And six yards of narrow satin ribbon for trimming a bodice. And perhaps some sprigged flannel—for Flora had decided to make Grace some nightdresses.

A message came from Skeetchestn to say that Grace was too ill for Mary to leave her. Flora knew that things must be very serious indeed. So she prepared a basket of things to take to Mary's home—jars of preserved fruit, fresh biscuits, a cold roasted chicken, clean flannel for poultices, barley water, and a jar of boiled sweets that she thought the children might enjoy. There was also a plain muslin nightdress for Grace—the sprigged flannel had not yet arrived—with a tiny matching bonnet. Flora had drawn pink ribbon through a border of hemstitching on both and she embroidered stalks of lavender in French knots among the smocking. George had saddled the grey mare, Vespa, before he left for the orchard and put her in the stall to be ready for his sister when Gus Alexander came by to collect her. For George had decided he could not leave his own work undone and asked Gus to accompany his sister to Skeetchestn.

He was a man she had seen from a distance, a man who kept his distance in fact, and she could not remember him present at a dance or a tea following a polo match. He was a labourer, employed by the Anglesey Estates, but he also did work

23

for individual orchardists; she had seen him pruning earlier in the season, for instance, and George implied that he often did repairs on the flume system and spoke of the man with admiration. When he arrived on his horse, a pretty chestnut mare who danced a little before obeying the command to stop at the gate, Flora introduced herself and quickly brought out her mare, accepting Gus's assistance in securing the basket to the pommel of the saddle.

"Miss Oakden, you must let me know immediately if you find the pace too fast or the heat too uncomfortable. My mare, not named Flight for nothing, would rather race than walk, regardless of the heat. I promised your brother I would care for you as I would my own sister." There was a tiny smile on his lips as he said this, a smile almost cheeky, which said, almost as clearly as words, that this was what one would say to a toff. It was a moment when Flora sensed something important although she could not then have said what it was exactly.

Riding away from the houses, Flora felt her lungs open to the morning air. It was not yet very hot, but the sun had warmed the rocks, the drifts of sage, and she could smell the lemony leaves. Gus rode ahead a little to open a gate, but once over the bridge, where they paused for a moment to watch the osprey in its nest on the bridge's high trestle, they let their horses trot along the road, side by side. Flora noticed how easily the man held his horse's reins, resting his hand on the saddle, and how the hairs on his wrists were golden. The tiny smile came and went on his lips quick as bees. He was handsome, with a profile such as one might have seen on Greek coins. His sleeves were rolled up to just below his elbows and the golden hair continued up his arms. She had never really looked at a man's arms before. Pale freckles dappled his skin. And when he turned his reins idly this way, then that, she glimpsed the underskin of his forearm, milky and clear. She looked away, hoping he hadn't seen her. And then her face was suddenly hot, her neck quite damp with heat; a little shudder worked its way across her shoulders in the way she had always thought of as someone walking over her grave. Flora put one gloved hand to her cheek. She could not believe that Gus Alexander didn't realize her agitation; how on earth would she explain herself? That she had grown quite warm at the sight of his wrists, the hair on them delicate as new grass? And how happy she was at that moment that she was not his sister.

Glancing back to the settlement, she could see teams of horses at work in the fields being prepared for planting. A hawk circled above, watching for the mice that would scatter as the horses approached. Far away, she could hear the sound of the train approaching. It would stop at Pennies to leave the mail and other provisions for the hotel. It was something to look forward to—letters from home, a few newspapers now months old but containing news of her county, the text of a particularly well-received sermon given at Chippenham, the program of a choral evening at Trowbridge, an afternoon of recitations in a home on the Royal Crescent at Bath, the price of wholemeal loaves at the bakery in Bradford-on-Avon.

Just before noon they reached Skeetchestn. They had followed the river and let their horses lope along its banks under sparse cottonwoods. Flora was easier now with the sight of bare arms and she didn't feel so tongue-tied. It was nice to listen to Gus talk. He noticed things, pointing out a clump of vivid yellow flowers he said were called balsamroot, and the tracks of a rattlesnake in sand along the river. There were neat fields of tall grass for hay, shadowy turns in the river where it passed under the red rock cliffs, a long gravel bar where some cattle stood ankle-deep in water, swishing their tails back and forth in a vain attempt to keep away flies. Gus asked a man sitting on a big rock where they might find Mary and Agrippa's house and he led them to a low cabin near some cottonwoods by the river. A little curl of smoke inched its way out of the stovepipe and a dog briefly barked, then returned to its cool nest by the trees. Mary came to the door. Three children clung to her legs and stared at the strangers.

"Mary, I know things are difficult right now, so I've brought you some small offerings. Can the children have a sweet?" Flora dismounted and handed her reins to Gus, who had indicated he would tie her horse before going off to talk to some men who were needed later in the week for ploughing.

The children came out to stand before her, two boys and a dear girl, all under ten. She gave them each two barley sugars and they solemnly thanked her. Then Flora turned to Mary, who still stood in the doorway.

"I'd like to help, Mary. Is there something I can do? Look, I've brought a chicken—the mean hen, the one whose neck George kept threatening to wring? He did, I'm glad to say, and I've roasted it for your family. Can I come in?"

Mary nodded and stepped aside. It was a very small cabin but cozy too. It smelled strongly of bitter herbs; Flora saw a pot of them on the stove, steaming. Mattresses were leaning against the walls to make more room for the day's activities. In a corner, near one of the two windows letting in a little light, Grace was asleep in a large rush basket. Her face was very flushed.

"Missus, Grace is worse. I'm afraid she will die. The doctor came, but he couldn't tell us she will get better. Agrippa has gone for the priest."

"Oh, Mary, I'm so sorry. But she's sleeping—that's a good sign, isn't it?"

"She can't eat or drink, Missus. Nothing stays down. She will die."

Flora unpacked her basket, putting the chicken in its wrap of greaseproof paper on the table. She unfolded the nightdress and bonnet and draped them over the back of a chair. Then she stood, holding the flannel cloth in her hands, turning it over and over. She was remembering the sweet smell of Grace as she carried her around the garden after her bath, the soft skin of her shoulders, her voice. The weight of Grace in Flora's arms had been something she had waited for all her life; that was how it had felt. But this was Grace's home, her mother, her family. Their knowledge of her was much more profound than an afternoon, a single bath.

"Are there dishes I could wash for you, Mary?"

"No need, Missus. My mother will help."

Agrippa came into the cabin, saying that the priest was on his way. If he was surprised to see Flora, he gave no sign and poured himself a cup of tea, indicating the pot to the women. Both of them nodded and accepted the mugs he handed to them. Putting his own cup down, he took Mary in his arms and held her while her body shook. She made no sound and quite soon pushed her husband away and finished her tea. Flora was not accustomed to intimacy between couples—her own parents never kissed, only embraced on Christmas morning when her father handed her mother the customary jeweller's box from London—and was moved to tears herself. She excused herself, putting her mug by the basin on the table. Outside, laundry from the household was spread over bushes near the water, clematis unfolding its white blossoms, serviceberry, chokecherry; so much of the linen consisted of Grace's bedding, stained with her illness. Gus was standing by the river, watching the children attempting to coax their dog to fetch a stick in the quiet flow. He looked at her and raised his eyebrows in question.

"It doesn't look good. Mary says she can't eat or drink anything and the doctor has given them no hope. I feel so helpless, as though there's something I ought to be doing. But they are so stoic and it is clear that they will cope with it as best they are able to. Agrippa went for the priest and now he's back." Flora reached up her sleeve for her handkerchief and dabbed at her eyes.

Gus said gently, "Ah, that's it then. The priest means it's very serious."

"Might it mean that they are trying everything? I hate to think of a child dying. Oh, anyone dying of course, but a child . . ."

"Lots of children die on the reserves, Miss Oakden. Well, not just on the reserves but perhaps more of them than white children. Agrippa and Mary lost one only a year ago. We have brought so many diseases to them, smallpox being the worst, I guess, but even measles or influenza will sweep through these villages, killing far too many people. My father . . ." and then he stopped, looking surprised that he had gone this far, and to a complete stranger.

"Your father . . ." Flora prompted, curious. One did not think of the men who ploughed and fixed fence posts as boys with fathers, young pups trailing the wake of an older man with a pipe, a shooting stick, the only kind of father Flora knew; they seemed to have sprung from the landscape fully formed, ready to work in their dungarees and worn shirts. "What about him?" She took some of the bits of laundry from the bushes and turned them so the stained parts would bleach in the sunlight.

"He's a doctor, you see, in Victoria. He's worked with Indian people a lot—a lot of them live near Victoria, in fact the whole inner harbour was until recently a village site—and it's made him bitter at our interference in their lives, not to mention the diseases we've brought, the foods we insist they eat."

"A doctor!" exclaimed Flora. She wondered how the son of a doctor had ended up living in the cluster of tents where the rest of the workers stayed, close to the fields.

"Yes, a surgeon in fact. You look so surprised!"

Flora realized it was rude to stare at him with disbelief writ large upon her face. She pretended to be very interested in two ducks idling in the shallows of the river.

Gus touched her arm. "Please don't tell others that I've told you this. The others in Walhachin, I mean. I'm a bit of a black sheep, you see. I left home at seventeen, much to the sorrow of my mother, and have made my own way since then. If people know about my father, they want more—the story of our unhappiness, our falling out."

"Out of kindness, surely?"

Gus guffawed. "That is a charitable way to look at it. There is nothing new in our story, however; it's the same as any other in which the father and the son can't see eye to eye on how the son will live his life. I am quite happy for now being treated as a labourer. It gives me a kind of pleasure to pull my forelock the way the toffs expect, them not knowing where I come from, that I was educated at a good school, know Latin, and all that. I decided it wasn't important to me so I don't want other people bringing it up."

He reached into his rucksack and took out a small silver flask. "If you don't mind drinking from the flask, I think you should have a drink. You look pale. The heat, of course, and the shock of what you've learned of Mary's child . . ."

Flora tilted the flask and drank a mouthful, gasping as the liquid burned its way down her throat. Almost immediately she felt its effect, a warmth in her limbs, the anxiety she had over Grace dissolving. She examined the flask, running her finger over the elegant monogram on its dull silver surface.

"My brother has never allowed me to drink whisky. I've just broken his rule," she told Gus, handing him back the flask.

He laughed, and took a long swallow himself. "This is a fine malt from Islay, Miss Oakden. I suspect it's the one thing upon which my father and I might agree. Anyway, you seem of an age to be making your own rules. And breaking the ones that don't fit."

In the quiet that followed their shared drink of whisky, Flora could hear only the river and the far-off murmur of children's voices. She began to forget why she was there, on the banks of the Deadman River, a few thin horses grazing among the cottonwood trees, the bark fraying away like rags. And then the wail from Mary's cabin, so piercing that both Flora and Gus immediately ran in its direction.

The door of the cabin was open and the wailing, not human, was coming from inside. It was Mary, but not Mary, it was a lamentation that could have come from an animal in pain. Flora stood in the doorway for a moment and then crossed the room to where Mary sat by Grace's basket. The flush was gone from the baby's face and when Flora reached down to touch her, the body felt cooler now. And she looked like she was no longer breathing. The baby's mother was wailing, then stopping to touch the small face, wailing again as the child remained as still as a stone.

Another woman pushed by Flora and took up the child, putting her face very near to feel breath or a heart beating in the tiny chest, then gently replaced Grace in the basket. She kneeled beside Mary and joined her in her lamentation. A tall man, a priest, ducked as he entered the low threshold, crossing himself as he moved to mother and child.

Flora went back outside. Two women approached from another cabin and began to chant, *Nesika papa* and *kloshe kopa*, a language Flora had not heard Indian people speaking before. Gus took her arm and said quietly, "They are speaking Chinook. That's the Lord's Prayer in Chinook."

"Chinook?" Flora asked. "But aren't they Shuswap Indians here?"

"It's a way they talk between different tribes and among traders and such. Not a language exactly—it uses words from a number of languages. English, French, various tribal ones. There was a lot of it around Victoria when I was a boy. Here, too, because the Oblate missionary Father LeJeune in Kamloops had a newspaper that used it. But you don't often hear it anymore. Those women were probably students of LeJeune, maybe at the school in Kamloops."

"I don't think we belong here right now, Gus," said Flora softly, and the two of them walked over to the river to wait for whatever might be required of them.

Back under the shade of the cottonwoods, Flora began to weep. She was remembering the warmth of Grace's naked body as she carried her around the garden, the child's voice like rustling leaves. She remembered the sight of Grace drinking from her mother's breast and wept harder for Mary who had given birth to the infant, cared for her and her siblings, and who had carried her, damp with fever, on her horse to Flora's veranda so that she would not lose a precious day's pay. She remembered drawing the bath for Grace, small tufts of cattail clinging to her buttocks until Flora brushed at them and they drifted away in the dry air. Is that what was left of Grace now, seeds on the wind? A faint odour of urine in a soft towel?

One by one, the people of the village arrived at Mary and Agrippa's cabin. The wailing continued, the prayers in Chinook, the priest coming out of the cabin and kneeling with the others. It was no time for strangers or employers to witness a family's sorrow. After ensuring that there was nothing they could do, Flora and Gus mounted their horses and quietly rode away towards Walhachin, following the river again for the cool air occasionally drifting up from its surface. Flora wept, taking a hanky from her sleeve to wipe her eyes. To lose a child! And it was not the first taken from them, the earlier child buried within its spirit house in the cemetery bowing both to the Christian god and to the God who dwelt within the red hills, the wash of the river over sandbars, the scent of sun-struck sage.

FOUR
1962

It was best to ride a bike alone on the narrow lanes through the cemetery. Trees leaned over some of the paths to make dark tunnels and you could smell their branches, a bitter smell, like cough syrup. When the other kids came on their bikes, there was always lots of shrieking and talk of ghosts—"Look! There's one now! It's reaching for you. Aiiiii!"

Certain areas were to be avoided because of the density of growth around the stone houses that Tessa knew were called mausoleums. There were other houses, lower, which her father told her were sarcophagi; the bodies were placed within them rather than being lowered into the ground in coffins. When she was with the other kids, Tessa would shriek too and pretend to have seen a white form hanging from a tree or to have heard creepy voices calling from under the new graves.

Alone, however, she was not afraid. Of course there were ghosts! It was a cemetery after all. They were not white shapes like children wearing a sheet over their heads. That was for Halloween. But she could tell when one was around. It was . . . well, it was like being in the same room with someone else. You knew they were there even if you didn't talk to them. Sometimes she did hear talking, though, and weeping, and crying (though it might have been the wind off Ross Bay in the evergreens). Sometimes the voices drifted over the graves like a flock of small quiet birds, a murmuring, a soft rustling. But there were no birds when she heard that sound.

And she heard the hidden water under the ground. Could

water be a ghost or was it only people who lingered? She imagined the water yearning for its time above the ground, when it tumbled in sunlight down to the ocean, alive with insects and tiny fish.

Tessa liked to sit on certain graves and talk to the dead children with their angel stones, their broken rosebuds (the Sehl children), and baby Campbell with his chair and booties. This was the saddest thing of all, really—to think of babies buried without ever having had a chance to do what she, Tessa, could do: ride bikes, read Nancy Drew mystery stories, toast marshmallows over a campfire while stars peppered the heavens. Sometimes she would slip between the iron bars of one of the mausoleums and sit on the stone bench inside where there might also be a little heap of scales from pine cones, the seeds long removed by squirrels. Once, she saw a rat carrying something into a hole in one corner of the inner chamber; when she poked a stick into the hole, she heard a long hiss within.

There was a tree with forty-seven trunks. It took a long time to count them, mixing her up until Tessa decided to take a spool of red thread from her mother's sewing basket and tie a piece of thread to each trunk as she counted. On a walk with her father, she asked him what kind of tree it was—he worked at the Experimental Farm out on Saanich Peninsula—and he told her it was an Atlas cedar, from the mountains of Morocco. When they returned home, they got out an atlas and he showed her where Morocco was.

"Is it the same atlas?" Tessa asked, pointing to the book. "Was the book named for the mountains or what?"

Her father thought about that for a minute or two. "I know that the name we use for this kind of book, an atlas, comes from the Greek god, Atlas, who held up the universe. Early geographers used that image as the frontispieces for collections of maps that eventually became known as atlases. I remember seeing one by a guy called Mercator, for instance—the big maps that you have in your classroom are based on his idea of how to represent the surfaces of landforms. And I bet those mountains in Morocco are named for Atlas too. Maybe they're thought to be similar to the image of him holding up the world."

As usual, her father knew everything and told too much. But this time it was interesting. So Morocco was far away, farther than Vancouver, where Tessa had been with her family, farther than New Brunswick, where her grandparents lived. Some of the Atlas cedars were blue, her father told her, and she kept her eyes open for a vivid blue tree.

Sometimes Tessa saw Miss Oakden walking through the cemetery, carrying a basket of flowers. She lingered in the area where the graves were that contained men who'd fought in World War One. Her father told her these were mostly men who'd fought and come home and then died because they'd been hurt too badly to get better. Most of the others who'd fought and died were buried in France and had poppies growing over their graves. This was why everyone wore the felt poppies on Remembrance Day, the ones with the pins that boys used to stab an unsuspecting girl in the arm before the teacher confiscated the poppies and gave lectures on respect. There was a tall cross in the corner near the graves, called the Cross of Sacrifice, to honour all the men who'd fought. But that wasn't the place Miss Oakden visited and put her flowers. After Miss Oakden had gone, Tessa went to see just what she had been visiting. It was by a stone, flat on the ground, with a few lines in another language, one she recognized from her father's plant books. Latin, it was called. There was a name: Augustus Alexander; she could read that. Tessa traced the lettering with her finger. Then the dates. She made the dates into a bit of arithmetic and realized that whoever this person was who'd been buried under the stone, he'd been dead a long time, forty-six years. Once, when Tessa said a hello to Miss Oakden as the woman sat by the stone and arranged a little cluster of flowers, Miss Oakden turned and Tessa could see she was crying. She hadn't wanted to talk. So now when the girl saw the woman walking in the cemetery, she left her alone.

There were graves that called out to Tessa as she passed them, pushing her blue bike along in front of her. The one that was stone but that looked like a stump, with a scroll hanging from a branch. Even the rope by which the scroll, also stone, hung from was carved from stone. It was the grave of someone called Hay. She liked that one because often the squirrels sat on it and she wondered whether they knew it was not a real tree, if that mattered to them. And there was the one topped by a globe with an anchor carved into it. These were all clues, she knew, to the people buried underneath, just as the mausoleums meant that rich people were buried there. And the graves that were decorated frequently with fresh flowers and that had their small plots swept regularly meant that the dead person had not been forgotten by the living. Or at least had living relations or friends who wanted to visit and pay respect. Some of these were the graves of children. No child Tessa knew had died, although there was a boy in her class at Sir James Douglas Elementary School who had leukemia and might die if the treatment that was making him fat didn't work. No matter that she didn't really like him. When he was well, he was a bully; she hadn't noticed that leukemia made him any nicer. But still, there was the matter of dying. When she asked her mother what might make so many children die, her mother asked if she remembered lining up at the church hall across the school for that shot in her arm, followed by a sugar cube soaked in something pink and sweet. She did, of course. She had to do this before she was allowed in grade one. The needle had hurt and she'd cried out and the nurse told her to stop being a baby but to think instead of all the children in the world who didn't have this chance.

"The diseases you won't get because of that shot and the sugar cube," her mother explained, "are all things that many children died from before those vaccines were discovered. A child might come home from school with a cold that could turn into something far more serious and by morning he or she might be dead. This happened to your grandmother's sister, for instance.

She was only four years old and died of whooping cough."

Later, when she was attending school, she asked, "Why didn't Donald get a shot against leukemia then?"

But leukemia was something there wasn't a vaccine for, which was why Donald had it and was now losing his hair. You could not catch it from someone else. It grew inside your body like a plant, carried in the cells of your blood, the marrow of your bones. This was not very reassuring to Tessa, who spent most of a week imagining that every little twinge, every small bruise, might be leukemia growing in her body.

FIVE
1913

Mary was back at work within a week, quiet, her eyes dull. Her hands, so capable, seemed almost to carry within them the shape of a child, a damp head, the unbearable softness of shoulders. Flora and George had gone to the child's funeral, a strange affair in which the priest was almost the only person who spoke. The Indian people were silent, their faces closed and distant. Someone told Flora that the real ceremony would take place when all the white people had departed. Mourning songs would be sung, Grace's infant carrier would be hung in a tree with some of her belongings in it, Mary would cut her hair. Only the family and members of the Skeetchestn village would be welcome at this later ceremony.

And Flora regretted that she had only had the single encounter with Grace, remembering how the infant laughed and touched her face. She had dreamed of the baby afterwards, even made the little nightdress that might still, for all she knew, remain draped on the chair like a tiny ghost. How could a child die so quickly? And yet when she went to the cemetery at Skeetchestn for the child's funeral, she saw many small crosses to indicate the deaths of many babies. If she closed her eyes, she saw them lying under the earth in their flannel wrappings, as though asleep, and the weight of Grace on her lap, more warmth than anything, was something she could not forget.

It seemed frivolous to play croquet on the hotel lawn or to sit by the Marquis' pool with a glass of Pimm's Cup. So Flora spent a lot of time walking alone on the road to Ashcroft, though never arriving. She was watchful for snakes. She took a book to read in the orchard in late afternoon rather than drink tea with other women. A wind nearly always rose cool off the river; she would place her book on her chest and think of Grace.

A package arrived from Wiltshire containing a framed picture. It was an ink-and-wash sketch of Winsley, the village near her family home. It wasn't until she read her mother's accompanying note that she remembered doing the sketch herself. *You were about ten, wrote her mother, it was the summer that the young man from Cambridge came to tutor George in Greek as he was doing so poorly in his studies. He took the two of you on many outings, do you recall, and had you sketch scenes while he worked with George on passages from Thucydides. You gave me this one as a gift, but I thought you might like to hang it in your new home, where you can be reminded of Winsley."*

And then Flora did remember, she remembered sitting on a bench by the turn in the road where the stone buildings leaned right to the edge of the road on the one side and where the vale fell down to the river on the other. She remembered trying to get both views into the sketch, not quite successfully, but the tutor had been pleased with her perspective and had encouraged her to apply soft washes of green (for the vale side) and yellow warmed with a tiny bit of red for the stone buildings (they were built of the mellow Bath stone that glowed in sunlight) when they returned home. Rose campion and deadnettle foamed on the roadside in the heat of the stone. She had done a pale wash of pink for those, even though the deadnettle had blossomed white. The feeling of the moment was caught—the heat (one of the buildings trembled a little, probably due to the unsteadiness of her hand using ink), the density of the plants, the uneven cobbling of the street between its two poles, one the natural water and fall of fields to the river, the other the work of man in stone and mortar. She had been exactly ten. The sketch was signed with her initials, and the date: 1901.

Flora had forgotten she could draw that well. Mostly what she did now were designs for needlework, but seeing her sketch,

38

clumsy in a way but with a care and attention for particular detail, made her want to sketch again. She sent to Vancouver for three tablets of watercolour paper—she remembered that it held up well to the washes and the ink—and a tray of watercolours. Ink she had, and a variety of nibs. She would try to make a record of this house, these buildings, the slope of the hills on the other side of the railway tracks, tawny as buckskins, the jaunty angle of the flume coming down their flanks.

Word had come that the Indians were down on the river, fishing. The Footners told George that it shouldn't be missed, the sight of them taking the huge fish from the water, the women expertly cleaning and splitting them to spread them out on pole racks constructed of willow and red osier to catch the currents of air. There were horses all around, the sturdy native ponies staked out or hobbled while children played among them, followed by dogs, a chorus of magpies in the wild cherry trees near the water adding to the sound of voices, shouts as fish were lifted in big nets; there was the smell of cook fires as meals were prepared to feed the huge numbers of people congregated and the medicinal odour of smudges fending off pests as the fish cured. And thunder as the ponies were raced on the flats, dust following them in clouds. Now and then a child cried out as a bare foot encountered a cactus in the dry grass.

People from Walhachin had a fire of their own and, in the embers, roasted potatoes, some of them traded to Indians for the marvellous salmon, wind-dried and chewy. Someone played a fiddle, someone else an accordion, and others drifted over to listen or to stand with toes tapping while a few couples danced as the stars came out one by one. Flora felt a hand on her elbow.

"May I have this dance?" It was Gus, smiling his ironic smile.

It was a Hesitation Waltz, sweetly plangent in the cooling air. Flora kept her hand lightly on her partner's shoulder but felt his own hand tighten at her waist.

"I hoped we might ride together again," he was saying. "I

know that might be difficult to arrange, but if I am able to do so, would you come?"

Flora leaned back to look into his face. She thought of the beauty of his forearms with their golden hairs. It pleased her to think of them lightly touching her dress. He was still smiling, but there was something else, a look in his eyes; she felt it right down her spine and into her knees. She was suddenly a little weak.

"Oh, yes," she replied. "Yes."

It c a m e a b o u t because her brother was busy. Too busy to think about a parcel that was waiting for him at a ranch near Savona. And Flora had been asking him if she might ride in that direction to explore a distant bench, to sketch aspens and late brown-eyed Susans. As it turned out, her brother told her, the reliable Gus Alexander had reason to ride to Savona, and she could accompany him, collect the parcel, and have some time to sketch. There was a brief argument about tacking up Vespa, the grey mare, with George saying with some irritation that he would do it and Flora insisting that she was capable of tacking up the horse she would be riding. George gave in, because he was so busy, and Flora put on her riding costume, caught Vespa easily, and led her to the stable, where she gave her a brushing and then slipped a bridle onto the horse's willing head, fastening the buckles, then placing the numnah, then saddle, onto the mare's back. She was fond of Vespa, who reminded her of the mare she'd left at Watermeadows, a dark bay Arabian, Seraphim, who had replaced the grey pony of her childhood. She'd ridden with her father; Seraphim was a strong-winded mount for hunting, bold enough to jump a watercourse. Vespa had something of the same ardent spirit. Flora buckled the girth loosely and led the mare out of the paddock to the shade at the front of the house to wait for Gus.

He appeared almost immediately, coming from the direction of the labourers' cottages, mounted on his calm gelding, Agate. Flora watched him approach, at ease in the saddle, almost like an extension of his horse. He jumped down and held both horses while Flora tightened the girth and mounted her mare.

"All set?" he smiled.

"I think so. I have this small rucksack only and George insists on a canteen."

They were away, riding towards Savona. The day had not yet become as hot as it would and there was a breeze coming up off the river. Gus knew a route that was shorter than going by road and took them through a small gap in the red hills by the Deadman River.

"There's a place on this trail where I almost always see snakes. Tell me, Flora, have you ever seen a rattlesnake?" There was a twinkle in his blue eyes.

Flora shivered a little. "No, not really. I've seen their tracks in the dirt and I found a skin once, and of course I imagine I hear them every time I go walking alone, but I haven't actually seen one. I'd like to, though. At least, I think I would."

"We'll leave the horses on the trail and just walk up into the rocks. Agate is the most reliable horse on earth—until he smells a rattlesnake."

They dismounted, and Gus produced a rope, tying both horses to a single pine tree with a little shade. Then he took Flora by the hand and led her up the talus slope, taking each step carefully.

"There," he pointed. "Look. Three of them, all asleep. That one on the far left is a young one. It doesn't even have rattles yet, just that little button at the tip of its tail. I think they're beautiful."

And they were, Flora decided. Two of them were olive coloured and the young one was more tan. They all had dark brown blotches on their back, with lighter edges. There was something peaceful about the way they slept on the rocks. There was a smell, not unpleasant, like leaves or mushrooms. Gus murmured that it would be best to let sleeping snakes lie, and they quietly returned to their horses.

It seemed to Flora that Gus kept his hand on her back a little longer than necessary when he helped her to mount; the place where it had rested was very warm. For a moment she felt short of breath. When the young men in England had danced with her, their hands encircling her waist for the waltz, she had felt trapped. There was everything in the action, and nothing—a negotiation that had everything to do with land and the certainties of money and nothing to do with this feeling: a response the earth might make to wind, or sun. A little shudder, the passing of a shadow over the light skin of water.

It took a further hour to reach the ranch where George's parcel was waiting for him—books the rancher was lending him about soil health and grafting—and after a welcome glass of lemonade on the shady porch, they continued to the bench above Kamloops Lake where Flora wanted to sketch. They found a grove of pines, surrounded by a profusion of brown-eyed Susans, a fringe of aspens leading to the lake. Gus led the horses down for a drink and then found a place to tie them in shade with a long rope so they could graze on the sporadic bunchgrass. Flora took out the lunch she had stowed in her rucksack—cucumber sandwiches, a pot of Gentleman's Relish, a few of Mary's biscuits spread with anchovy paste—and they ate in the shade of a pine, Gus spreading his overshirt first for Flora to sit on. The view up the lake was spectacular, the long blue water still under the sun.

Flora dipped her pen into ink and began to draw the lake and its aspens. The sky in this country always gave her trouble. How to imply its enormity—you felt you could see forever!—and its changing moods made possible only by a drift of cloud or the thunderheads that frequently appeared in late afternoon only to disappear again almost immediately. Thicker lines for cloud, hatching for pines, a place where she used a pencil to indicate possible colours for the wash.

She realized Gus was watching her. She turned to him and began sketching his face on a fresh sheet of paper. It was beautiful, she thought—the strong nose, the well-spaced eyes, and his mouth. She examined it with her pen, the curve and the slight droop of the bottom lip. She paused at the chin, wanting to get the sense of how it jut forward, like a challenge. Before she knew it, he was kissing her. She had never been kissed. Oh, a peck on the cheek by her father or nurse, the Frenchman who brought special water lilies to her father and who kissed her hand, but never by a man whose mouth she had just drawn, whose arms had made her feel light-headed.

His mouth was luscious, like ripe strawberries. Taking his lips from hers, he whispered in her ear, "Do you mind, Flora? I've wanted to kiss you since I first saw you walking across your brother's orchard months ago, looking like a girl out of a painting."

"Does it seem that I mind?" And they were kissing again.

It was a Saturday morning. Some of the orchardists were taking a day off, but the Chinese labourers were out in the orchards, hoeing the rows of potatoes between the small trees and making sure that bears had not damaged boughs, some of them propped with forked sticks. One orchardist had among his workers a couple, both Chinese, Song Lee and his young wife, May. The growing community had several businesses run by Chinese, one of them a laundry that was thriving. Song Lee came to Walhachin on his own from somewhere in the Fraser Valley. When his employer discovered he was married and that, unlike the other Chinese labourers, his wife lived not in China but with her parents in Vancouver, he gave Song permission to bring her to live in a tiny shack built of packing cases. She grew vegetables that she'd sell from a basket in front of her shack, a few chickens clucking nervously around her feet. When May first arrived, Flora bought early peas from her, a few lettuces, and some spring onions, and admired rows of tiny cabbage seedlings and the delicate ferny tops of carrots. May was a tiny woman with glossy black hair and a beautiful smile showing even white teeth. It was rumoured she was expecting a baby, though her slight frame revealed nothing. Or perhaps, thought Flora, the faintest swelling under her cotton jacket. It was so picturesque—the Chinese woman in her dark blue jacket surrounded by chickens, her baskets of vegetables looking exactly like a still life—that Flora went home for her Brownie camera and returned to take a photograph.

"May I take your picture?" she had asked, and after May shyly nodded, she snapped the pretty scene.

On that Saturday morning, when a young boy came running up from the orchards, shouting for help, Flora dropped her needlework and quickly intercepted him on the road.

"It's the Chinese lady, miss. She's been bitten by a snake! I'm going to Flowerdews to see if the doctor is at lunch there."

Flora let him continue on and she called Mary from the kitchen.

"What can we do, Mary? Do you have any experience with snakebite?"

"Put the kettle on the hot part of the stove, Missus," she said and ran down to the path by the river. She snapped some sticks from a young maple growing there and rushed back.

"This is good but depends on how bad the bite." She was putting the sticks into an iron pot and covering them with hot water from the kettle. "I'll let it steep for a few minutes and then we can go."

Standing on the veranda, Flora could see several people on their way down the orchards. Was the doctor among them? She couldn't tell. He was a man who liked his drink, and she hoped he hadn't begun on the many glasses of port he liked as an accompaniment to lunch. He wasn't a young man either and was semi-retired; most people chose to go to Ashcroft or even Kamloops for medical care.

Mary soon appeared with a basket on her arm. She and Flora walked as quickly as they could to where a small crowd was gathered around the moaning form of May Lee on the newly hoed earth of a potato bed. Someone had cut the lower part of May's skirt and had used some of the cloth as a makeshift tourniquet on her upper calf.

"It was a rattlesnake," a man whispered to Flora. "Evidently she was hoeing close to the rocks on the edge of the potatoes and it struck her hard on the leg."

Flora could see where the fangs had punctured the skin. The bare feet—for someone had removed her black cloth shoes—looked unbearably fragile, side by side on the dry earth. No one should have been looking at those bare calves and knees, pale and smooth, apart from a young husband. Already there were blotchy red patches all over May's lower leg, beginning to reach up past the tourniquet. Mary took out a flask from her basket and soaked a clean flannel with the tea of maple sticks she had made in that moment of quick-witted attention while Flora had wrung her hands and wondered what on earth might be done. Gently pushing Song Lee away from his wife, Mary applied the cloth to the punctured skin, pressing while May tossed her head and cried out. Flora knelt down with her and began to wipe May's forehead with another flannel. Her skin was clammy and cold. She was moaning and shuddering and she had vomited. Flora cleaned her face. She murmured reassuring words, but it seemed that May was beyond hearing, her eyes fearful and her pulse, or what Flora thought must be her pulse, a slow and distant measure against her finger as she held May's wrist. Flora gently laid her hand on May's abdomen and felt the briefest of fluttering, a butterfly on milkweed.

"Is the doctor coming?" she asked one of the bystanders. "And has someone asked that a car be available to take May to Kamloops?"

"He had to go to his house for his bag," was the answer. A car was in fact on its way. And then the doctor was there, puffing and brisk, his face flushed. Others were arriving too, Gus among them.

"Well, then. Snakebite, eh? Let's see what I have for that." The doctor reached into a battered leather bag and brought out a vial and a case that he fumbled open. A glass and steel hypodermic syringe lay in a bed of blue silk. He pushed Mary aside and bent down, wheezing with effort. He was very red.

"Calmette's serum," he announced to the group, as he filled the syringe from the vial. "It's an anti-venom for snakebite. We used it in India. Terrible snakes there."

He injected the serum into May's arm and, untangling a stethoscope from the bag, he listened to her heart, breathing heavily as he did so. He looked up.

"This young woman is in serious trouble. Has someone sent for . . . Ah, here it is. I will accompany her of course."

A car had arrived. Several men lifted May from the ground and arranged her in the back, where the doctor found room for himself. He located a respiration mask in his bag and fitted it over her face, pumping its bulb as the car pulled away. There had been no gesture to poor Song, who stood watching the vehicle leave with his wife inside, his hands helpless at his sides. He followed slowly on foot, uttering a single cry as the car disappeared over the bridge and up the hill to the main road to Kamloops.

Mary was putting the lid back on the flask and the others were leaving to return to the community. Flora felt a hand on her shoulder. It was Gus.

"What an awful thing for Song. Why couldn't they take him along?" she asked him.

"Well, at least *she* was taken," he replied. "I've been present when medical attention has been refused to Chinese workers because no one believed they could pay. But I have to say that this doesn't look good for May. Calmette's serum won't work for this."

"What do you mean? He said it was for snakebite and surely that was what bit her. Look, they've killed the snake. There it is, right there!" She pointed to a big rattlesnake, its head sliced off with a hoe, left on the side of the potato bed. Flies had already found it.

"Oh, yes, I believe that snake struck her. But Calmette's serum was devised for cobra venom. I know from my father that it is useless against rattlers. What Mary prepared will sometimes work. Later in the year, a poultice of baneberry might have been more effective, but there're no berries on the plants yet. We'll just have to hope that they get her to Kamloops in time for treatment. Dr. Aspern is a bit past his prime, I'd say, and the port has befuddled what sense he might once have had."

"He did have his case and came quite quickly," said Flora in defence of the old doctor. He had once been kind to her when she had been laid low with a fever.

"But he has no idea where he is, Flora. Surely that is evident? A medical man who doesn't know that snakes from the Far East are not the same as those in British Columbia? Or who seems unaware of the knowledge of people like Mary who live here and have some sense of how plants have medicinal value? I'm surprised, though relieved, that he didn't pull out a kit to cup and bleed poor May. It confounds me beyond belief that people have so little interest or knowledge of the actual place where they live. In India, I'm sure his feeling was that it ought to be more like England and that would suit everyone and solve the dreadful problems created by the natives. He is like something out of *Punch*."

May did not return to Walhachin. She was dead by the time the car arrived in Kamloops. Arrangements were made for her body to be returned by train to Vancouver, for her family to bury her in their own way. Song went down to the city for a week and then returned to work. Flora wondered about the child. It had died with May of course, but had it been mourned as its mother must have been mourned by her family in Vancouver?

Flora took Song flowers. She had been told that white was the colour for Chinese funerals so she made a bouquet of yarrow and traveller's joy, long tendrils of it, along with pearly everlastings, daisies, and a few pale asters. Song's eyes were as sad as anything she'd ever seen; he carried the flowers into the shack and then returned with four brown eggs, wrapped in a bit of newspaper with Chinese characters on it. On the wooden box where he had been sitting, she saw a little bamboo flute. Some nights Flora would rest on the veranda, eager for a little of the cool air off the river, and she would hear quavery notes coming from the direction of Song's shack. It was lonely music, a series of longing phrases but no response.

SIX
October 1913

George was away in the Okanagan, looking at orchards and talking to their owners now that the main harvest was over. He had been reluctant to leave Flora unchaperoned, but she insisted he go.

"Whatever could happen to me here with the community at hand?" she asked him. "I will draw and perhaps bottle some applesauce. If I ask her, Mary will stay overnight, in the box room behind the kitchen, though I can't think why I'd need her to."

And so he left, catching a ride with another orchardist. After his departure, Flora let it be known that she herself was going away for a few days. To Vancouver, someone suggested, and she didn't correct that impression. She packed her small valise. She was given a ride to Pennies and then left to wait for the train, which was due within the hour. As the car disappeared down the road towards Ashcroft, Gus appeared on Flight, leading his gentle gelding, Agate. Under her travelling skirt, Flora was wearing her jodhpurs, so she removed the skirt and folded it into her valise, which held only her nightdress, an extra blouse, and a sponge bag of toiletries.

"I can't believe I'm doing this," she confessed to Gus as she mounted Agate after tying her bag in among the saddlebags.

He smiled and released the reins he'd been holding while she arranged herself in the saddle. "I don't know when I've looked forward to something as much as this," he replied. "Now let's be off before the train comes and you're spotted from the window by a matron from Kamloops."

They touched their heels to their horses' sides and were off at a lope, up a trail along the flume and over the hill by the time the train slowed down for Pennies. Luckily it stopped to drop off freight so that anyone listening would think that Flora had boarded. Out of sight of the bench and its community, Flora felt hugely, wildly free. She removed her gloves and tucked them into one bag and flexed her fingers on the smooth leather of the reins.

Gus had asked to use the cabin that Agrippa's parents wintered in, up in the Back Valley. Over the summer he had become very friendly with Agrippa and had gone hunting with him earlier in the fall. The men stayed in the cabin then. Gus told Flora about its placement on a little lake, saying they'd fish for trout and walk barefoot in the sweet grass. To get there, the pair rode for a good part of the day, through grasslands, then aspen forests, the turning leaves trembling on their stems; finally they went up into higher country where the air already smelled of approaching winter, though it was still warm. Gus called it "flinty," a tang of rock in icy water, and noted the frost-damaged wildflowers they passed along the way. The cabin was waiting, its lake fringed with reeds and bulrushes where the remnants of blackbird nests clung to the tall stalks. Tattered leaves of water lilies floated on the lake's surface like saucers, stung by dragonflies. A loon watched from the opposite side, curious at the sight of horses.

"How beautiful this is!" Flora exclaimed as she helped unpack the gear. All around the cabin, tall grasses grew in soft abundance. Gus removed saddles and bridles from the horses and turned them out into a corral of peeled poles. They immediately began to graze on grass as high as their bellies, their tails fanning their rumps for flies. A small shelter stood at the far end of the corral. Above the low door of the cabin, a rack of moose antlers reached out to embrace those entering. Flora touched the surface, surprised at the granular texture.

Inside, the cabin was dark and smelled of mice. A startled bat flew out the door at the interruption of its sleep. Gus opened the shutters—there was no glass in the openings but screens of frayed mesh—and brushed mouse droppings from the table. There was a stack of pitchy pine by the stove, and he'd brought a few sheets of newspaper in a saddlebag for lighting the first fire. With the windows open and fresh air coming in, the place felt quite welcoming. Flora quickly picked a bouquet of willow boughs and a single yellow aster to place in a tobacco tin in the centre of the rough table.

The cabin consisted of a single room with pole beds built into two walls. There were no mattresses. Gus explained that fresh fir boughs were collected each winter, providing not only comfort but also some control against bugs. The table, the stove, some shelves, a screened cupboard with lard tins for flour and other staples, two benches and one comfortable chair made of woven sinew with a cushion sewn of calico filled with yarrow— when Flora sat on it to test its comfort, there was a sharp clean odour that did something to dispel scent of mice. Snowshoes hung from the rafters and a box of tools sat on the small porch, its handle gnawed by porcupines.

How little is needed, thought Flora, thinking of the busy enterprise that was Watermeadows. Or Walhachin, for that matter, with the accumulation of farm equipment, the regular deliveries of every manner of house furnishings, dishes, even a set of Meissen coming from a family home in England, arriving in a tea chest, the delicate items packed in paper, then nestled in straw like precious eggs. Panes of window glass necessitated regular cleaning, and curtains to keep out the night. And water lily roots packed in a vasculum with their promise of the familiar.

"I am going to cut some fir boughs. Why don't you take a bucket to the lake for some water? Then we could have a cup of tea," suggested Gus. So Flora walked to the lake and dipped the bucket in, filling the kettle when she returned and setting the bucket by the door. By now the fire was burning well, the stove pipe creaking as it adjusted to the heat. The incense of burning pine was lovely in the cooler air of the high valley.

Gus came into the cabin with an armload of sweet-smelling fir boughs and piled them onto one of the pole beds. He showed Flora the bear skin on an exterior wall of the cabin, the side they hadn't yet investigated. The animal's feet were nailed to the logs, its head was supported by a hook, and the skin covered almost the entire surface of the wall. Flora had not expected to touch a bear in her life. She marvelled at the coarse hair, the dry nose. She took the tea things out to the porch, and they drank from tin mugs while the loon swam back and forth as if to inspect them from all possible angles.

Flora knew from Mary that Agrippa's parents still spent every winter in the Back Valley, living in the old way, though even cabins as rustic as this one weren't used until recently. Gus pointed out a depression possibly twenty feet across, on the shore of the lake, and explained that it was the site of a kekuli or pit house. Poles would be erected to hold a roof of sod and boughs, and access would be by ladder through an opening in the centre of the roof where smoke also exited. Flora tried to imagine people coming up through the hole in the roof, out of the darkness and into daylight like this, the sound of grasshoppers and water lapping against the pebbles drawing them forth. Though maybe by the time of year when grasshoppers could be heard, the families would be living in the tule lodges Gus also described, sleeping in airy rooms created by bulrushes.

There was the time in the mown grass of the farthest orchard, the two of them lying down to the song of meadowlarks, clothing pushed aside, and there was this time, a naked embrace on the sweetness of new fir boughs covered over in homespun. The weight of their bodies, turning and lifting, released balsam from the crushed fir, a rustling of branches as though they lay among trees. Wind came in through the screened openings and cooled their bodies after they had made love in the early evening. They had now a small history of such encounters accumulating in their hands, the way they sought an area that responded eagerly, a particular texture of skin, a rough patch on a heel, the soft hairs of an area unknown to Flora before the time in the orchard. She was drowsy with pleasure.

They ate a meal on the cabin steps, balancing tin plates on their laps. Gus had taken care of the cooking, heating stew and a few biscuits on the stove, and pouring them each a measure of whisky in the cups they had used for their tea. By now the loon had come to their shore and drifted in and out of the reeds. Goldeneye could be seen out in the middle of the lake; bats were beginning to swoop from the trees. Flora had never felt so far from what she knew. When darkness came and the air cooled considerably, Gus brought out a blanket and wrapped it around her shoulders. She leaned against his legs. She could hear the horses snuffling in the corral and wondered if they, too, experienced displacement or whether it was all the same to them—home pasture or a corral in the Back Valley, river water or lake water in their buckets, human voices or loons.

She had never known anything as nice as talking after lovemaking. Face to face on the narrow bed, Flora offered the details of her childhood to her lover like a series of small gifts. The rocking horse saga, riding lessons, walks with George's tutor over Roman roads with appropriate fragments of poetry being recited, in Latin of course, as they scrambled over fields and along the river with the faint echo of old campaigns in their ears.

Hic tamen hanc mecum poteras requi
escere noctem fronde super viridi. Sunt nobis mitia poma,
castaneae molles et pressi copia lactis,
et iam summa procul villarum culmina fumant
maioresque cadunt altis de montibus umbrae . . .

. . . remembered Flora, having been taken by the tutor's ability to evoke those earlier times. She loved Latin for its hard, clean sound, even if she had difficulty in understanding exactly what it meant.

"Ah, Virgil," murmured Gus, "my favourite poet. I had so much of him memorized when I was at school. There was always a line or two of Virgil appropriate to an occasion. As now. Let me translate that.

Here still you may lie with me this night
on the green foliage. There are ripe apples for us
sweet chestnuts and an abundance of milk . . ."

He broke off for a minute. "*Pressi* is a bit of a problem. It's a genitive participle that goes with *lactis* and the phrase literally means "milk having been pressed." So cheese, I suppose. To go with those apples. Anyway, let's say an abundance of fresh cheese, then,

. . . and now in the distance the high gables of the farms smoke
and greater shades fall from the high mountains."

"How beautiful that is," murmured Flora as Gus translated the lines she had called up from memory.

"And poignant," replied her lover, "when you think that the subjects of some of the *Eclogues* are shepherds who have lost their farms to soldiers. Sleeping on green boughs instead of their regular beds! Though they sound quite happy with it, don't they? As we have been. At least they have apples and cheese and some chestnuts to roast, and though wine isn't mentioned, there is almost always drink in the Latin poetry!"

Gus shot a grouse for their midday meal next day, using an old gun hanging from the log beam. He cooked the bird with some chanterelle mushrooms he had hunted for in the woods beyond the lake and then in the rich fat, fried potatoes he had packed in his saddlebags. He swam in the lake, gliding through the rushes and out into the open water at the lake's centre. Flora watched him splash and plunge under the surface, wondering if she had ever been as happy as she was, sitting on a stump under blue sky, long skeins of geese passing overhead on their way south.

"Did you really say 'Dame's Bottom,' did I really hear you say that?" Gus laughed as Flora repeated a bit of history from her village. It was the second evening of their sojourn in the cabin; Gus had come up from checking the horses for the night to find Flora wrapped in a blanket on the porch, two glasses of whisky poured, eager to talk.

She slapped his arm. "I most certainly did not. I said 'Dane's Bottom.' From the Battle of Edgington, where Alfred stopped the Viking expansion and saved Wessex and England from the barbarian hordes. Dane's Bottom was the place where it all happened, or so we were told. A little hollow near the Kennet Avon Canal. You'd know that if you'd paid attention instead of trying to reach under the blanket!"

"So much more interesting if it *had* been a dame's bottom. But I suppose a pretty girl would never have been told such a thing by her brother's tutor."

"You really are incorrigible. Will you pour me a little more whisky, please?" She watched the amber liquid arc gracefully into her mug. Then: "We really could be at the end of the earth, couldn't we? So far from people. No lights. If you'd told me when I was packing to leave England that I would be spending a night in a cabin in a forest without a soul within miles, the only sounds being loons and . . . well, something large moving towards us . . . Oh, it's only Agate! Hello, Agate. Gus, you must have left the gate open. Would you like a little piece of my biscuit, Agate? Anyway, I don't know if I'd have believed you. I wish we didn't ever have to leave."

Gus leapt up to lead Agate back to the corral and then returned to trace the shape of Flora's face with one finger. "And if you'd been told that you'd be sharing a bed of fir boughs with a man, what would you have said then?"

She turned to him and kissed his ear. "I'd have dropped the blanket, just like this . . ."

She stood up naked in the moonlight.

". . . and I'd have led him back into the cabin."

SEVEN
May 1914

Many of the Walhachin men were taking part in training exercises as part of their involvement in C Squadron of the 31st British Columbia Horse. George would saddle his gelding, Titan, and Gus took Flight, his lovely chestnut mare, though Agate would be a more reliable mount, Flora thought. Both men sat tall and steady among the others in the village square, ready to head out in formation to one of the fallow fields where they would wheel and turn in the dust. A platoon of small boys, armed with lengths of stick held like bayonets, followed them on foot. Some of the men had been training for several years now, going to Vernon or Kamloops to join the other squadrons, coming home with stories of mud, bivouacs, and saddle sores. And dust! In Kamloops the training camp was located near the racecourse, rumoured to be the dustiest place in the entire Dry Belt. Hay rakes had to be employed to comb articles out of the deep drifts at the conclusion of the camp. A few men had been members of HRH Duke of Connaught's cavalry escort when he'd come to Vancouver in September 1912, and the Governor General had sent an official document professing his great satisfaction with their performance. Rumours of war were circulating throughout the Empire; C Squadron was determined to be ready.

An invitation came for Flora to spend a few days on the McIntyre Ranch in the Upper Hat Creek Valley. She'd met Jane McIntyre at a social in Ashcroft, and the two had become friends, sending letters and little mementos through the mail. Like Flora, Jane loved needlework and often described a new project, many of them inspired by the wildflowers of the valley where she lived. She was clearly enamoured of her home there; when the invitation arrived, Flora was excited at the prospect of a few days away. A vehicle from the ranch would be coming to Ashcroft for supplies, and if Flora could arrange to be there on the Wednesday, then she could travel up the Oregon Jack Creek Road with the ranch foreman. She took the train to Ashcroft and found a laconic Pete Richardson waiting for her in front of the harness-maker's shop, where various items were being left for mending. Pete hoisted Flora's valise into the back of the truck, along with a saddle, two sacks of flour, a small chest of tea, and various other parcels and boxes.

"I'd like to get us going, Miss," Pete said in his quiet voice. "It's a long piece of road and I want to drive it in the daylight. I always allow time for a flat tire or breakdown—that road, she's a rough one. Mrs. McIntyre asked me to make sure you used the pillows she sent."

He indicated a little stack of cushions on the seat where Flora would ride. She climbed into the truck and arranged the pillows at her back and bottom. She tied her straw hat firmly under her chin, and they were off.

Flora was surprised at how the climate changed as they proceeded up the long road that rose dusty from the sagebrush flats and feedlots by the Wagon Road near the Ashcroft Manor, up into forest, then above the valley formed by Oregon Jack Creek, cliffs on one side of the road and the green meadows below. Aspen shaded the road and the wildflowers were all later than down below, sticky geranium and penstemon and balsam-root brightening the verges of the narrow way. No wonder Jane's embroidery was so lovely, thought Flora, with this wild beauty as inspiration. Richardson was a man of very few words but occasionally pointed out birds—a kestrel sitting on a fence post, killdeer flying up to take attention away from their nests. Down below the road, they saw a black bear seated among the grasses with two cubs at play nearby. The bears looked up at the sound of the truck but didn't leave their patch of sunlight.

At various points along the journey, Pete would stop the vehicle and get out to figure out the best way to navigate a difficult section of road. In some places, rain had created washboarding; in other places, rocks had tumbled down a cliff-face to create obstacles that had to be pushed over to one side. Pete explained that he'd come down to Ashcroft from the other side of the valley, the lower side, collecting some equipment from an outfit at Cargyle, before driving down from Bonaparte. Every time he stopped, Flora got out of the truck and took deep breaths of the clean high air. How lovely this was. She was lately accustomed to take pleasure in the small beauties of the desert landscape—the brief yellow flowers on the prickly-pear cacti that surrounded Walhachin, and the pink bitterroot. She loved the dry heat and the low grey vistas or distant tawny hills, but this, oh this, was a kind of Eden, and but for Jane's invitation, she would never have known it existed.

When they reached the ranch, Jane was waiting at the gate on a tall black horse with a spotted rump. She was holding the reins of a saddled mare, a dun. Quickly dismounting, she tied each horse to a post on either side of the gate. She embraced Flora and told Pete to go on ahead; Allan was waiting for him by the barn to help unload the truck.

"Flora, I'm so happy to see you! We could see the dust of the truck for ages, and I thought how nice it would be if you could ride up to the house with me. I can show you things as we go and no doubt you have had enough of that truck!"

She reached into her saddlebag for a flask of cold water from which Flora drank gratefully. The ranch lay on the eastern side of the valley, its pastures sloping down to the road. Soft wind rustled through the aspens and pines growing in small groves to provide shade for the horses grazing there. The two women mounted their horses, Flora wishing she'd worn a divided skirt but managing to tuck up her gabardine in such a way that she was able to find her stirrups without too much difficulty.

"That mare has a very soft mouth. Just use your reins against her neck and don't pull her up too quickly," Jane advised.

Opening a gate into the side pasture with her riding crop, Jane led them away from the driveway and after closing the gate again, they let their horses lope up the gradual hill to a place fringed with pines, offering a view of far-off snowy peaks that Jane said were on the coast. Everything was so clear and fine that Flora felt her throat constrict. A magpie swooped down from a tree, followed quickly by another.

"It's as though we're on the spine of the world," Flora said quietly.

The ranch house was made of logs, covered in areas with clapboard; sunny yellow shutters framed some of the windows, and vines had been trained to grow up the southern side of the house to cool that exposure. White clematis tumbled in great frothy swaths from trellises while deep green Virginia creeper wound around the chimney. Jane's husband, Allan, greeted them as they rode up to the house, then took their horses away to unsaddle and turn loose. Jane showed Flora to a small pretty room on the second floor, tucked into one gable. Faded chintz curtains hung in the window, a white-painted iron-framed bed was spread with a quilt pieced from tiny squares of summer dress materials, a wicker chair waited by the window for reading or dreaming, and two small watercolours of the valley decorated the whitewashed walls. Looking at them, Flora was surprised to see them signed with Jane's name.

"I didn't know you could paint," she commented, looking closely at one of the pictures.

"My first winter here was a little lonely, I have to admit," Jane told her. "I wondered if I'd made a mistake in marrying Allan and leaving the bustling hub of Ashcroft! But then I found paints that had been his mother's and every day I saw those mountains and the pastures going on forever and far off, the coast mountains with their crowns of snow. And the birds—oh, Flora, the birds are extraordinary here. I've begun to keep a list, a life list

I suppose it would be, and most days there's something to add. Perhaps not a new bird but certainly a new behaviour, a nest, a moment that seems, well, momentous somehow! Of course we go down to see my parents in the town, and others too, and one day there will be children, God willing, so for now I have this luxury of space. My heart feels twice as wide as it did when I first came here with Allan after our wedding. I feel it expanding as we come over the rise on the Oregon Jack Creek Road."

Then laughing at herself for such a long and excited reply to Flora's simple comment, she left her friend to unpack, saying that they would have supper outdoors that evening.

When Flora woke in the flowery bed the next morning, it took a moment for her to remember where she was. From where she lay, from a gap between the curtains, she could see branches of aspen trembling in the early morning air; she could hear magpies and the creak of a floorboard as someone hesitated outside her bedroom door.

"Hello?" she called and was rewarded by the appearance of Jane carrying a tray holding a pot of tea and two cups.

"I thought I'd bring you tea in bed! And then I thought, But why don't I take a cup for myself too and then we can talk! What would you like to do today, Flora? It's going to be beautiful. I was up early to see Allan off—they're checking on some cattle in the upper pasture—and saw the sun rise. Not a cloud in the sky!"

They settled in on Flora's bed, sipping hot tea and chatting. Jane remarked on the lace edging the bodice of Flora's nightdress, asking was it Flemish? It was not. It was Honiton, coming from that area of Devon made famous for its bobbin lace and where Flora's mother went regularly to buy fine trimmings for her dressmaker to use on clothing for herself and her daughter. That led Jane to suggest a sewing activity they could work on under the shady trees a little later in the morning.

"I've just learned this method of making a camisole. I've been accumulating handkerchiefs, my mother sent me a box of them she found in Vancouver, so say you'll do it with me, Flora, say you will? It's no fun to sew these little gems alone."

"How could I refuse?" smiled Flora.

After a breakfast of warm biscuits—"Our Chinese cook has a very light hand with pastry and biscuits. These are almost a scone, don't you think? But I wish we could get him to realize that a piece of beef is not leather and doesn't need to be boiled for hours"—and dark bitter marmalade that gave Flora a small pang of homesickness for its resemblance to the preserves of the Watermeadows kitchen, the two women gathered sewing things and went out to the yard.

"Here, let's put this stuff on the table and then I'd like to show you around a little," said Jane, indicating a wicker table and chairs under a spreading tree. They walked to the big barn where sunlight lit the long central walkway between stalls. Most of the horses were turned out, but one mare and her filly remained in a box stall, awaiting (Jane said) the ministrations of a ranch hand for a gash on the mare's hock.

Another smaller barn was completely empty but for its hay-loft; it was the winter home of the milk cow and a few goats. Sheds held equipment and tack. Everything was neat and orderly; a pair of perfectly matched cats sat on either side of the gate leading into the nearest pasture.

"Allan's family has been here for two generations. Or three, now, with us. They came from Scotland, for the usual reasons, I suppose: a small piece of property and too many sons for it to be divided in any way that would allow for a decent living to be possible. Allan's grandfather couldn't believe that such large parcels were available here. The water rights were a little more difficult—Cargyles, for instance, were forced away by having their right to water reneged upon, and they went reluctantly because they had been first here and truly loved it—but really Grandfather McIntyre put so much labour into this ranch and hoped his sons and grandsons would carry on his name, continuing to care for this land."

"Which Allan is certainly doing," Flora exclaimed as she looked at the pastures stretching down to the dusty road, the supple poplars lining the driveway, the healthy garden. "And children, Jane? Are you planning to have children or is that too personal a question to ask? This place would be heaven for children . . ."

Jane said in a quiet voice that she'd had three miscarriages; although her doctor had told her there was no reason why she should not have a child, she wondered if it would ever happen.

"I think of those poor wee babies, a bit like ghosts now, and feel very uncertain about carrying a child to term. Allan is perhaps more optimistic than I am. He's also very patient, which I don't think most men would be. I said I was keeping a life list of birds and some days it seems that there is a death list also, of the lost babies. I wouldn't tell Allan that. He would call it morbid. But each time I was so excited to be expecting a child and then . . ."

Her voice trailed off, and she touched her eyes with a hanky. Flora had told Jane some weeks previously about Grace and how she had felt sorrow at the brief time that baby had spent on earth. Mary's sadness, the droop of her shoulders as she scrubbed clothes, dusted, sat alone in a chair with some mending: these spoke to a dimension of a woman's life that Flora could only wonder at. She had not known that Jane had anticipated birth and then had her joy taken from her prematurely. She embraced her friend. And of course it was Allan's loss too, for surely he had imagined himself a father, holding a child. A son who might ride these pastures as a father himself.

Flora had felt she had entered a rich and mysterious place with Gus, almost a secret world (and indeed no one knew of their meetings, certainly not of their lovemaking), in which she imagined the two of them were alone in the sensations they experienced on the boughs in Agrippa's family's cabin, under the apple trees, in coulees far from Walhachin. She wore both her anticipation and the memory of these encounters like a delicate garment, aware of its invisible weight upon her bare skin. She hadn't thought that others shared this mysterious pleasure and that it might develop into something else. A marriage would contain both a past and a future as well as the day to day. And the quotidian might include the possibility of children, both their births and their untimely deaths.

"We will not talk about this anymore this morning, Flora," said Jane, taking her friend's arm and leading back to the arrangement of chairs under the shady tree. "We'll make pretty underthings instead!"

Jane reached into her workbasket and took out a handful of light cotton. It moved a little in the breeze like thistledown.

"We take three of the handkerchiefs, fold them in half on the diagonal, and press them—I've done that already, as you can see—and then cut them along the fold. That gives us six triangles and we arrange them like this . . ."

Jane laid out her pieces of fine lawn like a puzzle on the tabletop, showing how the front and the back of the camisole would look.

". . . and then we sew them together with bands of lace in-between the sections, and look! My mother has sent a lot of lace, though none of it as fine as your Honiton. I've got these tiny pearl buttons we can use for a little fastening, well, what do you think, under the arm or down the front seams? And of course lace for the shoulder straps. Do you like them, Flora?"

"So lovely, Jane! I would never have thought of using hand-kerchiefs this way. Oh, what a good idea."

They began to sort through the assembled hankies, matching up plain ones with lengths of pretty lace. There was satin ribbon too, narrow widths in pale pink and blue, and Jane had the idea of threading it through some of the lace in order to create soft gathers to size the neck openings a little more precisely. They cut and then pieced their triangles together with the tiny stitches they'd learned at their mother's knees, silver thimbles aiding the work. They held up the camisoles to see the progress of their work. At one point, Flora held her camisole to her chest and danced under the shady tree while Jane watched, smiling.

Then, out of the blue: "You are looking remarkably well, Flora. It's almost as though you were in love . . ."

Flora felt heat rise from her chest to her face. Was it that obvious? She had thought of Gus as her own dear secret. Not that she wanted him to be a secret forever, but she could not think of how they might present their affection for each other to, say, her brother. Or her parents. She knew her brother respected Gus, but that would not necessarily translate to acceptance, would it? While still in England, preparing to come to Walhachin, she had heard that the colonies were classless, but she had not yet seen evidence of this. Miss Flowerdew would not allow men to enter her establishment unless they were dressed appropriately—Flora could not imagine Gus bothering to put on a collar or tie, though he must own such things. And there was an attitude in Walhachin not so different to what she'd left in Wiltshire, that labourers did not even really speak the same language as their employers, that women needed to be sheltered from such people, that a person's breeding was implicit in the care they took to remember such details as gloves and cards. Local ranchers were seldom invited to the monthly balls at the hall, there were mutterings about "trade" and "belowstairs" when certain names came up. Gus was apart from much of this. He was not Chinese, not Indian—those were obvious and had a place. His accent and vocabulary indicated an education, his table manners at the few events where labourers ate with their employers were curious for their excellence. No one could place him, quite. And he told Flora he liked it that way.

"Jane, is it so obvious?"

"Flora, you positively glow! Your skin, your eyes—you have the look of someone who has found out the secret of youth and beauty, which love surely provides. That little smile that plays upon your lips like a few bars of secret music. May I ask to whom you owe this bliss?"

"I will tell you, Jane, but you must promise me that you will say nothing about it, not even to Allan. There is someone special, yes, and I am not ashamed of him, but we are not yet ready to tell the world, not even George. Will you promise me, my dear and curious friend? Because quite honestly I am dying to tell someone."

Jane assented.

"It is Gus, Jane. Gus Alexander. He works for my brother from time to time, and of course other orchardists too. You will understand why it is a little difficult to make this known right now, but what you don't know perhaps is that Gus is not entirely what he appears. He comes from reputable people actually and has set out to make his own life. There is a past, of that I am certain. He is quite cut off from his parents who live in Victoria and whom he has not seen in seven years. But he is wonderful, and . . ."

Jane cut in. "Make no apologies, Flora. I have always liked Gus, as does Allan—did you know he'd worked here one summer, during haying? And Allan always felt there was no one like him for the breaking of young horses. Gus never called it 'breaking' though; he said he was gentling them, and watching a colt new to the saddle under him, it was easy to understand why. His voice, so calm, and he never wore spurs. Didn't need them. Horses responded to him gladly. And yes, you're right to acknowledge that there is a past. I think it involved debts of some sort. Something mysterious and rather dark. But there is also intelligence. He's extremely capable and, well, it must be said, he is devastatingly handsome!"

Flora blushed. She thought so too, of course. She remembered how she had gone quite faint at the sight of Gus's wrists, the undersides of his arms, that first day they had ridden together to the sad house in Skeetchestn where Grace was dying even as they let their horses lope along the Deadman River. Little did she know then that a man's arms were just a suggestion of his body unclothed, the beauty of the skin at the tops of his thighs, the curve of his buttocks. And that the beauty was accompanied by such pleasure as the man in turn admired the skin of the woman, touching it with tenderness. No one had told her of these things, prepared her for the way her body craved the weight of his body on top of her or the shape of it beneath her, ballast between her and the sky, a firm anchor between her and the earth.

"One problem, Jane, is my family. At least I think this will be a problem anyway. George may well like Gus as a worker but as a consort for his sister? I suspect not. And the fact that I have been meeting him secretly? Oh my goodness, George will be furious about that. But I am determined now to make my own decisions about my life, though I am still too nervous to tell any of my family that I am doing so! I am praying for more courage. Gus tells me I am developing a mind of my own. No wonder. If I mention a rule or an objection of George's to a particular thing, Gus encourages me to think about it for myself and break the rule if it suits me to do so. But not openly, not yet. So I will confess I've developed a taste for malt whisky. There. It feels good to say it!"

Jane smiled at Flora's confession. "Love does make us flout the rules a little, I think. And I, too, like the occasional glass of whisky. I've never understood why it is taken for granted that a woman would prefer Pimm's Cup. Ugh." She shivered extravagantly.

Gradually over the next few days, Flora found herself confiding more in Jane than she had ever done with a friend. A married woman, Jane could discreetly provide information to her friend, could answer questions Flora would never have asked her mother, a beloved but remote presence, even when they'd lived in the same house. Flora had vague but confused ideas about her body and its workings. Jane was able to set her straight on aspects of the monthly cycle, irregularities, and discomfort.

"It has always amazed me," said Jane, "that girls enter into womanhood without the simplest knowledge of any of this. Why weren't we taught these things in school? At least as important as the date Caesar crossed the Rubicon or Alps or whatever it was he did. I was lucky; my aunty Hortense is something of a suffragette, and she took it upon herself to tell me about reproduction.

She even had a little chart. I remember her quizzing me on, well, the ovaries. At our coming-out ball in Vancouver, one girl had her entire evening ruined for her when a red patch appeared on her white dress. She hadn't known to expect her monthlies, thought the whole thing was a terrible injury. And was of course mortified in front of a room of people, none of whom will ever forget. So an injury, I expect, is an accurate way to describe it."

Flora told Jane about her own coming-out season in London, spring and summer of 1909. She was one of a group of thirty girls presented to the King and Queen, all of them clad in white dresses with silk trains drifting behind them.

"Mine was Empire-line, with a draping I hoped would look Grecian. Silk, of course, and embroidered with seed pearls. I remember feeling grateful, when the dressmaker came to our house for fittings, that the season wasn't a few years earlier when my cousin was presented. Her dress was in the style of that year and made her look like an elaborate letter S."

"Did you feel a little like a sacrificial lamb, Flora, being dressed in white like a bride and paraded in front of that man? Our impression here in Canada was that he was something of a roué! There was talk even of mistresses—all those actresses!"

Flora laughed. "I didn't think that then. I didn't dare. It was just something we were groomed for, our season in London, where it was hoped we would meet the right young man and instantly become one of the hostesses behind the scene for the next round of girls. But I do see it now. My brothers were sent to school and expected to do something, even if it was the church, but I had a very casual series of governesses at home to teach me a little French, a little geometry, because of course I would marry and needed only to produce children and run a fine house."

"It was different here because my family couldn't afford governesses, so I went to school," said Jane. "And my mother wanted me to have more than she'd had, more possibilities."

"That's heartening, Jane. But you didn't have brothers, did you? It seems all the family hopes are invested in the young men.

But I did love to draw, and painted a little, and one of the tutors was very good at helping with lessons. My mother was pleased when I began to create designs for needlepoint. What I didn't know, to be quite honest, was how constrained my life was. I see that now, especially when I ride with Gus. These skies—well, I feel I can breathe in a way I never felt before. I don't remember noticing the skies before. Though there was one coming-out ball held in a house with a ceiling painted like an open sky, deep blue, with stars. The young girls in their gowns dancing like meadow flowers on slender stalks. And the King standing in his uniform. We were brought before him, as you say, like spring lambs."

"What was it like, meeting him? Them? Did he seem like the sort of mortal who might dally with an actress? And was she really as aloof as I imagine she was?"

"The King was quite fat, I remember, and yes, his Queen was aloof. She was lovely, though. And the whole thing was very quick—we were presented, they took our hands, mumbled a few words. She had an accent, of course, coming from Denmark. There were rumours among the young women, particularly those who lived in London and whose families were part of the King's set, rumours of his appetites, shall we call them?"

"What happened to your dress? Did you wear it again?"

"Oh, Jane, of course not. Did you ever wear yours again?"

Jane shook her head no.

Flora continued: "Mine was put into the wardrobe with all the other gowns, my mother's and my own, made for special occasions and never expected to be worn more than once. We kept them all the same, much as my father kept the trophies won by his horses and his prize water lilies. Proof of performance, I suppose. The shoes I did wear again, and the gloves with the beaded embroidery. No, the dress will be there still, at Watermeadows, beside a ball gown made for Mother for the presentation, cream silk, that one was, with black lace and jet bead, very extravagant, even for her. But not quite right for the next year and so put into the wardrobe with its sachets of cedar-wood and lavender to keep away the moths."

Then Flora was quiet, remembering the months that followed. The years. There were dances in London, and parties. A series of young men sized her up. She'd had no idea what to expect of courtship, but surely it had to be more than a clammy hand pressed to her back, discreet questions to determine what came with her. Land? Horses? A sizeable sum? She had not anticipated the stubborn voice that told her mother and father that she could not imagine a life with this one or that one. It was like another girl speaking, using courage Flora had no idea she possessed (but was in the process of finding again). Two years after her coming-out season, George was planning to come to Canada and Flora was still without a suitor, dangerously close to being considered too old—at nineteen!—to interest the young men with money, or prospects, or both. And perhaps a reputation for fussiness beyond what was reasonable. She was not quite a beauty, though she had a look that was lovely in profile, and wonderful hair. The men were eyeing the new crop of girls in London. And when she expressed an interest in joining George at Walhachin, there had been a collective sigh of relief. Already it had become known as a place where matches could be made. All those single men from good families, and so few suitable women.

EIGHT
August 1914

"Must you go?" she murmured against his shoulder. Her skin was flushed with sun and love; small droplets of sweat had collected behind her knees.

"Oh, yes, of course, Flora." He said it emphatically, as though there could be no question.

"'Of course?' I didn't think you were so fuelled by the promise of heroics as the rest of them." She turned so she wouldn't have to see his eyes.

He took her chin gently in his fingers and turned her face back to his. "Sweet Flora, it's not heroics. I don't have war fever. Absolutely not. And I'm not even convinced that any of us ought to go out of any kind of patriotism. The idea of this country means something different to me, I expect, than it does to the other men here at least, most of whom weren't born here. England calls to them as it never could to me. But I must go because it is my duty right now. I have shirked duty enough in the past to know that it is time that I paid attention to its demands."

He smiled at the young woman lying in his arms on a saddle blanket spread on warm grass in a little box canyon he had discovered. He brushed damp hair from her forehead, the delicate curls that had eased themselves out of her braided coronet. "You are so lovely. I will always remember you like this, even when we're old and grey together."

"Will we be, Gus? Old and grey together?" There were tears in her eyes. He touched them with his finger, and licked the salty taste. He kissed her.

"I will come back as soon as I can. I don't expect this to be a long war, no one does, and perhaps I'll even be home by Christmas. We could shock the community by appearing at a dance together, you in the obligatory gloves, I in a jacket and tie. I do own those things though I can't remember the last time I wore them. I expect the moths have been at the jacket—though being moth-eaten hasn't made a bit of difference to the nobs at the hall."

"I'll write to you every day," Flora told him, her hands on his forearms, his hands resting on the small of her naked back.

"I won't promise you daily letters in return, my love, because I don't know what is in store for me. But as often as I'm able to, I'll write. I expect there will be restrictions, perhaps even someone who will read every letter written by young men to their sweethearts in case vital secrets are being revealed. The secrets of the mess kitchens, the tents, the tin baths where we will be allowed to wash ourselves in a few inches of tepid water. I imagine there will be fleas."

They both laughed.

Gus continued. "We should have a code, shouldn't we, so you know if I am simply sitting in a camp eating and waiting or else on my way into the heat of battle. A line from Virgil perhaps?"

"You will have to write it down for me so I can compare. Your Latin is far superior to mine. Is there a bit about horses? I can always recognize *equus* when I see it. And now, too, *pressi lactis*, though perhaps horses are more appropriate to war."

"Something from the *Georgics*, then. Let me think. But before I think, may I adjust my arm? What you are doing with your hand is particularly fine."

Much later, after they had made love again in the privacy of grass and washed their bodies in the trickle of icy water entering the canyon from the main creek travelling down from the lakes on the Bonaparte Plateau to the Thompson River, after they had dressed and were tightening saddle girths and making sure Flora's hair was tidy, her clothing reasonably unrumpled, Gus turned to her over the back of Agate and said, suddenly, "*Sed nos immensum spatiis confecium aequor / et iam tempus equum fumantia solvere colla.* That will be it, Flora."

"And what does it mean? I recognize horses, of course, and something about distance, is it?"

"Well, let's see. Something like, 'But now, a huge space we have travelled / and time has come to uncollar our steaming horses.' When I send you this message, you will know that, hmmm, that . . . oh, please don't cry, Flora. I'll write it down for you, shall I?"

"Yes, I will memorize it so that I have it by heart at every instant. I'm sorry. I don't mean to be feeble. And now, speaking of collars, could you check to make sure I have no grass seeds on the back of my blouse? I would hate to be thought a woman who lies down in fields."

"I can't think of anything more appealing somehow. But here, let me just unthread this needlegrass from your sleeve. And now we should be on our way."

The box canyon became a favourite retreat. You could ride by it without noticing its entrance, a narrow gap between rocks, hidden by a hedge of Saskatoon bushes. Pushing aside the bushes, they would urge their horses through. The bushes sprang back, perfect camouflage. Once inside, it was like being in a room with a ceiling decorated with tumbling cloud. The creek for water, dry grass for a bed. Within its intimate space, they talked about everything, sharing details of their lives (though there was always some reserve on Gus's part regarding his life since leaving his family home), books they had read and loved ("When I read *Cranford*, I thought it amazing that a book about a quiet village in which nothing really happens could be so entrancing. It occurs to me that such a book could be written about Ashcroft, or Walhachin." "Maybe you will write it. As I recall, the narrator of *Cranford* is a young woman who has come to the village as a visitor . . . " "Oh, but I'm not a writer. I am keeping a journal, though, and perhaps when I am old and idle . . .")

The one problem was finding the proper excuse for Flora to ride off without arousing suspicion. She had her sketching and that was considered suitable, but generally her brother would encourage her to find someone to accompany her. Once the workload of the community increased in summer, with watering and fertilizing, her excursions were not so noticeable. And Gus found ways to absent himself too. Because he worked for many but for no one in particular, it could always be assumed that he was off on a job that took him away from Walhachin.

Within the box canyon's walls, wild baldhip roses and drifts of cinquefoil. Hawks nested at the cliff top and floated over the lovers like angels, their harsh call either blessing or warning. And once they woke from a brief nap to see the tracks of a rattlesnake that had passed close to their sleeping bodies, its scribble in the earth a text as mysterious as Sanskrit. And once after they had been absent from the canyon for some weeks, the stripped body of a deer that a cougar or a bear had brought to the canyon in secrecy for a long meal for itself and its young. All the flesh was gone; the ribs looked like the frame of a small boat, beached and ruined. Gus used his knife to remove the lower jaw from the skull, wanting it as a talisman to pack in his rucksack once the call came to travel overseas. He washed it in the little creek, rubbing at the remains of connective tissue with sand to scour the bone clean. One of the teeth was loose in its socket, ground down by the animal's diet of leaves and grass.

NINE
Late September 1914

A young woman dozed on a blanket under a tree in an orchard of apple-laden trees, her body cooler now that she'd loosened her bodice, removed her stockings. In the orchard it seemed as though everything might go on as usual—the apples picked, Wagoners, Jonathans, Spitzenbergs, Wealthys, and Rome Beauties finally come to maturity, loaded into bushel baskets, taken by cart to Pennies. Whatever happened in the distant world, the dogs would still bark as coyotes sidled too close to the chicken coops, sheets billowing in the wind, raising their cotton hems to the sky. Sage would release its scent to the brief rain, and oh, if she watched long enough, Gus might still ride between the trees to take her in his arm and murmur into her hair. Her face was hot. It was certain she carried a child.

Flora's workbasket was at her side and she took out a piece of linen, one of a set of a dozen napkins she had hemstitched and was now embroidering with a monogram in fine white-work, her initial F and the *A* for Augustus, married to the second A for the surname they would share once he came back to her. He had been gone a month, to Quebec with his regiment, which had been dissolved almost immediately upon arrival; most of the men had been absorbed into the 5th Battalion, but Gus had been invited to join men from a detachment of Rocky Mountain Rangers from Kamloops whom he'd known for a few years. There was also a connection, Flora was not quite certain of its details, with the Victoria Fusiliers, who were also part of this first British Columbia Regiment, the 7th Battalion.

She would not panic. Everyone said the war would not, could not, last long. George had gone too, leaving the house in her care and a detailed list of responsibilities to be divided among her, Mary, and the Chinese men who would be helping with the orchard. George had some concern about the flume but felt that enough able-bodied men, too old perhaps to go to war but certainly capable of maintaining the irrigation system, would ensure the continuity of water. For herself, Flora was willing to work hard, though how long she could depend on her energy and strength was a worry. Mary was pregnant again and came to work on her horse, her modest bulge usually concealed by an apron or the work pinafores that Flora left hanging for her behind the kitchen door.

The summer had gone on forever; that was how it seemed now. The flats above the river rippled with heat, and the willows along its banks trilled with kingbirds. Because of the settlement's altitude, evenings cooled off so that sleeping was pleasant in the screened rooms. Flora set up a bed for herself on the second-storey porch, draping it with a length of netting hung from a hook in the ceiling so she would not be troubled by mosquitoes in the early hours of the morning. She dreamed of meeting Gus among the trees, something she had done whenever possible. If she couldn't arrange to ride away, she'd walk to the farthest orchard grove, the one with tall tobacco plants between the rows of apple trees. In that long summer, she had taken to wearing as few underclothes as possible to make it easier to make love with him during their meetings. The first time he reached under her muslin skirt and realized she was bare-legged and clad only in a light envelope chemise, buttoned where it met between her legs, he laughed aloud. She loved his laugh. It held nothing back. And she, too, held nothing back on the days when they met among the trees and the tall grass, unbinding her hair and opening her mouth for his kisses. She had opened her mouth to his body too, each and every part, delighting in the textures upon her tongue—the rough skin of his knees, the velvet of his upper thigh. His shoulders tasted of salt. Who among her family and friends would have known this young woman, ardent and eager for the weight of one particular man upon her breasts? She had come to life, as plain trees quicken in spring, dressed in blossom and leaf.

The picnics with the other settlers had been lovely on the long hot summer afternoons after the men had departed. A wagon organized, food packed into baskets, one of the older men going on ahead by horseback to light a fire so that the children might roast potatoes in the coals. A small lake in the hills above the river might serve as a destination, or else the wagon would take the group to one of the gravel flats by the river, preferably one with shallows to allow for wading. Hampers were placed in the shadows cast by cottonwoods, paraffin stoves lit so urns of tea could be made, and beaded thermos flasks of lemonade were propped in the shallows of river or lake, protected by a small wall of stones. Children ran in the sunlight, their faces brown and freckled, while their mothers sat under parasols, some of them boldly removing their shoes.

Some families had returned to England, the husbands to regiments they were affiliated with in the home country, the families to wait out the war in familiar surroundings. They had been in such a hurry in August to return that some of them left entire households of furnishings, hopeful that the war would be finished by Christmas and they could return for the spring blossoms. Gus's horses were left in the care of a man who could not enlist due to persistent lung trouble. Flora would see them in the pasture, their lovely heads lifting as she gave them the whistle that Gus had taught her. Putting her face against Flight's neck was as close as she could get to the body of her beloved.

Mary was wiping the work table in the kitchen when Flora came in to pour herself a glass of water. She turned to Flora and met her eyes. In an instant, Flora realized that Mary knew of her condition. She dropped her glass on the floor and let out a small anguished cry. Mary put her cloth down and took Flora in her arms. There was a faint smell of smoke in her clothing, not unpleasant, and a firm support in her shoulders as Flora wept, then drew back to smile uncertainly. Mary continued to rub her neck, her shoulders, smoothing her hair with rough hands.

"How foolish you must think me, Mary. You've had enough babies to take it calmly, yet I am like one of the quail, silly and skittish. And for something as natural as having a baby."

"It will not be easy for you, Missus. I have Agrippa and he is not leaving for the war."

TEN
April 1962

Tessa's mother was feeding bark to the wood burner in the kitchen. "How is Miss Oakden?" she asked as she angled a particularly large piece of bark into the opening of the stove.

"She's fine. She sent matrimonial squares for the boys," Tessa replied, putting the package wrapped in waxed paper on the counter. "They got a bit squished because I rode my bike through the cemetery before I came home. What's for supper?"

"Macaroni and cheese. Your brothers have Little League, so we're eating later than usual. Set the table, please."

Tessa took the melmac plates from the cupboard and went to the dining room to put them around. The cloth was already laid; the napkins were kept on the sideboard, each in its own silver ring, gifts from their grandmother in New Brunswick. Once a week the napkins were washed when Tessa's mother did the laundry in the basement where the washing machine was set up beside two deep sinks of soapstone. When Tessa helped her mother feed the sheets through the wringer, she always took care to keep her fingers away from the rollers because a boy (a friend of a friend of a friend) had his arm drawn in by mistake. His bones were all crushed and never healed properly. That boy's hand still hung by his side, useless, all because he hadn't been careful enough. On the days when laundry was done, Tessa loved going to bed because she would have a fresh top sheet and pillowcase, both of them smelling of the wind. Last week's top sheet would have been shaken outdoors and then carefully tucked over the mattress to act as the bottom. You never got two fresh sheets unless you had an accident. Once, Tessa had dreamed she was trying to get to a toilet; in a panic, she kept trying every door to discover which one opened to the bathroom; each led to a hall, a broom closet, the stairwell to the basement. When she finally found the right door and sat on the toilet, the relief as she peed was wonderful. Waking, she'd wondered at first why her bed was damp. Then, in horror, she remembered her dream. She quickly got up, stripped her bed and took the sheets downstairs to pile by the washing machine, her pyjamas tucked inside them. She entered the kitchen, fully dressed though it was not yet seven, the time her mother usually called her to get up.

"I've already taken my sheets down," she told her mother, "so you won't have to do it."

"But, honey, this isn't washing day!" her mother exclaimed, starting to say something else, then thinking better of it. Tessa realized later that her mother must've known she'd peed her bed but didn't get angry with her. But she herself worried that it might happen again, that she might become a bed-wetter—a girl in her school was teased for this very reason and couldn't go to Brownie camp because she would pee her sleeping bag and there weren't washing facilities to deal with the accident. After her own accident, Tessa would wake herself up early to make sure her bed was dry. She began to swish only a tiny bit of water in her mouth after brushing her teeth in case the glass of water she usually drank at bedtime was the reason she had peed her bed. But it didn't happen again. Still, it was something to remember and worry over.

Once she'd set the table, she went to the window looking out onto Eberts Street. The sky was deep blue with pink across the horizon. The trees stood out like black paper cutouts. On Bushby Street, Tessa could see the headlights of a car illuminating the road. The car proceeded so slowly that it seemed not to be moving at all. Perhaps there was a man driving and a woman watching for a particular address, her eyes squinting into the dusk to make out the numbers on the front of a house. The park across the road stood empty, its swings hanging still, the ball diamond waiting. In just five weeks, the evenings would be light enough for all the neighbourhood children to gather together in the park to decide on a game—to divide into sides if there were enough of them for baseball, hide-and-seek, daredevil on the swings. Tessa loved hide-and-seek the best, especially when it got to be dusk and long shadows were cast across the park by the monkey puzzle trees and the cedars. Then a girl could flatten herself against a shadow and not be seen until the seeker was almost on top of her (this happened once and she never forgot, it was that thrilling), then two girls could hide in scraggly privet bushes between the park and the backyard of a house angling over from Bushby Street, the smell of the privet bitter and sharp.

"We're starved! When's supper?"

Tessa's brothers, Mick and Teddy, bounded in. They were eleven and nine, loud and sweaty, having ridden their bikes from the school field where ball practice was held on spring afternoons. Their mother directed them to change their clothes and wash their hands. Supper was ready. It would just be the four of them tonight as their father had to work late at the Experimental Farm.

"Do you have a game on the weekend?" she asked, spooning macaroni and cheese onto each plate and adding a helping of salad. "Mick, will you pour milk, please? And carefully. I mean it. This is a clean tablecloth."

"We play View Royal. Their field. Can Dad take us? And maybe Petey and John too?"

"We'll see."

After supper, Mick and Teddy asked if they could go out to play with the other kids and were told yes, but to be back by eight.

"Are you going with them, Tessa?" asked their mother, beginning to wash the supper dishes in the old aluminium pan.

"They didn't ask me. But can I go across the road?"

Her mother nodded, and Tessa ran to put on her old runners. She also put her flashlight in her back pocket as it was dark in the shadows away from the streetlights. She was thinking of water, of the stream running underground through Bushby Park, meeting another arm of it coming down through the cemetery, just beyond the park, then trickling into the sea below the breakwater. Or this is what she had worked out so far. Maybe she could make a map of its route. They were learning about maps at school, and she liked figuring out things she knew in real life from the way they appeared on maps—the roads, the parks, one map even showing the Experimental Farm on Saanich Peninsula, indicated by a little row of trees. You couldn't see everything, of course, not the houses and the other buildings, not the cars on the Pat Bay Highway, or the fences, or the horses leaning over their rails at the farm across from Elk Lake. But you could imagine yourself here, enroute, matching the names on the map to the real places. You could almost imagine a train on the little tracks on the map that led up the Island to Nanaimo or boats in the expanses of water.

She lowered her body to the grass in the far corner of the park, checking for her flashlight first to make sure it was at the ready. Tall boards separated park from yards, and mint crept from the garden on the other side of the boards to flourish in the damp earth. This must be the stream, thought Tessa, this must be where it is underground because the grass is always wet here. Ruefully she rubbed at the damp patch on her dungarees. Her mother would not be happy; she'd only worn these pants for a day or two and already they were soiled. She thrust her head into the mint to listen.

Yes, she could almost hear the water. Or was it her own blood rushing around in her head? She listened. Water, she thought. And then was certain—it was gurgling and ringing. How far from the mint could she lie and still hear it? She backed up, on her knees, and then pressed her ear to the ground. It was like hearing rain, from a distance, a dripping, an echoing. She kept backing up, still listening, still hearing the water in its course under the park. All those days when the park had been crowded with children playing ball, hiding in the bushes, running races back and forth across the grass, a stream had been running under their feet. When Ricky Anderson pumped his swing higher and higher until it flipped over the bar from which the row of swings were suspended, Ricky falling with a great shout and a flailing of arms to the cement underneath and cracking his head open (you could still see the blood stain, a faint rust mark on the cement), the stream trickled underneath as the children screamed and various parents ran to help. It was something to think about, how water just kept on doing what it had always done, no matter the activity around it. And Tessa dug her fingers into the damp soil, feeling the tough stolons of mint criss-crossing just under the surface, eager to spread. She wondered if they followed the route of the creek, the small nubs of stems emerging from the soil like road signs, leaves unfurling, flagging the course of a hidden waterway.

Riding a bike along the quiet lanes in the cemetery, she thought about the fact that underneath the grass and tree roots were bodies, some of them skeletons by now, and the more recent burials still recognizable as people. Mick and Teddy knew more about this than she did, and they said worms and bugs ate the flesh until only bones were left. It took longer now that people were buried in special coffins, but that was what happened. As though to prove it, they buried two of Mick's hamsters—both died within three days of each other, of old age—in the backyard, one in a cigar box and one just wrapped in Kleenex. Four months later they dug them up. Most of the hamster wrapped in Kleenex was rotten, its skin and fur gone, with maggots everywhere, and most of the one in the cigar box was still in quite good condition, though the smell made Tessa throw up by the compost heap. They had conducted a little run of burials then—birds that had broken their necks flying into the window, a squirrel run over near the breakwater, jellyfish washed to shore and stranded in the sun. Even Tessa had been buried in the sand under the monumental works, her head sticking out so she could breathe.

Her brothers told her she would have to stay there until she died. She remained perfectly still, trying not to worry. She could hear her heart thumping through the sand, her pulse racing in her neck in time to her heart. Was it possible to be buried alive, in sand or in a coffin? How long would it take to die? Panic began in her chest, the flutter of her heart racing. Her feet felt numb. She had to pee. She could hear the men in the building above her and supposed if she screamed, someone would come down and help her. But then children might be forbidden to play in the monumental yard. Or her mother might be told and then she would be in big trouble. Just when she thought she would have to give up and pee into the sand (which had already begun to smell of cat), she heard her brothers laughing as they returned for her, Teddy digging her out with a piece of board and Mick pulling her by the arms until she stood up, her knees shaking. They knew she wouldn't tell.

Going back to the house with the stream still ringing in her ears, Tessa saw Miss Oakden's porch light shining through the dusk. Hers was one of the houses backing onto the park, though not close to the route Tessa thought the stream must follow on its way to Ross Bay. She had never been in that backyard, but even in the falling light she could see through the space between the boards that there was a small pool with some potted plants around it and something growing right in the pool itself, large shiny leaves spreading over the surface of the water. They caught the light from the kitchen window, where Tessa could see Miss Oakden washing dishes, looking up occasionally from the sink to gaze out at the gathering dusk. She looked sad. As she leaned against the fence, Tessa discovered there was a loose board. By working it a little on its nail, she found it could be moved aside like a shutter to make an opening wide enough for a skinny girl like herself to enter the yard. She would ask Miss Oakden first, but this special gate would eliminate the need to walk around the block if she were to visit her friend. It could be their secret. And she wanted to see the pool the next time she visited.

PART TWO
Memorial Crescent, Fairfield

ELEVEN
1962

Tessa begged a large sheet of chart paper from her teacher, Mrs. Barrett, and found an area in the basement at home where she could spread it out, held down at each corner by a brick. She was also allowed to bring home one of the blue-covered classroom atlases. She struggled to understand some of the explanations: contours, projections (there was that Mercator guy again); but some of it was really interesting. A map could show crops, populations, zones for climate and agriculture and mining. Some of this was helpful. Tessa laboured over scale until she understood that it was a way to show how the real distances between places or objects could be presented in a relative way by using a ratio. They had learned about ratio at school, so it was a matter of thinking about things above and below a line. If she kept that in mind, it was easier to imagine the distance between her street and the Cross of Sacrifice in inches instead of in yards or miles.

Tessa tried to think of the best way to begin her map, to include as much as she could. She wanted to trace the route of the buried streams, position her favourite graves at the cemetery, some of the trees she loved best (the Atlas cedar with its forty-seven trunks, of course, and some pines—one her father said was a red Japanese pine and another, from the Himalayan Mountains). She looked both places up in her borrowed atlas and realized how far the trees were from their native soil and air. She wanted to include her street, and May Street, and Memorial Crescent where Miss Oakden lived. Also the Moss Rocks, and

Moss Street too because that was the way she usually walked to school, and Fairfield Road because her classroom in the Annex looked onto it. The old turreted house on the corner of May and Memorial. She knew there would have to be a legend; she would need to work out a scheme for this before she began to draw the map.

Among the books on the shelves in the dining room she found one with old maps. She particularly liked the maps drawn by Samuel de Champlain. He included little drawings of fish and mammals, mountains, trees, sailing ships in the oceans, and even crops. This was so much more interesting than the usual maps that divided Canada into provinces with broken lines, stars for the capital cities, and elevation shown by colour with a legend explaining how each five hundred feet above sea level shaded from green through orange to pink, with three shades of blue below sea level. She decided that de Champlain was a person to learn from when it came to making maps.

Tessa made a pad of old burlap potato sacks and lay on her stomach on the cold basement floor to plan her project. Even though she felt such urgency inside herself to begin, she chewed indecisively on the end of her pencil. Finally she decided to lightly sketch in certain areas on her map, to mark out the territory. There was no point in going beyond the cemetery, past where the Cross of Sacrifice was, that far corner near where Hollywood Crescent began its meandering to Gonzales Bay. Tessa's mother sometimes walked with the children to the Gonzales beach on hot summer days, but the streets and houses between Eberts and that beach were like a foreign country. Tessa knew no one living there; the children from those streets attended another school. This map was about her own street, her route to school, the monumental works, and the graves. And underneath it all, the buried streams. So she carefully made a line around a patch of white paper, taking up about a third of the entire area. This would be the cemetery. Fairfield Road would be the top boundary. But what about compass details? She would have to borrow her brother's Cub compass and take her bearings the next time she went over on her bike. It would be a kind of orienteering, wouldn't it?

TWELVE
December 1914

The train was late. Flora stood on the platform at Pennies with her valise and trunk beside her. She tucked her scarf in a little more snugly; the December wind was cold, coming off the bench above the river and carrying sand in it. Flora's cheeks stung—from wind, and sand, and tears. She had never felt so uncertain about anything in her life.

She hadn't heard from Gus for a month. A letter had arrived from England in late October, from Salisbury. She was surprised to learn how close he was to her family home at Watermeadows. She thought about asking her parents to have him come to stay but then realized how many questions that would cause and how few could be answered. Best to wait, perhaps, and take him there herself, a ring upon her left hand.

Letter Three: *We are in the shadow of the great Stonehenge,* he wrote. *But the gods who guard those stones have done nothing about the weather. It was lovely when we first arrived but has rained ever since. And I've never seen anything like the rain here. Our tents leak, there is talk of huts but nothing has come of it yet, and the horses, well, I feel for them most of all. Mud fever, dreadful problems with their feet . . . It is hard to train in mud. And Flora, you've never seen mud like this. It sucks your boots off! And yet we are told we are not disciplined enough and require serious drilling to make real soldiers of us. Ha.*

She wrote back to tell him of the unborn child she carried within her body, and a reassuring letter had come back very quickly to say she should not worry, he would do what he could, and if she needed to leave the community, she should think of his family home as a place of refuge. He would write to tell them to expect a letter from her, or some sort of contact, and he trusted they would write to her. He was now at a camp called Lark Hill and he said it was utterly bereft of larks. Instead, the tents and a few huts the men lived in were surrounded by mud. There was a lot of illness, which he had, until then, avoided, though many men had already died. They had yet to cross the English Channel. The King had inspected their regiment. Training went well. The weather was terrible and the food barely edible.

But then no other word. Each day she'd go to the post office. There were letters from her parents, a catalogue or two, invoices for fertilizers and agricultural equipment, but no letter from Gus. And she had begun to receive looks from women in the townsite, pointed looks at her expanding waistline (it was no longer possible to flatten her stomach with binding under her skirts). Invitations to join the other women for whist or knitting bees—socks were particularly needed among the troops and the women prided themselves on the quality and abundance of their socks—ceased.

And then she had been cut from inclusion in any social event, shunned in the post office as though she were invisible. A comment had been made, in a mocking voice, as she walked away from a fruitless quest for a letter—"Well, if we come to grief, I am certain it will not be the fault of Mary"—and she learned how spite could be carried in a heart like a wasp in a hidden place, ready to sting when least expected. There was no one Flora could turn to with her secret, which was not a secret any longer, but which had a story, a history, and she hoped a future. Jane McIntyre might have listened and comforted, but Jane and Allan were on an extended trip to San Francisco, in part to provide Jane with a chance to recover her health. And Flora could not present such awkward, ill-timed proof of her ability to both conceive and carry a child to her friend, weakened by another miscarriage.

Flight and Agate stood by the fence, waiting for their master, their coats ungroomed and their wise eyes patient. *But now, a huge*

space we have travelled / and time has come to uncollar our steaming horses.
The lines had begun to make a queer kind of sense, these horses bare of any tack, their saddles forgotten, standing by the fence listening for their master, the distance between Lark Hill and Walhachin and the far fields of France unfathomable.

Just when Flora had become so desperate that she was sleepless with anxiety, Mary made a suggestion.

"The Sisters might help, Missus. Where my brothers and I went to school, in Kamloops, at Le Roux Point. We write sometimes. They might help."

Flora was moved that Mary was thinking of her situation. "Thank you, Mary. It's so close though, Kamloops. I wonder if I might not be better off going farther away from here. I can't bear being shunned, and so many of the people living here are in Kamloops regularly."

"The Sisters have another place too. In Victoria. I have a letter with both addresses. Will I give it to you? I believe Gus Alexander's family is in Victoria."

Flora grasped at the small hope that the nuns might take her in, give her some tasks to pay for her keep. The money her parents sent, the clothing allowance, would surely cease when they learned of her condition, though a small trust from her grandfather would continue, she thought. A letter was sent to the nuns, and they replied that she should come and they would see what might be done. There was a home in Victoria for women who found themselves in Flora's position and inquiries would be made on her behalf. Something about this did not sit right with Flora, but she put it out of mind, reasoning that now she had a plan, a destination, and she would work out the details. Mary agreed to forward letters and of course Flora would let Gus know as soon as she had a new mailing address.

The train finally appeared on the rails to the east of Pennies. Flora checked her pocketbook again to make sure of her small amount of money and the letter with the directions to the convent. She had as well the address for Gus's parents' home written on a card. Dr. and Mrs. Robert Alexander, St. Charles Street, Victoria. She had been expecting a letter from them in response to the letter she had written to tell them she was coming to Victoria, but nothing had arrived. She would contact them, she thought, once she was settled into some kind of home.

She was lucky to have a seat to herself, on the left side of the train, where she sat pressing her face to the glass to watch the progress of the river down below. Everything looked so cold—the rock slopes, the grey hills, singular pines, the turbulent river. Flora nestled farther into her coat, moved her fingers in their gloves to increase circulation. She had a flask of sweet tea and a packet of sandwiches, made for her by Mary.

At Lytton the train stopped to take on more passengers. Flora had never been in the small town before. When the conductor suggested that those on the train might want to stretch their legs—the train would be stopped for an hour—she adjusted her scarf securely around her neck, pulled her cloche low over her hair, and disembarked to see what might be seen.

An Indian woman was sitting on the train platform, surrounded by baskets. Flora stopped to look at them. The woman was bundled in layers of sweaters over a woollen skirt, a kerchief wrapped around her head and tied at the back, gypsy-style. She smiled up at Flora.

"Your baskets are beautiful," Flora commented. "Did you make them all?"

"Yes," the woman replied, vigorously nodding. "All mine."

Flora knelt, with some difficulty, to handle a spruce-root basket with an intricate rim. It had leather straps so it could be worn on the back, and it was worked with a detailed design of some darker fibre. Holding the basket up to her face, Flora inhaled its odours of tree and dried bark and a dark winy smell.

"For berries," the woman explained.

That explained the straps, the faint stains on the interior. The basket was beautifully made, the woven work tight and smooth.

Flora knew she had to have it and reached into her reticule for her money. She had no idea what to offer but simply held coins in her hand and let the woman choose. What she took did not seem enough. The woman's hands were gnarled and leathery and cold—when she reached into Flora's palm to take the money, her fingers were icy. On impulse Flora removed her gloves and placed them in the woman's hands, saying, "I'd like you to have something of mine too." The woman smiled and took a small grass basket from her collection, imbricated with chevrons of a deep red reed. She tucked it into the larger berry basket, and the two women nodded at each other with satisfaction. The Indian woman then placed her hands on Flora's stomach like a blessing, nodding and smiling with such approval that a warmth began to spread through Flora's body.

Flora walked the main street of Lytton where four thin dogs watched her from the step of the gracious hotel. A hospital, a store, a new-looking Catholic church (St. Ann's, was this a portent? wondered Flora), some tidy houses. There was a place she could stand and watch the two rivers converge, the clear Thompson meeting the murky Fraser—a man walking by with a small boy held firmly by the hand told her which river was which—and then the combined waters gathering force for their long run down to the sea. Flora had grown to love the Thompson River during her residence at Walhachin, its sinuous muscular rope winding down below the house, its scent in all weathers. There was a place where the children of the settlement bathed in summer; a breakwater of large boulders had been constructed to create a deep quiet pool. Flora bathed there too at dusk on summer evenings when the silver flies made a screen she would pass through before lowering her body into the flinty water. Once, she had seen a strange creature coming down from the rocky shore to the pool; when she'd watched it for a while, she decided it must be a toad. Though a toad did not entirely make sense for the desert landscape. Asking someone later had produced the information that it had probably been a spadefooted toad and that it was not uncommon to see them after sunset when they left their cool underground holes—they dug these themselves with their curiously shaped feet—to drink in the safety of the dark.

Flora leaned over the fence that ran a distance along the bench to see how long the Thompson kept its own riverness, a colour resembling old bottle glass, before being lost; its lighter water was visible for a time and then she could see only the dark rush of the Fraser River.

Back on the train, still with a group of seats to herself, Flora settled in for the run down to Yale. She reached for the basket she had placed on the empty seat beside her, examining its fine work, the imbrication like crewel embroidery, and then she took the small basket out of the larger one to look at it. She removed the lid and peered inside. To her surprise, there was a tiny pair of fur shoes within.

She held the little shoes in the palm of her left hand and brought them to her cheek. She wondered if the soft fur was rabbit. They smelled smoky, with a faint whiff of dried grass. There were ties of sinew to tighten or loosen the fit; attached to these were opaque beads that she realized were made of quills. She tucked the shoes back into their basket and wiped a tear from her eye. How odd, she thought, that the first thing she acquired for her child's layette was a pair of shoes made from the body of a wild animal. And yet so soft, so warm to the touch. Grace would have worn shoes like this, she thought, and remembered again the weight of the child against her shoulder, the dampness of her feverish cheek.

Flora took out a bag of handwork she had prepared for the long train ride to Vancouver and then the steamship across to Victoria. She was still working on her dinner napkins. She had finished three of them; they were folded in the bottom of the cloth bag in which she also kept skeins of silk floss, a pair of golden scissors shaped like a crane whose long beak snipped the delicate remnants of floss, and a little wooden case for her needles. She stitched quietly while glancing up from time to time to watch the landscape pass, the flinty slopes above Lytton becoming more verdant as the train approached Alexandria and Yale, though it was December. She supposed these were evergreens she was seeing out the window. The lamps in the train flickered as they passed through the dark tunnels, and Flora finally put her handwork away, on impulse tucking her cloth bag into the berry basket.

She fell into a reverie, head back on the plush rise. So many matters to think about, to settle in her mind. What would she tell her parents? It was only a matter of time before they'd hear she had left Walhachin in disgrace. Someone at a hunt meet or the grouse season in Scotland or at a garden party in Pewsey might say something that would announce to all present that Flora Oakden had brought shame upon her family. To pre-empt this, however briefly, she had sent a telegram saying she was going to Victoria by train on a matter of business. But her parents knew Charles Paget, the Marquis of Anglesey, and surely their paths would cross now that he was back in Wales. They also had other connections with Walhachin. Only a matter of time.

Certain families had already returned to England at the outset of the war, thinking it best to wait things out with relations and the security of the King nearby. Those families did not really think Canada a civilized country, not quite, despite Miss Flowerdew's pretty sitting room, the presence of the famous Paderewski piano in the community hall, the golf games and the polo matches on the Thompson bench. Walhachin might be a small pocket of decorum in a dusty landscape, but it was a landscape populated by Indians and farmers who did not know how to hold a teacup.

As Flora dozed, she felt again the warmth of the Indian woman's hands on her abdomen, assurance that she carried a gift worth blessing. Warmth penetrated her body, despite the chilly draft whistling around the windows of the compartment. She woke, held still in the comfort of that touch, and she poured herself a mug of tea from her flask, tea prepared for her by Mary.

It seemed so long ago now, so far away. Mary had said that the nuns might arrange a home for the child, once born, and that Flora could return to Walhachin again. This happened occasionally with Indian girls who had got themselves into trouble without marriage. It was especially possible if the father of the child was white. Sometimes a child might even be taken by the man's extended family, particularly if it was a little boy. The girls would go back to their villages, emptied of disgrace. They might eventually marry. Or else they'd find work as cleaning women or hops pickers or processing fish in the canneries on the coast.

But one thing was becoming clear to Flora, as though sleeping in the moving train had allowed for a clarity she could not discover in her own bed under George's roof: she decided she would try to find her own way in Victoria. The farther she travelled from Walhachin, the less she felt she should conceal her condition or feel shame for the child she carried in her body. She and Gus had loved each other, loved each other still (she believed this), though letters had ceased to come (there was surely a reason) and marriage had not actually been spoken of in the soft grass of the orchards, the fragrant boughs in the Back Valley cabin, the sanctuary of their box canyon with its ceiling of blue. The thought of staying in a convent no longer seemed like an ideal solution. And Gus's parents had not replied to her letter. Perhaps she would make contact with both the nuns and the Alexanders; they might be able to help her find work of some sort. But she did not want to be hidden away like a shameful secret. Her baby, conceived in love under trees, in warm orchard grass, was something to welcome and cherish. As though to confirm her new confidence, she felt a flutter of tiny feet against the walls of her womb. She tried to think of other women in her situation—she supposed *fallen* was the term—and could only bring to mind one serving girl at Watermeadows who had been seduced by a gardener who had then refused to marry her. Both had been dismissed by Flora's father, the girl with a small cheque and the man with a good reference.

THIRTEEN
Late 1914

The new CPR terminal in Vancouver almost overwhelmed her with its hubbub. She must have looked lost because she was quickly taken in hand by a helpful man who determined she could board a steamer that very day to Victoria—"Very timely, miss. A three-hour journey is all it will be!"—and he arranged the transfer of her trunk and assorted bags. Flora could not afford a stateroom so she sat in a lounge on a rattan chair, drinking tea and watching small islands pass by the windows, some of them wreathed in mist. She discouraged conversation by keeping her eyes focused on the windows or her teacup. She didn't want the necessity of explanation.

Stepping onto Wharf Street with a boy trundling her baggage on a handcart behind her, Flora stopped to get her bearings. So this was Victoria! Named for the late Queen (Flora's father's brother had been decorated by that Queen for valour in the Boer War), its streets clean and quiet. She was directed to the Empress Hotel after a phone call ensured that a room was available; the boy pushed her baggage down the causeway and across to the hotel's generous stairs. They were met by a hotel bellhop who transferred her trunk and valises to a trolley grandly bearing the hotel's insignia. She pressed a few coins into the boy's hand before he took his handcart back to await another traveller.

Her room was small but comfortable, with a view of the Inner Harbour and beyond. She stood in the window and looked out at the steamers, the bridge just visible. The legislative buildings were the most impressive part of the view, taking up one entire end of the harbour.

Flora spent an hour going over her finances a day later. With her small trust fund she could just about survive if she bought no new clothes and found somewhere to live where she could prepare her own meals. Her calculations led Flora to a discreet conversation with the woman who ran the hotel tea room. The woman poured Flora another cup of India tea from a Spode pot and they chatted for some time about England, discovering shared touchstones—china patterns (Flora's cousin owned a set of the Spode), Salisbury Cathedral, and certain areas of wild grassy Dartmoor covered in spring with pheasant's eye narcissi. She was directed to a house on Memorial Crescent where a widow fallen on difficult times took in lodgers. At Flora's request, the hotel clerk called ahead to alert the widow to her arrival.

Flora found her way to Fairfield, then Memorial Crescent. The house, directly across from a cemetery gate, was lovely—a low pink-shingled building with trellises surrounding it and a big orange cat on the picket fence who greeted Flora with so much enthusiasm that she felt her eyes prickle with tears.

"My dear, I see Rufous has greeted you. I am Ann Ogilvie. Welcome to Hollyhock Cottage."

It was a soft Scottish voice. Flora felt two hands clasp her own between them and saw two bright blue eyes smile into hers. Mrs. Ogilvie was a woman in her middle years, fair-haired and sturdy. She wore a high-necked blouse garnished with a large cameo at her throat, with a paisley shawl around her shoulders. She led Flora into a parlour where a warm fire burned in the grate and a low table was set with tea things. Rufous had followed them into the house and wrapped himself around Flora's ankles, purring so loudly that both women laughed.

"A cat is never shy about its affections. And generally they are very good at assessing character as well . . ." She looked at Flora with a smile. "You must tell me where you've come from while I pour you a cup of tea. Two lumps?" She paused with the silver tongs until Flora nodded.

"I wonder if you know of Walhachin . . ." Flora began.

"I do indeed. The man who designed most of the houses, Bert Footner, was in the same regiment as my late husband. They were in South Africa together, though Phillip, my husband, was lost at Paardeberg and Bert went on to design bridges, I believe it was, in the Sudan after the war was finished. There is occasionally news of the other men and I'd heard about Bert's new project. But what on earth led you to Walhachin? I am not wrong in placing you in the West Country?"

"What an ear you have for accents! Wiltshire, in fact. My family home is Winsley, near Bradford-on-Avon." And Flora told her about her brother, their orchard, and then how almost all the young men had rushed to enlist as soon as war was declared. With eyes downcast, she told of her sweetheart, among the men gone with the 31st British Columbia Horse.

"Forgive me for saying this so soon, but you are expecting a child."

Flora felt her face go warm. "Yes, I am. Sometime late this spring. Before I knew it to be the case, my sweetheart left with his regiment and we never married, although I fully expect us to when he returns."

She paused. But had to say it. "I would understand if you did not want to have me live in your home."

Ann Ogilvie looked at her appraisingly. "I will tell you frankly that it will not be easy for you in Victoria, but you will not find me to be a harsh judge in this. I lost my husband so soon into our marriage that we hadn't yet had children and I am left with such sadness that nothing of him continues with me apart from memories. A child would have been a solace, though difficult to raise alone, on a limited income. As it is, I have memories and photographs, as though they could ever be enough . . ." She gestured at the photographs that covered the mantel, the small tables at either end of the large rose-coloured sofa. Flora leaned to look more closely at the ones on the mantel. A tall man in regimental uniform mounted on a fine dark horse. A garden with the same man seated on a wicker chair, holding a teacup, plate balanced on one knee. A wedding photograph, a younger Ann Ogilvie in a pretty dress and the tall man in formalwear, smiling for the camera as they paused on the steps of a church.

"Let me show you the room I have available." Ann Ogilvie led the way down a hall hung with striped wallpaper to a room facing the back garden. It had a bay window with a seat made cozy by chintz pillows. A brass bed, a dressing table, a high oak chiffonier—seeing the Axminster carpet on the white-painted floorboards, Flora was reminded of her room at Watermeadows.

"This is lovely," Flora murmured as she touched the quilt, Dresden plates pieced with flowered cottons. She looked out the window to see a wintry garden, trees bare of leaves but a few of them hung with suet bags. Chickadees darted among the branches. Turning to her hostess, she asked, "Are you certain you want me here, knowing now that I am going to have a child? And knowing nothing about me?" And she held her breath while she waited for the answer.

Ann Ogilvie's response was to take Flora by her arm and gently lower her to the window seat against the pillows. "It will not be easy for you, my dear, but I've said I will not judge you. You need a friend, I think, and a home. Like Rufous, I am inclined to trust my first impressions. And to tell you the truth, I am a little tired of hearing all the glory talk of the war right now. The IODE meetings to knit socks and to utter platitudes are sickening to me. I suspect there will be fewer invitations with you under my roof—I did tell you I was going to be honest!—and although I assure you this is not why I am offering you the room, I will be quite happy to absent myself from those meetings."

Flora's face registered surprise so Ann continued. "I know I tend to get a little shrill on the topic of war, the way men rush to them and those of us at home wave the flag and how a few years later, there is another war, the flags waving again, and far too many men slaughtered in the wake. I would rather knit small bonnets and blankets."

"I think men see it as their obligation to serve their King," Flora said uncertainly, a little shocked to hear someone speak so bitterly. After Gus's declaration of duty, and the bunting all around the post office in Walhachin, and everywhere she'd looked here too, Flora thought war was a given expectation for men in general and certainly Englishmen most of all. The men of Walhachin had hastened away as if their lives depended upon their prompt response, as if God himself were watching to see how quickly they rose to their responsibility to King and country.

"Ah, but will their King actually fight? I doubt that, my dear. Nor will the grandees who have decided this thing must happen. Generals tend to settle themselves in some safe, comfortable place and consult maps, never missing a meal. But I know my feelings are not the norm so I will bite my tongue, for now in any case, and tell you how much I hope you will take my back bedroom and live in my house!" She smiled an open, generous smile and led Flora back to the sitting room.

It seemed almost too perfect. But they quickly agreed on seventeen dollars a month for the room and for meals, which Flora understood she would help to prepare. Then the two women had more tea and made arrangements for Flora to come to join the household the next day.

"Will you tell me about those beautiful stones on your fireplace hearth?" Flora asked, looking at four large stones arranged on the slate, one of them like an orange crystal, with chunks of something else within it.

Ann smiled and bent to the hearth, taking up two in her hands. "This one is gypsum," she said, holding out the orange crystal for Flora to examine. "Look at the fossils in it. See, a scallop shell and there, just at the edge, a complete ammonite."

Flora held its weight in her hands, turning it over to see the fossils. She'd seen them in rock before but nothing like this rich orange, shot through with limestone. The ammonite looked like a small sleeping creature in the stone. It reminded Flora of amber beads her mother wore sometimes, several of them containing tiny insects.

Ann handed her another rock, this one polished and heavy. "If you look closely, you can see a segment of fish scales and a tiny bone. Just there."

"They're so lovely. Did you find them here?"

Ann was quiet for a few moments, holding the gypsum to her heart. "No, they come from your part of the world, actually. From Blue Anchor, near Watchet, on the Somerset coast. Phillip and I went there for our honeymoon—an aunt of his had a cottage that we borrowed—and we spent most of our days on the beaches and under the cliffs, amazed at the sheer number of fossils there. I remember our baggage being loaded onto the train when we went back to London and the porter saying, 'Very heavy, Miss. Do ye have rocks in 'er or summat?' They've accompanied me wherever I've gone."

Deciding to save carfare, Flora walked back to the Empress Hotel. Along May Street to Cook Street, then down Fort: Victoria was a pretty town, though Cook Street seemed very much in transition. Obviously there had been farms along the street. A few fenced pastures remained, and marshy areas with the remnants of skunk cabbage, their fleshy leaves broken by frost, bordered the road. But now newly built houses were everywhere, Tudor facades and stucco, new and clean on their mucky lots. Little tea rooms and shops materialized as Flora walked down Fort Street. Open spaces with surveying stakes showed that change was in the air.

"Will she have you?" asked the woman in the tea room at the Empress Hotel, not unkindly, as she poured steaming tea into those delicate Spode cups the colour of eggshells. And Flora was able to tell her yes, realizing that the woman had known all along of her condition, her situation (her fingers bare of rings, the absence of a husband's name), that Ann Ogilvie might not be the person to whom every young woman could be sent.

Waking a few days later, her first morning in the white-floored room, Flora was surprised to hear singing. She wondered if she was dreaming. She lay in her flowered bed hearing scales and arpeggios as someone, Ann Ogilvie almost certainly, warmed up her voice. Up and down the scale, to aye, and then to ah, and then to oh, and to ee, stopping and repeating. Then the voice began to sing a piece that Flora remembered from a concert at the Albert Hall on a trip to London during her coming-out: surely this was Handel? The recitativa "Frondi tenere" from *Serses*, boldly sung, and then the beautiful aria about a plane tree's shade? "'Ombra mai fu, di vegetabile . . .'" The voice was lovely, reaching the highest notes of the aria without any difficulty. Stopping. Ringing one piano note as though to remember pitch. "'Caraed amabile!'" Flora wept in her bed, an eiderdown around her shoulders as she listened. The music contained within it memories sweet and far away from this pink cottage opposite the cemetery where she had a room—but for how long, and what would happen to her? The enormity of the future, with its unknowns: Flora felt lost in her bed, thinking of this. But then a few more bars, the same words: "'Ombra mai fu, di vegetabile, soave pui . . .'" It was reassuring somehow to listen to such praise for trees in the midst of her anxiety.

When she came out of her bedroom to use the toilet, Ann peeked out from the room at the other end of the hall.

"Good morning, my dear. I hope I didn't wake you? I always try to practise in the mornings because one never knows what the day will bring. How did you sleep? Were you warm enough? Later in the day, I will show you the linen cupboard where you will find extra blankets and things."

Flora laughed. "Warm enough? As though there could be any question with that mountain of eiderdown and blankets. It was perfect. Thank you. And so nice to wake to Handel! I'd forgotten that piece, but it was a good reminder of how grateful we should be to trees. In Walhachin one longed for leafy plane trees in summer. Or an avenue of pollarded limes. Apple trees take such a long time to come to maturity. Ours provided such a little shade. So to hear that aria, bringing to mind memories of, oh, I suppose completely English glades . . . Thank you so much, Ann. Not just for the singing but for, well, everything."

"It's my pleasure, Flora. I will go back to my piano and my music now. You will find tea in the kitchen—it's on the hob—and a place set for you in the dining room just beyond. Go through the French doors and you'll see."

Flora settled into the household with ease. Ann had routines THAT were not to be disturbed. Her singing, for instance. She had trained as a singer in London, before her marriage, and had enjoyed a brief but happy career as a recitalist. And she continued to perform in Victoria when possible. She practised every morning. And she insisted on fresh sheets every week; Mondays were always laundry days. She welcomed Flora's help with this and was not surprised that Flora had never actually washed a sheet— "Why on earth would you have? I'd never done laundry myself until Phillip died and suddenly there was so little money, not enough for servants. But I rather like to wash bed linens, in part because they are so lovely hanging out in the garden like clean ghosts and the scent of them when they are ironed and returned to the beds! Heaven!"—and showed her how to use a mangle to wring out the water after the final rinse. The two of them did this together, their dresses wrapped in coarse aprons. They hung the sheets from the line, clothespins between their lips, each of them taking an end and pegging it in a kind of domestic dance, arms raised and faces uplifted.

Every morning Flora checked the mailbox to see if a letter had arrived. There was one, posted in early February, and her heart turned as she opened the envelope. He was writing from Avonmouth, waiting to be transported across the Channel to the Bay of Biscay, and then the Loire. For some reason, she kept hearing "The Raggle Taggle Gypsies" as she read his brief letter, the refrain playing in her head like a lament: "And the other sang, Bonny Bonny Biscay Oh!" She would have to look on a map to see where he was now. Somewhere over there.

Letter Five: *Sweetest Flora*, the letter began. *Where I am now, when you read this, is anyone's guess. We are preparing for the Continent and I think that ultimately means France, or Belgium. We are told almost nothing. Thus far I have been camped in a muddy field at Lark Hill as I mentioned. Never was a place less happily named. It seemed that every man but myself came down with a particularly nasty bug and the problem of keeping warm and dry was the thing on everyone's lips. It is difficult to remember sometimes why I was so ready to come here. It was to end by Christmas, that was what everyone said. By now you will have met my parents . . .*

Flora broke off reading here with a pang of guilt. She had not met them. She had written to them and received no reply. This caused her considerable uncertainty. Should she write again? Should she simply appear at their door? And she had put them out of her mind in her effort to fit into Ann's home. The two women spent a portion of each day sewing a layette for the baby; in that homely work Flora found a kind of peace. She had not wanted to interrupt it.

She continued reading. "*. . . and I wonder what you make of them, them of you. I cannot believe that they would not love you at first sight, as I did. Or at least my father. About the matter of which you wrote to me. I can only say I will return to you as soon as I am able. Know that I think of you often and remember our time in the Back Valley as something approaching Eden.*"

There was more. Descriptions of weather, a leave he had taken in London with a group from his battalion, little observations about the English countryside that pulled at Flora's heartstrings because he was so close to Watermeadows. Gus had teamed up with a fellow who had been studying archaeology at the University of Toronto and who was happy to have company on rambles around Wiltshire in search of ancient sites. Gus's observations brought specific memories to mind for Flora because one of her brother George's tutors had taken the two of them on as many outings as their father would permit. Stonehenge, the smaller and less-frequented Avebury, an avenue of stones leading to the

Sanctuary nearby, and the long barrow at West Kennet. And Gus had also managed to get away for long walks. With much of the camp waterlogged, it was possible to simply absent onself from the training that was so often cancelled due to weather conditions and illness on the part of the officers as well as soldiers; anywhere else, he said, there would have been serious disciplinary action but no one noticed. He described seeing the white horses cut into hillsides, particularly the impressive one at Westbury on the perimeter of the Plain where the troops were situated. More than a few afternoons were spent in a pub on Endless Street in Salisbury. Gus had entered the cathedral in Salisbury too, and was moved to tears at the sight of the tombs of knights who had fought in the Crusades in thrall to the early kings. *It was their feet, Flora, that touched my heart. Seeing the effigies with those feet that had walked on soil so far from their homes. I don't know why but I thought of my childhood home then with some great longing.*

Then Gus expressed impatience at the delays in getting the War Office to decide that the Canadians were ready to proceed to France. *All a kind of snobbery*, he wrote in Letter Six. *We are not quite gentlemen to them. This is what it boils down to. But I think losses are higher than what anyone expected so I think it's safe to say that the colonials might well be needed sooner rather than later. And Lord knows at times I think anything would be better than the mud of Lark Hill.*

At first Ann made little polite noises about what was happening overseas. And then she began to talk more stridently about the war. Flora had never heard someone so angry about the conflict. In Walhachin, men drilled for years as though in anticipation. When the call came, they were ready to leave within a day or two at most, the actual tangible work they had committed themselves to for so many years quickly put aside for the more abstract considerations of duty, their lovely laden trees abandoned to Chinese labourers and women, to men too old or disabled to wear a uniform. That did strike Flora as sad. But this anger, from a woman who had direct experience with a war, her bitterness and her contempt for the leaders: Flora was shocked at first but then grew to see what Ann meant as she listened to the older woman's opinions.

"On February 1, Flora, it was the fourteenth anniversary of my husband's death at the Paardeberg Drift battle. There is no grave for me to visit, no monument in the cemetery across the road."

"I hadn't thought of that, Ann. Of course you would want a place in which to focus your grief and then your sense of honouring your husband."

Ann continued, as though she hadn't heard Flora's words: "There are these photographs of course to remind me of who he was and what I've lost. And what other women lost, other families. Phillip had elderly parents, a sister. Some of the men were fathers. All of them were sons. That is my immediate loss."

She turned the edges of her sleeves back, smoothing the fabric with her long fingers. She took a deep breath and continued. "But also there is the larger thing, for me in any case, of what we lost as a society, by allowing Kitchener to order the burning of houses, the enforced gathering of women and children into those camps where there was such terrible hunger and illness. So many died, Flora, and I believe that England has that blood on its hands to this day. It's utterly immoral. No amount of high-minded rhetoric will persuade me otherwise."

This was not something Flora knew anything about. An uncle of hers had gone to South Africa with the Duke of Edinburgh's Regiment and fought at Mosilikatse Nek; he'd returned with various souvenirs—a spear, the leg of an elephant made into an umbrella stand—and a medal, for Distinguished Conduct. Nothing had been said about camps.

"And as for a monument," said Ann, "I would give anything for my husband himself to be in my bed at night, to take me in his arms and dance me to dinner. Or bring me nosegays of sweet violets from a street vendor as he did during the year of our courtship. I can still feel the warmth of Phillip's hands as he pinned the little bouquet to my bodice. Oh, Lord, I pray that one day men stop this way of settling differences."

She wept as she finished, tears running down her cheeks as she peeled potatoes for their dinner. It was Flora's turn to comfort her; the two of them stood in the kitchen while the rain echoed Ann's tears on the windows, water coursing down the clarity of glass.

When the letter arrived, only a few lines—a greeting, a comment about the weather, and then, *Sed nos immensum spatiis confecium aequor / et iam tempus equum fumantia solvere colla*—it caught Flora completely by surprise. His name, preceded by love. She kept tracing her finger over his signature as if to keep him safe.

She wrote the difficult letter to her parents, giving them some information of her condition, her new home, details of Victoria that she hoped would soften the blow a little. She described the gardens, so English in their plantings and order, and the shops where one could buy tartans and Irish linen or order china to replace broken pieces. A telegram came in response with a brief message: *Extremely disappointed. Stop. George has failed us. Stop. Henry has enlisted. Stop. Father.*

She summoned her courage and wrote another letter to the Alexanders, telling them that now she had grown to learn the streets and neighbourhoods, she realized they were only a short distance away.

FOURTEEN
January–February 1915

"They have invited me to tea. Tomorrow," Flora told Ann. "But I am afraid I will be turned from the door." She laughed nervously. "Mrs. Alexander sounded polite but stern. Yes, Gus had written to tell them I would be coming to Victoria, and my reason for leaving Walhachin. Yes, they received my letter. Yes, they would agree to have me visit. Then directions. A time. That was all." She took a deep breath. "I think I will walk if this sunshine holds. I must say after two winters in Walhachin, I did not expect British Columbia to have such mild weather. Look, Ann! There are snowdrops in your garden!"

"Yes, and before you know it, there will be daffodils too. Don't worry about tomorrow. What do you say we walk down to the water?"

The door was opened by a grey-haired woman in a severe dark blue dress. A man was behind her, tall, with the blue eyes Flora knew from his son. She was taken to a sitting room where a fire burned.

"I cannot tell you we are happy about this," the woman began, but her husband cut in gently.

"Perhaps you could pour Miss Oakden a cup of tea, my dear, and let her get her bearings."

Flora sat in a deep leather armchair and was handed a cup of tea, the pattern the same Royal Worcester that her parents used for afternoon tea. She thought she would not mention this. Both of Gus's parents watched her as she drank her tea, taking in her good clothing, her features, the unmistakable fact of her pregnancy. She waited for them to say something, then put her teacup down.

"I know I must present something of a shock to you. I am a shock to myself. I was living one kind of life and now find that I must learn to live another kind entirely. But I must assure you that your son and I loved each other, love each other still. When he returns home—Oh, I hope it will be soon!—we intend to marry. This is not to say that I planned to have a child, not like this, but I cannot say I am altogether unhappy with it either."

Dr. Alexander spoke first. "We have not seen our son, our only son, in five years, and then only briefly after an absence of three years. It is a source of regret to me that hard words were spoken on my part, and he took my anger seriously and disappeared. We had no idea he was working in Walhachin. The last I heard was a rumour of his presence in a gambling establishment in San Francisco. So to receive a letter from a training camp in England with the information that there was a young lady in the picture who might contact us, a young lady expecting his child . . . You can surely see that it came as a surprise. You come as a surprise, Miss Oakden, and it will take time to adjust."

"I wonder what your own parents make of this," Mrs. Alexander broke in crisply. "Have they disowned you? It would surprise me if they haven't. I am the mother of two daughters and would not hesitate to call them to account if such a thing occurred in our family. Which it wouldn't."

Flora wanted to rise from her chair immediately, find her coat, and leave. She did not know what she expected, but it was not this woman's chilly assessment. Instead, she thought for a moment, then answered. "My parents are puzzled, of course, and I suspect rather relieved that I am so many thousands of miles away. They blame my brother, with whom I lived in Walhachin, for not keeping a closer eye on me. They won't acknowledge that I am an adult woman who must take responsibility for her own actions. And I expect they hope the whole thing will be taken care of somehow and never spoken of again."

Mrs. Alexander sniffed, as though in complete agreement with the long-suffering Oakdens, while Dr. Alexander looked thoughtful.

Flora continued: "Although I may wish that Gus and I married before he left, I have no doubt of his love for me and I know he will return to me and our child. As for such a thing occurring in your family, I can only assure you that your son did have an involvement in the making of this child. He will do the right thing. I am certain of that. But if you haven't seen him for five years, perhaps you have no idea of the man he became in his absence from you. In truth, it is eight years since you have known him. And now I have taken enough of your time. I will say goodbye."

She struggled to her feet and moved as calmly as she could towards the anteroom where her coat was hanging. She let herself out quickly and walked down the hill, her cheeks hot at the memory of the words spoken in her lover's home.

Back at Hollyhock Cottage, Flora gave Ann only the briefest of accounts of the meeting. Then she excused herself and went to her room to rest. She had walked back to Memorial Crescent at such a pace, fuelled by both anger and hurt, that she had worn herself out. She fell asleep with a knot in her heart that weighted her body to the bed like a stone.

A gentle knock upon the bedroom door. "Flora, a note has come for you from that awful man. Shall I bring it in to you?"

Ann handed Flora an envelope of heavy cream linen stock, her name on it, her address, in a strong black script. "By Hand" was written across the bottom. She opened it.

My dear Miss Oakden,

You are perfectly correct. We've no idea of the man our son has become. Will you tell me about him? I should like that very much. I apologize for our treatment of you in our home earlier today. My wife is too bewildered and unhappy to think clearly or lovingly about this, but I would like to see you again to try to make amends for our incivility. May I come by at your convenience to take you out to tea? Sincerely yours,

Robert Alexander

He had not said anything directly unkind. It had been Gus's stern mother. So Flora agreed to the tea for the next week. He arrived in a car, an immaculate Model T, and he was solicitous as he helped her to the passenger seat. He drove carefully along May to Cook and then to the city centre, where he parked his vehicle in front of the Garden Tea Room and held the door open for Flora to enter. On the drive he had only commented on the houses they passed, the progression of plants—she was surprised that winter was so mild here, even milder than Wiltshire where their pond occasionally froze to allow skating—his medical practice. But once inside, seated at a booth below walls trellised with lathe and swags of ivy trained through and among them, he made a formal apology for the way she had been treated at his home. Flora accepted without additional comment. He was a man who didn't do this often, she deduced, didn't admit he had been wrong. It would serve nothing to make things worse. She reminded herself that he was her lover's father, the man responsible for much of who and what his son had become. She remembered Gus's reflection about the malt whisky that his father enjoyed, as did his son, and she smiled.

"Will you share the thought that makes you smile, Miss Oakden?"

"Only if you will call me Flora. And it is only an observation that Gus once made about whisky, that the two of you shared a fondness for the Islay malts. It was the day when the child of the Indian woman who cleaned for us died. I was very upset. Gus offered me a drink from his flask. A day I remember because it was the first of my brother's rules that I broke, and I was surprised at how little guilt I felt, particularly as the whisky had such a fine mellow flavour."

Robert Alexander chuckled delightedly. He was surprisingly easy to talk to. Over tea, cucumber sandwiches, slices of Battenburg cake (which he joked would soon have to be renamed, just as the Royal Family's name, Saxe-Coburg, was rumoured to be in the process of being anglicized, both because of their association with the Hun: "Mountbatten? Is that change enough, do you think, Flora?"), he asked about her background, her family, the adventure in gentlemanly apple-growing undertaken by her brother. He was hungry for information about his son. Flora told him everything she knew, even the names of the horses, and then she realized how much she didn't know: where the entire past five years had gone, for instance. She knew of his two years on ranches and farms, but before that there had only been hints: a mine in Colorado, some time at sea. His father was aware of a brief stint teaching at a one-roomed school in the northern part of the province. Talking about him made him seem closer. His father absorbed every word.

On the way home, the doctor ("Please call me Robert. It does not seem appropriate to suggest myself yet as father-in-law, but one day we will talk about that.") asked if he might take her to tea another time. Flora agreed. She liked him and felt at ease in his company. What was left unsaid was that Mrs. Alexander would not be part of the outing.

Flora thought she would set up maternity care in preparation for the birth of her child, and to that end, she visited St. Joseph's Hospital by the convent of the Sisters of St. Ann. It was the Sisters themselves who operated the hospital. She had contacted them in the weeks after her arrival in Victoria because she felt she should follow up on their invitation to come to see them once she arrived. There had been a meeting with a Sister in a tidy room overlooking extensive gardens and orchards where she was given the impression she should arrange to stay in a home for unwed mothers to which they would be happy to refer her. Arrangements would be made for the Christian adoption of her child after its delivery. The Sister was kind but obviously taken aback when Flora replied that she had no intention of giving her baby up, that she and the baby's father would be married as soon as the war was over, and that although irregular, she felt her situation did not present insurmountable difficulties. Clearly the Sister thought otherwise.

At the suggestion of the Sister, Flora arranged for an appointment to see a doctor. He was very severe. It was his opinion that she had no choice but to take shelter in the home for unwed mothers, deliver herself of her child to the good work of the orphanage, and come to an agreement with God afterwards. She left in tears.

Ann was a great consolation when Flora returned to Hollyhock Cottage. She made a simple meal of scrambled egg and toast and carried the tray in by the fire; she poured them each a glass of sherry.

"Why on earth should you need to use their hospital at all, Flora? Babies are born at home all the time. And you *have* a home, here, with me. We will find a doctor who will take you as your patient, not lecture you, but who will come here to do what is necessary. I think you must know I am looking forward to this child as much as you are. I will help in any way that I am able to."

"Oh, bless you, Ann. I have to say that I left that doctor thinking that I was truly a fallen woman and that I ought to give up my child to the mercy of . . . well, the orphanage, though I can barely say the word. Listening to you restores my faith in myself somewhat."

Ann smiled and threaded a slice of bread onto a toasting fork. "I love the smell of toasting bread! Have you seen the Protestant orphanage, by the way? A beautiful location, all hilly, surrounded by oak meadows, but the building itself . . . Oh, my Lord. Red brick, and a sense of chilly foreboding, like something out of Dickens. I've always imagined faces at the windows when I've passed it, and little screams for help, but I suppose that is my imagination at work!"

When Robert Alexander arrived to take her for tea the next time, Flora found herself telling him about the consultations with both the nun and the doctor. He surprised her by offering to assist with the birth.

"Like your friend Mrs. Ogilvie, I am inclined to think that most babies can be safely delivered at home. I have assisted hundreds into the world myself. And I would be honoured if you should require my help. No need to decide now but know that I am available. Of course you will keep your child, Flora, and one day it will be a story to tell your grandchildren. They will not believe that their grandmother had such a time of it in very proper Victoria!"

FIFTEEN
Mid-April 1915

She did not know at first why she was awake. Still night. The dark windows unlit by any dawn. She was sleepy for a moment, then felt pain beginning in her abdomen, intense pain that lasted only a few seconds but that gripped her body fully while it lasted. She waited. A few minutes later, there was another. Less intense this time. Then another. She rose from her bed, put on her wrapper, and quietly went to the kitchen to make herself a cup of tea.

Ann entered the kitchen, asking, "Is everything all right, Flora?"

"I think today will be the baby's birthday," replied Flora, turning to smile at Ann, then suddenly consumed by another pain.

"Have you had the pains for long?"

When she could speak again, Flora told her that she wasn't certain, only that she had been brought out of sleep by them.

"I will call the doctor now and see what he would like us to do."

She spoke into the phone, then turned to Flora. "He asks, has there been water?"

"No, but the pains are coming a little more often . . ." and with that, she sat heavily in a chair and held her stomach with both hands as though to confine the pain and what might come after.

Ann spoke into the phone again, then replaced the receiver on its small cradle.

"He is on his way."

As she had been directed, Ann began heating water in a large kettle and taking extra towels and clean rags to Flora's room. She padded the bed with old sheets. Then she chipped some ice off the block in the icebox and dampened a washing flannel with cool water to bathe Flora's forehead, which was beaded with perspiration.

Three hours later, Flora was cradling a tiny howling daughter, wrapped in soft flannel, exhausted but exhilarated to have such tangible evidence that she had been loved by Gus. The baby was blue-eyed, with her mother's fair hair. You could not say yet about the nose, which was as small as a nose could be. As soon as she had been handed the child, after the cord had been cut and the tiny body cleaned, she gave her the name that she had been holding secret until she knew the gender. George for a boy, Grace for a girl. The room was lit by morning sun; a pear tree bloomed outside the window like a welcoming committee.

"May I?" asked Grace's grandfather, reaching to take the bundle. "She is a fine baby, Flora. And look, all ten toes and fingers! You have done well, my dear."

"If only . . ." Flora started to say, then stopped herself. Robert Alexander would know, without her telling him, what she longed for in those precious moments following her daughter's birth. He patted her hand awkwardly, the other arm hand firmly holding his granddaughter to his heart.

There were times, holding the new Grace against her shoulder after a feeding, when Flora was reminded of the Grace she had known at Walhachin—her gurgle, her skin, the damp warmth she had left on Flora's lap when the two of them had fallen asleep in the rocker. And only a few days later, that earlier Grace was dead.

Flora sent a letter off to Gus almost immediately. *You would love her fingers, she told him. So small and perfect, and the soles of her feet, which have never touched the earth. Your father says she has your nose, but it is truly so little that I don't know how he can say that. But she is clearly a comfort to him. I don't know if he doted on you but he surely dotes* on his granddaughter, stopping in so regularly that we have given him a key in the event we are busy with laundry—there is so much, I never would have dreamed such a tiny infant could need so many nappies, so many nightdresses. As a family we are perhaps unorthodox—a widow, an unmarried mother, a father so far away it might almost be another world, and a grandfather who has somehow accepted not only the child but also the household in which she lives. And cries! Oh Gus, her cry would break your heart.

The rabbit-skin booties were a delight to lace onto Grace's tiny feet, the fur soft against soles that had never touched the earth, never left a print in soil or snow. No item of clothing pleased Flora as well, though Ann had knitted sweaters of wool light as swan's down and Flora herself had smocked nightdresses sewn from flannel sprigged with nosegays of primroses and clover. When Flora put the booties on Grace's feet, she remembered the Indian woman's smile and the touch of those hands on her stomach like a blessing. Did she cast a spell upon me? wondered Flora. Because, riding the train down to the coast, she had woken from her brief sleep with the utter conviction that there was no shame in carrying the child of a man she loved with her whole heart, knowing that she would make her own way and not seek shelter with those who might want to take her child from her. The booties were proof of that moment.

Early June 1915

"Robert Alexander has telephoned, Flora," said Ann, coming out to the garden where Grace slept in her pram under a tree while Flora wrote letters at the table. A letter to her mother, a letter to Jane—she wrote but did not expect them to answer. "He is coming over. He sounded very serious. I hope there's not bad news. I will stay out here with Grace so you can see him in the sitting room. I put the kettle on and the teapot is warm."

He was at the door within ten minutes. Flora knew it was something awful when she saw him through the glass. He came in and hung his hat and his walking stick on the coat rack.

"There is no easy way to tell you this, Flora," Robert began, taking Flora's hands in his own. "No easy way. A letter has come from the Front, from Gus's commanding officer. Gus was killed in action at Festubert on May 24. That is near Artois, I gather, a terrible battle, coming quite soon after Ypres." His voice broke for a second, then he recovered himself. "The letter speaks of his bravery. As yet there is no body."

"Could it be a mistake?" asked Flora, knowing that it couldn't. She felt a shiver running down her spine, a sensation her mother always referred to as "someone walking over a grave."

"I do not believe it to be a mistake. I sent a wire to someone I know in Ottawa, an aide to the Minister of Militia and Defence, Sam Hughes, and he replied within the day to say that indeed there were casualties as the 5th and 7th Battalions took significant ground at Festubert and that my son's name was among those confirmed dead. Perhaps you should have a little brandy, my dear."

Flora sat down and felt a glass being pressed into her cold hands. She was urged to drink. A fire surged down her throat and into her stomach, making her eyes water, but it was warm; after a second mouthful, she did feel less faint. Her hands were still cold. She began to weep, quietly at first, but then great sobs wracked her body. The doctor handed her his handkerchief and she held it to her eyes, pressing them as though to obviate sight completely. As though to obviate her life itself.

After a time—it might have been a few minutes, it might have been an hour—she remembered her guest. She composed herself. Wiping her eyes, smoothing her hair, she turned to him.

"I am so sorry, Robert. For you and Mrs. Alexander, who have not seen him in so long, as much as for myself, and for Grace, who will never know him."

They talked for a time. Flora listened to her lover's father remember his son's childhood not a mile from where they sat, how he loved to take a lunch in his knapsack and walk for hours in any direction with his compass and his notebook (Flora remembered his note-taking on their own adventure in the Back

Valley where skies had been described, birds accounted for, guesses made at geological formations), coming back late in the day with eyes shining and clothing covered in dust and grass seed. It was different then, much of the land still held by the HBC and not subdivided, though there were farms here and there. The hillsides were brush-covered and threaded with small creeks. She wept again to think of the young Gus wandering among the Garry oaks with his eyes skyward, taking in the blue distances.

When he took his leave, Dr. Alexander embraced Flora for a long moment.

"I am most grateful to you for letting me take you to tea that day. And for the gift of Grace."

She watched him pull away from the house in his dark car. And then she walked slowly to the garden to tell Ann the news. And to take solace from the sweet damp smell of Grace's neck, to tighten the little laces on the rabbit-fur boots to keep her child's feet warm.

In her bed that night, Flora could not sleep. She relived every moment she'd spent with Gus, from the ride to Mary's cabin on the Deadman River when she'd almost swooned like a Victorian maiden at the sight of his forearms and their soft hairs to the few stolen nights in a cabin by a lake, reed-fringed and loud with blackbirds. There were thrilling encounters among the dry grass in the orchards where her body had fused with his by the ardour he knew how to awaken in her. The hidden canyon where they had picnicked by a little creek and reclined on a saddle blanket while hawks made lazy circles in the air. On one of those occasions, Grace had been conceived.

Subsequent days were difficult beyond imagining. So much of the pain of the past year was endured with the hope that Gus would return, they would be married and make a home together.

"How will I bear it, not just for today, but for the days that will follow?" she wept to Ann one evening after dinner.

"You must, Flora. For Grace and for yourself. And it will

become, oh, not easier, but something that doesn't stab at your heart every minute as I know it must now. Try to walk. There is something about the seafront, the wind, the sound of waves: it somehow cleanses the thinking. You will want to think your way through this as well as feel your way. Not that you could help the latter, but it will be good to try to think what it means as well. I will make sure Grace is safe. Just walk, whenever you feel you can't do anything else. Between the spray of the tide and your tears, who is to know if you cry?"

Flora walked. In all weathers—and early summer always brought its fair share of wind and rain as well as clear sunny days—she would walk the waterfront, make her way through the lanes in the cemetery, climb the pretty streets to the high places where she could see the Olympic Peninsula on a cloudless day or else dense banks of fog on an unsettled one. It was as though she was looking for Gus, for his presence in the city of his youth. Looking for herself as she might have been, had she known him then. She would come upon lovers walking on the windy break-front, the woman leaning into the man, and her heart would constrict. Or an old woman putting flowers into an urn on a grave in the cemetery, proof that grief had its own long lifespan.

She climbed the stony hill locally called Moss Rocks and sat with her back against a warm outcropping, looking far out to sea. Shooting stars and bleeding hearts grew in clumps as lovely as any garden, and she was surprised to find both pink and creamy late erythroniums still blooming as well. And nodding onion, long-spurred violets, a tall blue flower which Ann told her was camas, and the sweet-scented Nootka rose. Once, as she sat among the rocks, she had watched two tiny lizards mating in a dry cleft and found herself weeping at the beauty of it, the long dignity of their effort.

For a time, she avoided newspapers. She did not want the raw numbers of losses, the small triumph of a victory in the Ypres salient. She wanted to keep the one thing she knew about the war clear in her mind so she could examine it from every angle.

Sometimes on her walks, Flora entered Beacon Hill Park and stood on the highest point where the wind blew almost always. The early summer plantings were blooming. Ducks were on the ponds with their young behind them in untidy processions. Beautiful Garry oaks stood in groupings on mossy rises; willows overhung the water. Flora discovered one pond with several water lily plants holding the chalices of their yellow flowers above the water. If she got close enough, she could see the stigmas like small umbrellas and the flies at work underneath. It was an unexpected moment to remind her of Watermeadows and she returned with Grace in her pram to have the solace of familiar flowers and ducks.

Dr. Alexander stood on the step, tidy as ever, his hair brushed (hat in hand), tie neatly arranged, small wire-framed spectacles magnifying the blue of his eyes (Gus's eyes). He held a package.

"Flora, this has arrived. I've read it only long enough to know that it belongs with you, though I should like to be able to borrow it occasionally. Will you let me hold Grace while you look at it?"

Flora took him around to the back garden, to chairs arranged by the little pool, and handed her child to its grandfather. She looked at the cover of the book he had given her and then at him.

"I was of two minds. It will upset you, I know, but you will want to know its contents as well. It is Gus's journal, you see, sent by the lieutenant in charge of his platoon. At first they had no idea it was his, then one of his mates read it during a leave and knew at once."

It was a green cloth-covered book, stamped with Canadian Pocket Diary on the cover. Inside was his name, his regiment, and a note: If found, return to Dr. Robert Alexander, St. Charles Street, Victoria, British Columbia. Flora's hands trembled as she held it.

"I will look at it a little later, I think. Shall I bring tea to the garden? It is too lovely a day to be inside—and Grace's pram is just around the corner. If you hold her, I will bring it here. Oh, Ann, how lovely—I was just going to bring out a tray."

Ann appeared through the trellised gateway with a japanned tray holding a pot of tea and cups, a little dish of lemon slices, and a plate of thin ginger biscuits. She put it on the wicker table and exchanged a few words with Dr. Alexander, who was cradling the drowsy infant in his arms. Flora went through the motions of pouring tea, offering lemon, biscuits, with the chilling knowledge that Gus's journal was waiting for her.

"There is a packet of letters apparently that will come later on. Mostly from you, I would think, though his mother and sister also wrote. And some other items of a personal nature. Clothing, I think, and . . ."

His voice broke and he stopped, took a handkerchief from his pocket and wiped his eyes.

"Excuse me, my dear. And a penknife, with his initials. I know the one because I gave it to him myself, for his twelfth birthday. It had been my father's, who was called Alastair, and it seemed particularly fortuitous that Gus had the same initials. Lovely bone handle and a blade that held an edge."

"It must have been the knife he used to . . . oh, this will sound peculiar but it was so appropriate to the place and the moment. Please don't think of your son, of me, as cruel or maca- bre, but Gus cut the lower part of the jaw off a deer skeleton that we found in a place we liked to ride to, a box canyon near Walhachin. It had been scoured by weather and insects and was quite clean. Lovely really, like ivory. He said it would be an anchor he would take with him to the war, something to keep him mindful of home. Anyway, he used a pretty knife to do that particular thing. You should know how careful he was with the knife. He kept it very clean and oiled; it was always in his pocket. It obviously meant a great deal to him."

Robert Alexander looked both startled and relieved. "How odd you should mention this, Flora. There is something else, too, you see. That very thing, in fact. His lieutenant said it gave them a bit of start to find it in Gus's haversack—apparently some men take rather, hmmm, unorthodox souvenirs and that was what gave them pause. But it was then determined to be the jawbone of an animal—a deer, thought some of the hunters in the platoon. The lieutenant wondered whether it might be better not to send it at all but to dispose of it at his end. But it rather sounds as though it was important to my son."

His anchor, thought Flora, taken from that beautiful ruined vessel, the opened body of the deer. Aloud, she said, "Yes, it was important. Almost sacred, if you don't mind me saying that. I would like to have it if at all possible."

"I will say that we would like it sent back then."

She could not bring herself to open the journal. She'd read the letters he'd sent to her over and over again, in part because he wrote in a voice he had intended for her, things he wished her to know, to share with her, as they had shared thoughts and secrets in the box canyon—oh, less than a year ago! It would be different with a journal though. A voice not intended to be heard, speaking the secret language of the heart. And so the journal was a privacy she was not willing to intrude upon. Not yet.

Robert brought the package containing the jawbone of the deer. Holding it in her hand, Flora remembered how they had found the skeleton in their favourite place. At first she had been repelled by it—a young woman brought up in a garden designed by a student of Capability Brown had no precedent for the bones of an animal dragged to a place by a predator—but Gus had shown her the beauty of it, how it resembled the frame of a small boat, ribbed and bleached. And she had run her fingers along the jaw once he had removed it from the skull, remarking how the bone felt like ivory. "And what's ivory," her lover asked, "but an animal part? Tusks, Flora, and teeth. I've known sailors to use it as for scrimshaw, carving beautiful pictures into it that they filled with ink. And of course there are cameos. Piano keys, my sweet! They're ivory! No need to be squeamish about something so beautiful and so practical." Grateful to have it restored to her (so little, too little), she gave the jawbone pride of place on her dresser, alongside her silver brush and mirror set, and the little woollen strawberry where she kept the pins for her hat.

SIXTEEN
Late July 1915

Ann was away to consult with someone who wanted her to sing at a function. This offered Flora an unexpected privacy, a sense of space, which she felt she must use somehow. Grace was sleeping; the only sound in the quiet house was the ticking of the grandfather clock in the hall and the hiss and snap of the fire in the grate, built to stave off unseasonable damp. Flora took out the green diary Robert Alexander had delivered to her months earlier and put it on the low table in the sitting room. She had not felt brave enough to look at Gus's journal before, but now in Ann's absence, she wanted to touch the pages that he had touched. The empty house, her sleeping child, gave her courage.

"What will you tell me?" she asked the book. And then she opened it.

It was in part a journal, in part a sketchbook. She turned the pages slowly to look at the sketches first: a train carriage filled with men; two men played cards, another strummed a banjo. The date told her it was the journey to Valcartier when the men were filled with the optimism that they would be home within a month or two. By Christmas for certain. And then there were sketches, some incomplete, of ships—this must be the trip overseas, Flora thought, those hammocks the only privacy a man would have. Oh, and Stonehenge! She recognized a number of scenes from the sketches done while the battalion was encamped on Salisbury Plain. The long barrow at Kennet. The cathedral in Salisbury City. A little sketch to the side of quite a detailed one of the cathedral showed a tomb, with an effigy. A note in tiny handwriting below it: *William de Longespee, half-brother to King John, adviser on the Magna Carta, captured in France, returned to England, died in 1226, given everlasting life in stone.*

Flora stopped turning the pages. She had been in that very place, in Salisbury Cathedral, and had looked upon that very tomb, with George's tutor. George had wanted to know about every tomb, every knight of old, in every churchyard or cathedral they visited. She couldn't remember much about William de Longespee but did vividly recall that a very old man, not a priest or anyone like that, had shown them the interior of the cathedral. When they paused by that particular tomb, with the sleeping stone man on top ("Waiting for the Resurrection, he is."), they were told that a hundred years earlier the tomb had been opened. William de Longespee was only bones, but the perfectly preserved corpse of a rat had been curled up in his skull. It had seemed a horrifying story to tell a young boy and his even younger sister, but the old man had said, "Worms, rats, it don't matter to the dead now, does it? Even as they wait for their moment with God." The tutor had walked his charges briskly away.

And now here was the tomb, with the knight asleep upon its plinth of stone. Something the two of them had seen at different times but as though together. Particles of the air in that high cathedral might have entered each of them, been exhaled, then waited for the other's arrival. Their feet on those ancient stones. Their eyes gazing up to the workings of the clock. I was there waiting for you, my love, thought Flora as she looked at the sketch. All those years ago I was waiting for you though I never knew your name.

And here was France, shown in detailed sketches of villages, long avenues of poplars stretching to the horizon, a tiny bird drawn lovingly as it perched on a fence post. A few quick portraits of other men, his fellow soldiers, she imagined, one of them cleaning a rifle, another sleeping—brief but clear glimpses of those men. She imagined Gus leaning against a tree and observing them, detached, but interested.

This has been home. It was a drawing of a cave dug into the side of what must be a trench. Sandbags composed the walls. The roof was branches shored up by boards. A pile of blankets was held off the floor (which looked like there were puddles on it) by duckboards. And on that pile of blankets, a man slept with his head cradled in his arms. Gus's note said how bad the little hovel smelled—sweat, the latrine bucket, fumes of cordite. And how rats would scuttle back and forth along the trench, in search of food. *They like best human flesh*, wrote Gus, *and grow fat and sleek on this diet. We keep an eye on our comrades while they sleep*, he added, *because the rats have no fear*. He had seen them eating eyes and the liver of a corpse. The horned beetles were not so bad, but he hated the sight of slugs climbing the sandbags and sides of the trenches, leaving their thin scribble of silver. And the frogs—here was a sketch of a frog sitting on a boot sticking out the water like a bulrush. He wrote that frogs at least were companionable, their throats working as they observed the world.

And here was a field bereft of crops, of trees, barbed wire between the viewer and the view. Oh, Flora's throat caught—surely that was a body on the hatching of earth? More than one. And that—a horse with its side opened to the sky? In Gus's tidy hand, a note: *this was a field, beyond it an orchard. These were men with lives forsaken for this. This horse should have been ploughing, these men holding women in their arms. I should be holding Flora now and not crouched by this carnage, waiting for an order to creep out to pull the bodies back so they might be identified and buried.*

Little crosses in a muddy ditch. Burned trees. A team of horses struggling to pull a wagon holding a gun battery and a stack of shrapnel shells. Gus's note said that the six horses simply could not drag the wagon through the quagmire, there should have been ten at least, and of course they were easy targets for German shells. He would never forget the screams of the struck animals as they sank into the mud. Nor of his comrades wounded and waiting for medical help. A donkey bringing rations along a trench, its face calm and oddly wise. A man carrying another man past shell holes and collapsed fences.

She had not noticed the book falling to the floor. How was it that such horrors happened—were still happening—to fine Canadian men, to French men, to English boys like those she had known in her village, and that the world was unaware? How could anyone have prepared those young men for the sight of rats eating their comrades? Or for the sight of shells blowing horses to pieces? She had grown up near the home of General Henry Shrapnel, whose invention of exploding shells had been instrumental in winning the Battle of Waterloo; she had seen the stone piers of the gateway leading to the general's residence near Bradford-on-Avon with shells embedded in each pier, had ridden by on her own mild mare, never imagining that shrapnel might be put to such purposes. Yet why had she not imagined? The linkage from bomb to rats eating a young man's liver had been hidden in the language of duty and obligation.

"Robert," she asked when next she saw him, "what did you make of Gus's journal? You read it and seem calm and able to function. Yet I hardly know what to do."

"To do, Flora?"

"How can we go on living as we do, knowing what is happening to our men overseas?"

The doctor was thoughtful but emphatic. "It is war, Flora. Not a picnic or a holiday. Our men are there to serve their King. They know their duty."

"But . . ."

"I think you must try to think of the larger good, my dear. That if men like Gus had not gone, the Germans would have been free to take over whatever little nation caught their fancy. Of course it is terrible to think of the damage done. I don't think there is any other way however. I am not a believer in appeasement. It has never worked. I wonder if it might have been easier in past times when there were not telephones and telegraphs to transmit news so quickly. A runner bringing news from a battlefield seems to me almost more bearable. We at home are bombarded with daily news of the losses and I think it might detract from the high and noble work that our men are performing."

"I cannot agree with you, Robert. There is nothing high and noble about what these sketches depict. It is sorrowful and shameful to me. But not noble."

"Then we must agree to disagree, my dear Flora. You have every right to interpret the war in your own way. I think our ages and perhaps our genders mean that we see with different eyes. But let it not blind us to those shared things we also hold dear— your beautiful child, the memory of my son, our hope at least that this war might conclude sooner rather than later and that it might bring the promise of peace. To the small nations as well as the powerful ones."

In the days that followed, Flora struggled to keep the horror of what she had seen in Gus's notebook at bay. In the cozy home she shared with Ann, the trenches of France and Belgium seemed so far away. And yet. And yet.

When she talked to Ann about Gus's sketches, her friend was not surprised.

"I've told you, Flora, about the conditions of the camps in the Transvaal, where women and children were herded by the British so that they would not provide food and solace to the enemy. In other words, their husbands and the fathers of those children. How so many of them died of starvation and disease. Scratch the patriotic rhetoric and this is what is hidden underneath. And our young men joined up so quickly and so willingly to fight the Kaiser."

"Would they have gone, Ann, if they had known that such things were waiting to happen?"

"Some would say, Flora, that it has always been thus. But I think that we can and must hope for human beings to find other ways to settle border disputes and acts of aggression. How can we call ourselves civilized otherwise?"

Some nights Flora lay in the white sheets and imagined herself back into the cabin in the Back Valley, her bare body against fir boughs wrapped in homespun, crushed in the arms of a man who now was dead in France's soil. What a distance he had gone from her and how ironic that she had moved into the landscape of his childhood while he had moved far beyond it into a country unknown to her. For a time they had occupied a box canyon, protected by walls of stone and the smell of wild grasses in the dry air. Like William de Longespee, Gus would soon be bones, and then dust. But that good knight had come back from France where he had gone in service to his king and had been buried in the church of his own parish. And Gus, in a place far from his home. When she remembered the shape of his body upon hers, pressed into her flesh, it was though she carried the effigy of him, privately, unseen by any but her.

"Have you thought about what you might do?" Ann asked in response to Flora's comment that her allowance had been severely reduced. A letter had come from England, her parents complaining of frozen assets, certain funds unavailable, her trust fund from her grandfather included. What was not said loomed large between the lines.

"I have. As you know, I tried the hospital, which seemed the most likely place for a gentlewoman trained in needlework and little else—I was willing to clean, work in the laundry, make dressings—but am deemed a fallen woman, it would appear."

Flora laughed as she remembered the nun's grim face, tight lips explaining that an unmarried mother might not be the best choice to mop floors for those suffering illness or convalescing after childbirth themselves.

"I was walking Grace around the block this morning and stopped to talk to nice Mr. Stewart at the monumental works. I told him I didn't expect to find the mayor working stone with a chisel! But he said he likes to keep his hand in at the business. I admired the piece of pink granite he was cutting and then he asked out of the blue if I painted. Not really, I said, although I have developed patterns for needlepoint and have had some training in design, however sporadic. I sketch, I told him, and have tried my hand at colour washes over India ink. It turns out an acquaintance of his is very short-staffed and needs someone to paint fireplace tiles. I know just what he means. You have plain tiles round your fireplace, Ann, but you must have seen the beautiful ones designed by, oh, William Morris for one. Another William—de Morgan—, Charles Vosey, and another Charles, Charles Rennie Mackintosh. Flowers, emblems, even frescoes. Do you know what I mean?"

"Indeed. The house up the road, the big one with the turrets, has a beautiful fireplace in the main sitting room with iris and daffodils on its tilework. Where is this place, Flora?"

"Quite some distance, I'm afraid. Out Douglas Street, but on the streetcar line so it would not be too difficult to get there, though certainly something of a journey. I am to see the man tomorrow, if you are able to watch Grace for me."

Ann smiled. "A pleasure. You must take some time to make some sketches of possible designs. He will be impressed that you've come prepared. I will happily write you a character reference, you know that, and I expect Dr. Alexander would as well. Now, I've just received some new sheet music. I've always wanted to sing Gluck. Why don't you have a cup of tea while I see what I can do with this aria?"

Flora sipped her tea and listened to Ann as she began to find her way into the music. She played a note, found it in her voice, tried a little phrase, almost tentative in her articulation. It was Italian she sang: "'Che faro senza Euridice?'" She stopped and pronounced Euridice three or four times to correct the stresses. Then, "'Dove andro senza il mio ben . . . Oh, Dio! Rispondi!'" It was a glorious piece, thought Flora, and suited Ann's voice beautifully.

"Tell me what you're singing, Ann," asked Flora when the latter paused, pushing back a loose strand of hair from her forehead.

"Well, the opera Orfeo is the story of Orpheus, you know, and his bride Euridice. See, I keep using the pronunciation I remember from school, but it's different in Italian. I need to make a note on my score. There. She's bitten by a snake, dies, and goes to the underworld. He follows her and is able to convince Hades and Persephone that he should have his wife back. He does this by singing so beautifully that they can't resist. But the arrangement he makes is that she follow him back to life but he must not look back to see if she follows. She interprets his reluctance to look at her as an indication that his love for her has died. But eventually she does follow and he does look back."

"Oh, there are echoes of the Bible, Ann, and Lot's wife turning to a pillar of salt!"

"I would think this story predates the Bible by some many centuries as it comes to us from Greek mythology. Very old indeed. In the Greek version, she is lost to him forever. But in Gluck's opera—I have the synopsis here!—it appears that the character of Love allows for a happy ending."

Flora was quiet. She kept a tiny flame of hope alive inside her own heart—that Gus's death might have been a mistake, that he was even now wandering the fields of France, perhaps with loss of memory, and that he would be found and returned to her. That the body already found and buried, with her love's own belongings in the tattered pockets, was someone else, some other woman's beloved, or no one's. This was beyond what was reasonable, she knew, but still it was there, the spark.

And then: "What do the words mean, Ann?"

Ann looked at the sheets and thought for minute or two. "I'm not truly fluent at Italian, you know, and I can't begin to make a word-for-word translation because accommodations would be needed for meter and rhyme. But something like this: 'Live without my dear Euridice? Live without my Euridice? How can I? Sorrowing, where can I go?' And then some repetition of that, for the sake of the aria. Then he implores Heaven to tell him, as Euridice's true love, where on the earth he can go without her. He will have to wander the earth without her. Oh, my dear Flora, I didn't mean to make you weep. Please. I'm so sorry."

Flora wiped at her eyes with her handkerchief and smiled at Ann. "You will think I am crying because of Gus and of course that's part of it. But I was remembering a sweet Chinese couple who worked in the orchards at Walhachin. The young bride, a delicate flower called May Lee, was bitten by a rattlesnake. She was taken to Kamloops to the hospital, but no one thought to include her husband, Song, in the vehicle. He watched her leave with the saddest face and then after she died—the drunken doctor in the community gave her a serum that was useless against rattlesnake venom. Mary, my Indian helper, who actually knew something about snakebite, was pushed aside with her potion of maple tea—well, after she died, he lived alone in a shack made of packing cases. Did I mention she was expecting a child? I remember touching her small abdomen and feeling the faint flutter of the baby before they took her away. Song would sit outside his shack at night and play a bamboo flute. It was the loneliest music I've ever heard."

There was the sound of Grace waking and Flora went to her, hearing Ann singing as she changed her child's nappy and tickled the soft plump belly. She remembered May in front of the shack, chickens around her feet and that brief swelling under her cotton jacket, her baskets of vegetables so beautiful in the fierce sun. Somewhere she had a photograph and would look for it.

It was a beautiful fall morning when Flora set out for Douglas Street and the manufacturer of fireplace tiles. The chestnut trees were losing their leaves, their conkers strewn along the road. She found the place easily, a brick and tile manufacturing works, after a streetcar ride of almost an hour and presented her letter of introduction from Alex Stewart. James McGregor read it quickly, gave her sketches an appraising look, and took her to a workroom where the materials for tile painting were collected on two long tables. A system of kilns was located in a yard at the back of the building. Stacks of bricks waited on pallets for removal to work sites; smoke rose from one of the big-bellied kilns to indicate firing in process.

"Let me show you some samples, Miss Oakden. Here are some that are created by a method we call tube-lining."

He handed her a tile, a lovely full rose in deep pink on a

green ground, to examine. "You see the line of colour here? It's applied with a special tool, like those women use to decorate cakes and such, I'm told."

Flora peered closely at the tile, holding it to the light. "Now, here," he continued, "feel the edge of this with your thumb, you'll notice that it's raised? Well, glaze is pooled into the surface areas behind the dams formed by those lines. Very labour-intensive and expensive, but some architects insist upon them. Sam Maclure is very happy with our tiles and plans some rooms around them. We can do them a little more reasonably than the alternative, which is to order them from England. And now of course shipping will be restricted for some time due to the war."

Taking up another tile, just as beautiful, James McGregor asked her whether she could see a difference. And she could, immediately.

"The surface is less textured," she told him. "I can see that it's more like a painting, with a very highly glazed surface. None of the ridges that I can feel with the others under the glaze. I'm guessing that these require less intensive work?"

He looked at her approvingly. "You've a good eye, Miss Oakden." He looked at her sketches again, noting the details and the way the shapes filled the fields. He looked up. "I don't mind telling you that I am more comfortable with men in my work-shop, but the war has taken many of my best glazers and artisans. We have never had a woman. This place would normally be a hive of activity. Shall we give this a try, you working here? I have some orders for specific designs, but in time I will welcome suggestions from you too. I can tell that you have some sense of filling a space. Have you painted much?"

"No," she answered, "not very much. But I've done a lot of needlework and could never find patterns that I liked so I began to design my own. I've sketched of course and studied colour theory on my own. For a time I had ceramics lessons from an artist in our village in England. I know a little about glazes and kilns, though I have to admit not a great deal. I would very much like to try this."

Terms were settled: Flora would begin the next week. As she walked home to Memorial Crescent after being let off the street-car on Fairfield Road, she felt a kind of optimism she hadn't experienced for months. Gone was the terror that would wake her in the nights sometimes, a child first active within her and then sleeping in the bassinette beside her, that the world would turn its head from her in disgust. Some did, to be sure. She was accustomed to a certain kind of sniff when she entered a shop, a sweep of a skirt as a matron removed herself as quickly as possible from Flora's proximity. As though what I have is contagious, thought Flora. And what do I have but love, and now grief? And a lovely daughter to remind me of both. And surely grief has spread among the families of those who have lost their lives in the war like a terrible plague. You would think people might be more forgiving, having lost so much themselves.

It was true that Grace was lovely. At six months she was plump and healthy, eager to smile and be tickled. It was a pleasure for Flora to take the child into her arms and bury her face in the soft neck smelling of talc. It was a lot of work to have a child. There were nappies to launder and feedings to prepare, long nights when a new tooth emerging caused Grace to cry fretfully in her cot so that Flora would take her up and walk her within the room or out in the garden if the weather permitted so that Ann's rest would not be disturbed. She wondered what she would do without Ann's help, though, for the other woman seemed as infatuated with Grace as was Flora. She would take the baby out for long walks in the pram to give Flora a break and was constantly sewing a little bonnet or pinafore or knitting a jumper. Some mornings, Flora would wake and realize that Ann had come in quietly to remove Grace so that Flora could have a longer sleep. Lying in her bed, she would hear Ann singing to the child in the kitchen, her beautiful voice producing children's rhymes and lullabies to Grace's delighted chuckle.

Grace had something of Gus in her, apart from blood. It was his eyes, their blue distances, the way they held a face in them and made that person feel the only beloved on earth. Both the child's grandfather and Flora noted them.

Ann was willing to provide child care so that Flora could take up employment at James McGregor's workshop. She insisted it would give her pleasure. The days would be long ones, Flora needing to leave at 7 AM in order to make streetcar connections to allow her to arrive at the workplace on time. Ann would practise her singing during Grace's naps. The extra income from Flora's job would pay for a girl to help with the heavy cleaning. But Flora asked, and was granted, a work schedule that would give her Mondays free so she could continue do the household laundry with Ann. She had grown to like the act of hanging out the sheets in the garden. In all the years of her girlhood, it had not occurred to her to wonder at the process by which the clean linen was brought to her bedroom and fitted onto her bed. Or how her petticoats were carefully washed and starched, or the tiny pin tucking on her bodices and shirtwaists pressed. The first one she ironed in Ann's kitchen she had to dampen and press at least four times before she got it right.

Flora found the work at the pottery physically demanding but so interesting that she would use her time on the streetcar home to sketch possible designs for tiles. At first she had been asked to apply colour to tiles already designed—a beautiful set of linked roses, in deep pinks and reds, with leaves glazed in dark green. These were moulded tiles, the glazes applied with brushes. The standard glazes were kept in large tubs with numbers to indicate their formula. She asked to watch the preparation of the glazes, a long process that was fascinating in itself. Feldspar, flint, soda, potash, lime, oxide of lead—these were fired to white heat, then the liquid glass was suddenly chilled in water. It would harden into pieces that were ground in rubber-lined cylinders, with water, to make a thick liquid called "slop." The various colours were obtained by adding staining materials to the slop, the metallic oxides used—copper, iron, manganese, cobalt, uranium—giving particularly deep and beautiful hues. She was told that the purpose of the glazes was not just aesthetic, although the beauty of a glazed tile could not be denied, but served to seal the pores of the biscuit so that it was impervious to dirt and could easily be cleaned. The hygienic factor was important. Different types of clay required different glazes. Some would crackle at too high a heat while others would form bubbles. Some formed crystals, but these were considered desirable for certain pieces.

Flora asked lots of questions. The chemistry interested her, the way two discrete elements combined to create a third unique and unexpected effect. How heat brought out beauty. The elderly man, a Hungarian called Nagy, who did most of the mixing, taciturn for the most part as he moved around his building, scooping powders and consulting his notebooks with formulas worked out like something from an alchemist's workshop, was pleased by her questions.

There were meetings with James McGregor and architects from around the city to discuss particular tiles for particular applications—the usual fireplace surrounds, bathrooms, foyers. After a few months of employment, Flora was encouraged to attend these meetings; she had demonstrated unusual skill in both the glazing of the tiles and their design. After a walk through the oak groves of Beacon Hill, she tried her hand at replicating the blue camas she had seen there, huge drifts of it, and those tiles proved very attractive, so much so that McGregor asked if she would try to design a range of tiles using wildflowers as a motif. When spring arrived, he assigned a man to drive her to places where he thought she might see the flowers he had in mind—the vivid orange Columbia lilies, the delicate nodding fawn lilies, the tall wands of magenta fireweed. She worked hard at these designs, often sitting at the table for hours at Hollyhock Cottage once Grace had been put to bed. So much depended upon the space. Increasingly she realized that long stems and leaves that could be made to flow in a slightly geometric way worked best. She spent hours studying the designs of the Scot Charles Rennie Mackintosh, who brought a very clean style to his work.

One architect tiled an entire foyer with Flora's camas. When she went to look at the results, she was thrilled to see that the effect was a little like coming upon a massed planting of the blue flowers—a room filled with light and the airy flowers with their slender green leaves. She remembered the glass house she had been taken to as a child, with tanks of white and blue water lilies, the wicker chairs covered in a chintz with a pattern of water lilies, and thought there was something of the same feeling in this sky-coloured room.

EIGHTEEN
1917

A year passed. Flora's parents had resumed some contact with her. George had been killed at the Battle of the Somme, and her older brother, Henry, who'd been a captain in the Royal Wiltshire Regiment, had also been killed, in Gallipoli.

Both brothers. She hardly knew what to think. George, with whom she'd shared a home, and whose fussiness irritated her but who was kind, generous, and protective. She recalled him sitting on the veranda at Walhachin, in lamplight, drinking his small measure of whisky while moths dipped and found the light, the shadows of their wings huge on the shingles. His smell—shaving soap and wool and cotton. The sight of him coming home across the grassy plateau on his tall gelding Titan, tired but never slouching in the saddle. He was so proper, was George, but as hard-working a man as she'd ever known. She wrote to her parents, sending her memories of George as a consolation, as if anything could be.

She knew that her father in particular would be devastated by the loss of Henry even more than George. Watermeadows had been meant for Henry, the oldest son. He had been her father's joy, an ardent walker who was interested in prehistoric sites and who made maps and kept a life list of birds. A letter from her mother told Flora that her father had given up on his water lilies and that the gardens were becoming overgrown and neglected because it was simply too difficult to find labourers.

So many didn't return, Flora, her mother wrote, *and the ones that did don't want to do this kind of work any longer, it seems. We have had a terrible time* finding staff for the household. The young women all left to work in factories and the like once there was a call for workers to replace the men who'd joined up. Now the village girls all go off to be typewriters or nurses. I have no maid of my own any longer and have had to cut my hair because I simply could not find someone to pin it up for me. In any case, we can no longer afford to pay anyone what they require. We have Mrs. Sloan still of course, but she can't do everything—she has nowhere to go, no one to go to, her son was killed at Gallipoli too, I don't know if you'd heard? This is why she stays with us, though she lives in our house now, the dower cottage roof beyond repair. A kind of loyalty I suppose. And old Tom Higgins is too crippled with arthritis to maintain even the kitchen garden. I think he stays because of the cottage. Where else would he live? We've had to close the entire western wing of the house. I don't expect we will ever entertain the way we once did in any case so have no need for all those bedrooms. I have been terribly indisposed by the headaches all autumn and am of no use to anyone.

They did not ask about Grace. It hurt Flora to write her own letters back, with news of her daughter and her work at the pottery, and to have no response to this information at all. But she kept up the frail contact to maintain a connection with what increasingly seemed to be a dream, a world where she had been part of a large household, a cherished girl, with brothers who cared for her and once brought her rocking horse home across the fields. She grieved for that girl as much as she grieved her brothers' deaths.

Her father wrote sad letters in which he did not mention his water lilies. He had taken to rowing on the Kennet Avon Canal near home and mentioned swans and their fierce faces. He said his investments had failed. He talked of selling some of the meadows, the ones farthest from the river, to someone who wanted to grow oats. ("He has assured us he will fence the area carefully, and will not tolerate the Hunt using our hedges as jumps into his fields. He thought this might placate me and certainly I pretended it did—we need the money, I hate to say . . .") His once careful handwriting had become untidy, the pages occasionally blotched with ink, as though a tear had fallen into a sentence and dissolved the words.

I've sold my hunters. I have no heart for riding to hounds, chasing down foxes. We gave your mare away, he wrote, to a little girl in Winsley. Although Seraphim is somewhat long in the tooth, the girl was delighted. I've seen her riding on the Bath road and was reminded of you, Flora. How far away you seem. How far away you are. I walk the property these days with the vision of my sons in my mind's eye, before all this dreadful business with the Germans began. To think that there will not be an Oakden to continue on at Watermeadows causes me anguish. Perhaps one day you will return. Someone will have to care for your mother. I took her to Marienbad for two months just before the war broke out and sat at a table drinking a very nasty mineral water while she went through treatments, but we returned home in the same condition as when we set out for the Continent. I feel incapable of being her husband. What a thing to tell my daughter. And yet there is no one else.

How far away Flora felt too, but with no desire to return to the postwar Watermeadows. She felt she could not bear the close, dark rooms with her mother lying prone, *sal volatile* at hand and a damp cloth over her eyes. Or the empty stable. Or the ruined gardens, overgrown and untidy, a lame old man hobbling around with a wheelbarrow, unable to keep up. It was not a daughter they wanted, really, but someone devoted to Duty. And perhaps most of all, she could not bear a fence being constructed to replace the hedge where she had a secret gap that she used to move between orchard and meadow, each world utterly enchanted, the one with bees and birdsong, the other with foxes and hedgehogs, and the memory of her brother George returning from the swampy area near the river with her rocking horse over his back. There was no place there now for the woman she was and she wanted nothing to interfere with her precious storehouse of memories of the girl she had been. The war had taken too much that was valuable and she would not allow it to take this from her too. Though she conceded to herself that of course it had taken these things but she needn't have that confirmed with an actual visit to what she had stopped thinking of as home.

And was her father being forgetful or did he simply not acknowledge that Flora had a child who was in fact an Oakden?

Not the offspring of one of the beloved sons of course but a child, a continuation of blood and name, a child in which to place hopes and to fill with stories of the past? Out of sight, out of mind, she supposed. And what did he think might happen to Grace if Flora returned to care for her mother? A child at solitary play in the long corridors, the tangled gardens, unacknowledged by a silent grandfather mourning the loss of his sons. No pony, no uncles to lift her into the air, no loving governess to shadow her every move.

In one of her pensive moods, when Grace was sleeping and Ann out on errands, she began to draw water lilies, not as they grew in the tanks and ponds at Watermeadows but as they might decorate tiles. She drew the beautiful Egyptian blue lotus cradled on the deep green leaves, she drew the sweet-smelling British alba, the bright sun-coloured water lilies from the lake where she had spent an idyllic few days with Gus in that autumn of 1913, their horses grazing in the knee-high grass while they made love on a mattress of fir boughs, the heady resins scenting their bodies. She included the sinuous stems and indicated glazes to make the leaves glisten, the flowers as close to their natural colours as possible—the pink of N.'Ortgiesiano-rubra' edged with deeper rose, as though dipped in the most intense pinky-red pigment in the paintbox, the tropical red of N.'Devoniensis', named in honour of the Duke of Devonshire by his head gardener, Joseph Paxton, a talented hybridist as well as the man who helped to coax Victoria regia to bloom at Chatsworth in the first heat of excitement of its cultivation in Britain. These were stories Flora had grown up with, and she drew with yearning for a life lost and a time vanished.

James McGregor was pleased with the water lilies when Flora showed him final versions of her initial drawings. By now she knew just enough about the glazing formulas to suggest combinations that would result in the vivid, rich colours she had in mind. As background, she envisioned a blue, something deeper than the Ming Turquoise but not cobalt; she would work with Nagy to find the perfect hue. Cobalt lightened with copper oxide? Perhaps they would experiment with oils and salt to find a texture that would be pleasing. More tin oxide to give some of the lilies an opacity. She planned panels as well, for a bathroom wall, or as an exterior feature, perhaps to be placed within a brick facade. Well, she drew them but did not imagine she might actually ever develop the sketches to actual working plans.

We gave away your mare, he'd written, and suddenly Flora wanted to know what had happened to Agate and Flight, Gus's horses at Walhachin. Wanted to know about the apple trees, the curtains she'd chosen for the sitting room of the house she had shared with her brother, the roses he was coaxing to grow, those delphiniums the colour of the sky. Perhaps when Grace was older, they might make a trip by train to see what was left of that life. In the meantime, she might write to Jane McIntyre again (she had tried some months earlier but had no reply) in her paradise in the Upper Hat Creek Valley, to see whether her old friend might want to renew their relationship.

Some evenings she sat with her work basket, the one she had bought in Lytton with its faint stain of berries on the interior, and thought about sewing. There was often mending, to be sure. Grace's clothing, her own stockings to be darned, her bodices to be repaired and trimmed, some with a little of the Honiton lace she had kept from the days when her mother still sent her parcels with notions and newspapers and Shetland hoods. What she wanted was something else, the pleasure of the needle passing through fine fabric, leading its trail of thread, silk or linen or crewel-wool, flowers forming in the wake—bud to bloom, wild bouquets of colour. She remembered sitting with Jane under the shade of a wide leafy tree, making handkerchief camisoles trimmed with pretty lace. They had talked of love and children; Jane had agreed that Gus was handsome and worthy. After Flora had returned to Walhachin, she had worn her camisole when she and Gus met in the orchard to make love under an apple tree heavy with green fruit. Later, she'd picked out grass seed from where it had entered the fibres of her garment when she'd been pressed into the ground with the weight of Gus upon her body.

Jane, she wrote, *I know it might be difficult for you to know me now—I did write earlier this year but had no response but I am determined to try again. I would love to have a few lines from you. I have been remembering our day at your home, making the camisoles under the trees. I hardly dare ask if there is a child yet, but of all women I know, you are the one who should have them to love and attend to in your paradise.*

A letter came back. When Flora saw it on the hall table, arriving back after a long hard day at the pottery, she could hardly believe it: Jane's elegant script on a heavy cream envelope! She waited to open it. There was Grace to greet and Ann to sit with at the table for a half-hour's catching up on the details of the day—what Grace had eaten, how she had made an attempt to pronounce Rufous, how they had walked to Clover Point along the water and noticed a seal following their progress.

"I will just finish a few things in the kitchen, Flora, and Grace is happy with her dolly, so why don't you change your clothing and have a few minutes to read your letter?"

Flora sat in her window seat with its calm view of the garden and opened the envelope. A letter—and a photograph! Jane and her husband, a baby in Allan's proud arms, stood by the front door of their home, tendrils of clematis framing them. Both smiled broadly. Tears came to Flora's eyes as she held the evidence of her friend's new happiness. She unfolded the pages.

My dear Flora, the letter began, *how wonderful to hear from you! I've thought of you so often and wondered if we might be in contact again. As for your earlier attempt, I can only say that I did not receive any letter or I'd have replied at once. I asked in Walhachin for news of you, but, as you can imagine, no one would speak of you, except Mary, who thought you were in Victoria. I must confess that I meant to try to find you, but as you can see from the photograph, I find my hands full these days! We were blessed with young Thomas ten months ago, I hardly believe it still, but he is robust and bonny, as his grandmother says. You will wonder why Allan is home and not overseas. It's his heart. He has a problem with it (scarlet fever as a boy), gets tired easily,* and must be careful of what he does. He is of course glum that he can't be with the men in Europe, but people need meat too, and his work here is important. But, Flora, you've said so little about your life in Victoria! Please write and tell me more. Do you have a photograph of Grace? And—oh, I hesitate to ask this—is there news of Gus? I know the 5th Battalion suffered terrible losses at Ypres, and after, but I think Gus was part of another regiment? Perhaps he had better luck.

There was more. Jane wrote of the weather, mutual acquaintances, changes in the towns below the Hat Creek Valley—Ashcroft and Walhachin and little Clinton to the north. And then: Flora, this might seem delicate, but I want to say that I wish I had, well, counselled you a little more honestly during our last visit. If I had been less discreet, I might have told you that there are ways one can prevent a pregnancy if one is engaged in an intimate relationship as you so clearly were. You have paid a big price (I won't say too big) for something so natural and wonderful. But then your child must give you so much happiness too so perhaps I am speaking out of turn.

Jane, Flora wrote back that very evening, you could not possibly speak out of turn. I am so happy to have your letter with the photograph evidencing your great happiness. And it grieves me to tell you that Gus was killed in 1915, on May 24, at Festubert, just weeks after Grace was born. I don't even know if he knew of her birth. We would have married. I cannot regret Grace, who is all I have of him now, apart from memories. I minded terribly when I began to be shunned in the community, but I have made something of a life for us here, with the help of a wonderful woman who took me in and who is a second mother to Grace. Oh, it is too little to call it "help"—it is entirely due to her that I have any kind of life at all. I am thinking that one day I should like to take Grace to Walhachin, to see what is left of my house there, and to ask about Gus's horses. Do you know what happened to Flight and Agate?

The letters flew between the Upper Hat Creek Valley and Memorial Crescent as quickly as the steamships and trains could carry them. No, Flora had no photograph of Grace, but one was arranged: a man Ann knew who came to the house and took shots of a wide-eyed girl staring into the strange object with the hood and flash, her mother holding her and smiling not at the man who operated the camera but at her friend who would look into the photograph for news. And would find her friend changed, as the years change a face, cause the little lines of happiness or sorrow to form around the eyes, the slight disappointment in the lips, unkissed for much more than a year, though still with the shape of another mouth like a shadow across them.

As for Gus's horses, Allan asked our foreman and it seems Agrippa took them finally when it was clear no one had time for them at the settlement. He bred Flight and there was a filly, high-stepping, just like the dam; Allan said she would make a good polo pony if there is ever a team again at Walhachin. Flora, let's keep in touch. We will probably come down to Vancouver in the spring, and I would love to come across the water to see you and your Grace. Can we try to do that? And if you would like me to look in on your house, by all means let me know. I could easily arrange a trip over to Walhachin on one of our trips down for supplies. Allan has taken to driving to Kamloops for particular things now that the road's been improved. We like the change, though Heaven knows not much actually changes from our place to Kamloops. Some of the ranches have been abandoned, but there's hardly pleasure in that—the barns open to the weather and wagons without their wheels collapsed in the yards. It would be a nice side-trip to drive over the bridge, though, and onto the bench to see what might be seen. And to find out the news!

It was no small consolation to Flora to have Jane's letters, her old affection alive in the words, the memory of their after-noons at the ranch a balm to the abiding grief in her heart, a time when it seemed that anything might be possible in those golden days that seemed to have no end. If she closed her eyes, she could almost see the wildflowers on the road as she drove up the Oregon Jack Creek Road with Pete Richardson, windows open to the asters and fringe-cups, stork's bill and blue penste-mon in garlands on the roadside, black bear cubs at play in the soft meadows.

And if it did not happen that the waters would be crossed between the mainland and Vancouver Island in the next year, Flora felt that other barriers had been crossed, as important as a strait or canyon. A friend who had provided a peaceful room under gables where the windows looked out to mountains and the high pastures of the Upper Hat Creek valley had again offered solace, news of horses, the possibility of connection to a younger self, carefree and happy, sewing under the spreading shade of cottonwoods. The bodice of handkerchiefs, worn only for a lover in dry grass, remained in Flora's chest of drawers, wrapped in soft tissue, a sprig of southernwood tucked into the empty opening where her throat had once been kissed right to the edging of fine lace, and then below.

Flora, wrote Jane, we took a run over to Walhachin on our last trip to Kamloops, over the bridge with its osprey nest. The same osprey, do you suppose? Lots of changes—and few, if that doesn't sound capricious. Things look much the same. The houses for example, though the attempts at gardens in many have been abandoned; the hall is mostly used as a packing shed for the apples. I gather that labourers are hard to find and there has been a lot of trouble with the flume. It's mostly the women who stayed and the Chinese and a few men who are too old or else, like Allan, have some health difficulty to prevent them from enlisting. You'll remember Charles Paget, of course? The Marquis? Well, he's with the Royal Horse Guards in Egypt, an aide-de-camp if you please! So the Anglesey Ranch looks a little forlorn. There's talk of money difficulties. At any rate, I went to your house. Almost everything had been packed up and removed—that rather sniffy woman at the post office said your parents had asked for this to be done. Why are the women who work in post offices so often this type? Alert to anything that might be construed as misfortune or scandal? There were still bits of this and that in your house—I've taken some things back with me to hold for you. But this I am sending because it moved me to tears. It's dated, Flora. 1901. You must have been a child and yet look at how you've managed perspective. And the loving eye noticing things—the plants, the beautiful stonework. I didn't want it left in your house because the woman at the post office said that times were changing, there had been one or two occasions when items had gone missing from locked houses. And this is too special to have it disappear. And I've taken the liberty of digging up a small root of water lily from your brother's pool. I don't know if it will survive, but I remember that you said he was eager to grow them and although this bit has survived, I don't imagine it would go on much longer without any kind of care.

The root was very dry. But when she ran an edge of her

thumbnail over its surface, Flora saw that there was life in the tuber still. She decided to plant it in Ann's garden pool to see what might happen. And she found a hook in the box of work tools that Ann kept in the back pantry and fastened it to her bedroom wall. There she hung the little sketch, unwrapped from its careful packing. She could see it from her bed, where, if she almost closed her eyes, she could dream her way back into Winsley where the road wound its way around the buildings on its way to Bath.

NINETEEN
1962

Past the Hungarian house, past the monumental works, right to the gates of the cemetery (she didn't want to go home too early because she might get in trouble for coming back alone; she remembered her mother's request that they stay together). The day was warm, but the lanes were shady and cool. She could hear crows in the pines, their shaggy nests visible in the high branches. It was as though they were talking, the tones of their voices changing, becoming excited, then lowering to a mutter as Tessa walked under their tree. She sat on the edge of a small grassy grave and ate her candy, one piece at a time, making it last to the little seed within the jawbreakers. She had chosen two of the marshmallow bananas—they were two for a penny—and bracketed her snack with those. Finishing the bag, she let the last banana melt in her mouth, a wonderful feeling as the soft marshmallow innards of the candy turned grainy and slid down her tongue. She sighed. Bees droned in the flowering shrubs. She could hear the waves in Ross Bay hitting the breakwater so she knew the tide was up. She wandered over to the hedge separating the cemetery from Memorial Crescent and saw that Miss Oakden was sitting in a wicker rocker on her front porch. She waved and the woman waved back.

"Come and have a visit, Tessa," called Miss Oakden.

So Tessa left the shady cemetery and joined her on her porch. Two cats sat on the railings, facing one another, dozing in the sun; they were as still as carved lions at a gateway. And the roses were newly out, full and sweet-scented. Tessa remembered the pool in the back garden, seen through the fence from Bushby Park. She asked if she could go and look at it.

"Of course you may. If you approach slowly and quietly, you might see one of the frogs that have decided my garden is a good place to live. You must look carefully on the leaves of the water lily because those little frogs blend in so beautifully. Go ahead. I'll come in a few minutes. I believe you'd drink a glass of lemonade if I brought one to you."

"Oh, yes, please!" replied the girl, taking the steps down two at a time, opening the white gate at the side of the house and entering the garden.

The pool was even better than Tessa had imagined from the other side of the fence. It was quite large, perhaps ten feet across, and surrounded by stones streaked with lichen and softened by moss. A path of cobbles ringed the pool so you could walk slowly around its circumference, spicy pinks and mother-of-thyme tumbling over the cobbles. Best of all were the broad leaves covering the surface of the water because on the leaf closest to Tessa was a small dark green frog. She carefully knelt to the ground. The frog looked at her unblinking (could they blink? she wondered). There were four leaves in all and when she looked closely, she saw that three of them held frogs. In the centre of the leaves was a big pod, a flower not yet opened.

The woman had come up behind the girl and touched her gently on the shoulder. "My dear, the lemonade is here. And I see you have discovered the frogs."

"They're so beautiful, Miss Oakden. Are they always here?"

"Ah, well, I can't tell you that they're always here but certainly frequently. They're tree frogs, you know, and they have the ability to change colour somewhat to blend in with their background. When they creep through the wisteria leaves around my porch, they are a much lighter green. And see, look there! That one has a pink stomach!"

Tessa looked closely. It did! She put her finger on one edge of its leaf, and the frog moved backwards on its green platform.

She loved the way its front feet looked like tiny webbed hands, fingers long and animated. She watched until she remembered the lemonade that was waiting on a table under an apple tree where she sat with Miss Oakden. She looked around her. Two apple trees, with gnarled old branches, the remnants of blossom still clinging to some of them. There was a willow in one corner, roses along the fence, a pergola covered with honeysuckle like a tunnel of flowers. It was not like any backyard she'd ever been in. Her own had some flowers but also an area where her brothers practised pitching, a banged-up fence where they fired shots with their lacrosse sticks, a tree with a rope her brothers climbed with. It was not uncommon to slip on dog poo because their dog hated to leave the yard on rainy days, and no one liked cleaning up after it.

"What is the flower that is beginning there in the middle of the leaves in the pond?" she asked.

"That is a water lily, sent many years ago from my father's garden in England to the first home I lived in when I came to Canada. I'd settled with my brother in the Interior; he dug a pool in our very hot, dry garden, insisting he wanted to grow some of the water lilies our father loved. We had one plant of the native water lily that grows throughout British Columbia, the yellow one, but my brother wanted this one, which is native to England. It's pure white and very sweetly scented."

"I think I've seen water lilies in Beaver Lake. Yellow ones, like you said. My dad took us canoeing there and we paddled right up to them. There were lots of flies in the flower."

The woman smiled. "Yes, there would be. That is partly how the plant reproduces, by attracting insects into the shelter of its sepals. It is a wonderful plant for creating shady cool areas for fish to shelter under in warm weather, and of course you've seen how the frogs love to bask on those wide leaves."

Dragonflies hovered over the surface of the little pool, one landing on a lily leaf and remaining perfectly still, the delicate fretwork of its wings visible in its stillness. Tessa sipped her lemonade, crunching a piece of ice and chewing the sprig of mint that had garnished her drink.

"If you go into the kitchen, you will find more lemonade in a jug on the counter. Help yourself to another glass."

Inside was cool and dark and smelled of wood polish. Also lavender, which Tessa knew from the sachets her grandmother sent from New Brunswick. Through the living room (which Miss Oakden called a "sitting room") with its fireplace and a hearth with two large stones on it. Bending to look at them, Tessa saw that one was imprinted with shells. She knew about fossils from the encyclopedia at home. Into the kitchen: on the table was a tin box with papers inside, photographs it looked like, and envelopes wrapped with ribbon. An arrangement of photographs on the table, laid out like the games of Patience her mother sometimes played, a game her father also liked but he called it Solitaire and said his intention was to "beat the Chinaman." It didn't seem right to look for very long, but there was a photograph of a man on a horse and another one of a house. Some trees, not very big. A woman who looked like the people you saw in Chinatown, only she was in front of a little house, with some chickens. She would have liked to see more. She wondered whether the man had been Miss Oakden's husband.

"Did you have a husband, Miss Oakden?"

The woman was quiet for a long moment. Then, "No, my dear. My sweetheart died before we had a chance to be married. He never saw our daughter, whom I'm certain would have given him much pleasure. But luckily his own father lived not far from here. He was a wonderful grandfather to my Grace."

"Did your daughter play in Bushby Park?"

Miss Oakden smiled. "There was no park there when Grace was a girl. Like you, she liked the cemetery and she loved to go down to the water and skip stones as her grandfather taught her to do."

"It's a nice name, Grace."

"Well, I named her for another little girl, an Indian baby

155

whose mother helped in our house in Walhachin. She died of a fever. When my daughter was born, it seemed a good idea to honour the memory of that child who spent a day with me once and whom I never forgot."

"I think I'd better go home now, Miss Oakden. But thank you for the lemonade. And for showing me the frogs!"

"Goodbye, Tessa. Come and visit me again. I can't promise that the frogs will be here but I think they won't have gone far."

One of Victoria's leading architects, Tom Lamb, a former disciple of Francis Rattenbury, who regularly came to James McGregor's firm for tiles, saw Flora's water lilies. He admired the single tiles she had actually coloured and fired, which were given pride of place in the front window of the business; he wanted enough for a bathroom mural, his client having viewed the canvases of Monet's ponds and lilies on a trip to France before the war. He had been captivated by their qualities of light and reflection. Undeterred by the controversy surrounding the Impressionists as a group and Monet's work as perhaps the most significant example of the aesthetic, he had decided to bring something of it to the new home he was planning in Victoria's Rockland neighbourhood. He had bought a small Monet canvas, more an oil sketch, of water lilies and hoped to work the theme into his home.

"What do you think, Miss Oakden? Shall we tell Mr. Lamb yes? Of course we will not provide single tiles to be applied willy-nilly but an actual panel with an overall design. Your design."

"I'd like to try, sir, if you think you can spare me from the regular work. This will take some plotting and working out. I can do some of the design sketches at home, of course, but I think I will need to spend time with Mr. Nagy figuring out the glazes and what is possible in terms of colour with the firings we will need to use for a bathroom tile."

James McGregor smiled at Flora. "You underestimate your worth, my dear. The architect has seen your work and has asked for you specifically. I think it is safe to say that this will bring in more income to our firm and to you personally—we will talk bonuses at some point soon—than the regular work that I am happy to delay for a time. Please consider any time you spend on sketches to be part of your workday and leave me a record of your hours for payment. If you would like to come in a little later in the mornings, please do so, if you find it more congenial to sketch at home."

"I'm grateful to you, Mr. McGregor. And very excited about this commission! I'll begin straight away, shall I?"

It was a challenge to think in terms of a piece larger than a single tile, a little daunting although she had been hoping for the opportunity to do something grand. She'd had this feeling before, anticipating a square of linen and a basket of silk or crewel yarn. Those results, while pleasing, had never been quite what she'd hoped for. A pillow cover, after all, with a blue lotus or a tangle of wildflowers, was not much to devote one's creative urges towards. But an entire ceramic panel! Flora completed many panels of sketches, contemplated them, then discarded each one in a frustrated moment. She went to the local library to look at reproductions of Monet's water lilies and fell in love with the dreamy washes of colour, the reflected images in water, the lovely arch of a bridge across the canvas. What a wonderful composition, she thought, the bridge framing the view below. She arranged the pages on the table top in the airy reading room of the Public Library on Yates Street, the smell of wood polish clean and bracing. This was the work of someone who had looked carefully at individual water lilies and then the effect they had massed and blooming profusely in still water, bright air. It was a new way of seeing, attempting to offer the impression of how the images were a process of emotional response to something beautiful, not just the things themselves. And how light filled each canvas! But they were conceived in a painter's mind, to be worked in paints, another thing altogether from the disciplines of clay and fire. With tile, she would have to think in terms of space and interruption, of trying to subordinate light to her own purposes.

Flora worked on a panel of one hundred and twenty tiles, ten wide, twelve in length, each the six inches by six inches standard pressed-clay biscuit, framed with a border of narrow edging tile. She planned the tiles to be tube-lined but saw an example in a journal of a British designer's unique slip-trail technique, using a finer applicator for the slip than the tube-lining tools she was accustomed to but still drawing with slip of a firm-enough consistency to serve as dams between the colour fields. She experimented until she was able to use it for the fine "drawing" she needed for her panel. The effect was more painterly, she thought. She consulted at length with her friend Mr. Nagy and his alchemical recipes for colour.

"I'll want the leaves to have really high gloss. I know that there's some range in the copper oxides. How can we predict just how green the glaze will be, and how bright?"

"Ahh, well, I will try to stabilize with tin. And there are the silicas. And a soda frit, we will try that."

"What can we do to get a really milky white? Maybe with just a touch of yellow. Or cream really."

And it would be feldspar, quartz, some whiting, talc. Or magnesium carbonate to make the finish silky.

She wanted richly coloured glazes, some of them heightened with gold lustre, particularly to detail the golden stigmas in the centres of the open blossoms, and a few of the lilies themselves, modelled on the native luteums.

Nagy made a number of small batches of glazing media, each carefully recorded—the amounts of cobalt and antimony, of copper oxide and cadmium, in concert with the kaolins and feldspars. Flora experimented with many small tiles that she painted with glaze, at varying concentrations of pigment to slip, and Nagy fired them and kept careful records of temperature, time, and condition of the kiln. The test tiles would come out and the two of them would examine them carefully, noting each tiny flaw—shivering, crawling, pitting, pinholing. Occasionally a tiny blister would form, or pocking. Nagy would mutter and make notes.

"Can we deepen this a little, Mr. Nagy?" she asked him when the dark blue was almost right but with a tendency to wash out at the borders of the tiles.

He nodded and went back to work, adjusting his formula, making the glaze more alkaline. The next attempt was perfect.

When she found not just the colour she wanted but also the depth—she wanted the water to hold light and reflect it, she wanted the lilies themselves to be saturated with their hues—then she kept those small practice tiles on her work table as an inspiration.

The trick was to get the pattern to flow naturally from one tile to the next, and in order to guard against the likelihood of at least one tile cracking as it was fired, she made three of each, painstakingly measuring and adjusting to ensure that each was the same. It might have been easier to stencil the tiles or hand-paint them rather than the trickier slip-trail method, but she wanted depth and a sense of a second dimension, the glazes pooling in their contained areas and echoing water or deep green leaf or the drenched crimson of N. rubra. The narrower framing tiles she worked with a lattice of brown-glazed bamboo, letting edges of it nudge into the main panels at intervals; this meant careful alignment of tiles with an allowance for their mortar, the ideal result being that the eye would not stop at the thin mortar line but see the whole panel as a framed tableau of highly glazed ceramic.

Everything she knew of water lilies went into the panel— their stately presence in the calm water, the delicate dragonflies stitching petal to leaf (the beautiful Persian blue for the body of the insect, a gauzy grey, highlighted with gold lustre, for the wings), a field in the distance green with summer. In the air, a haze of morning sunlight. She arranged a stand of bulrushes to one side of the panel, the leaves heavy with the weight of a yellow-headed blackbird and its nest, and the shadow of a fish under one polysepalum. When she was bent over her drawings and notes for glazes, when she was moving the implement containing the coloured slip across the surface of a tile, easing the line into a golden stamen, a shapely reed, a ripple in the surface of the still water, she was back in her childhood, walking the watermeadows with her father, observing the marshy pools, or else inspecting the tanks of overwintered hybrids, alert to the new growth of leaves, the emergence of a bud, rising from the water like the head of a small mammal, the stalk supple and hollow. And she was sitting on the porch of a rustic cabin, wrapped in a blanket, a mug of tea in her hands, watching the dragonflies at work on the surface of the lake, blackbirds trilling from the rushes. Her heart would fill as she worked, memory informing her sense of design, longing and loss enriching the colours, the juxtaposition of flowers and water, a dusting of pollen on the arch of a leaf in one corner.

Flora stood with the work crew in the newly plastered bathroom, deciding on the exact placement of her panel. The client, a pleasant man who had been more than delighted with the design and now with the tiles themselves—he had seen them arranged on a large work surface and had been full of praise for the execution of the design, the colours, the movement of lilies in the calm water—was also present. Earlier consultation with Tom Lamb, the architect, determined that the tiles were sufficiently light enough in weight that it was not necessary to apply them first to a thick support that would then be securely hung by means of screws. Instead the tiles were to be fixed directly to the wall with a highly adhesive mortar. The wall had been marked carefully with builder's chalk, a grid to indicate how the tiles would be fixed to the surface with mortar, each square on the marked grid corresponding with a tile, each numbered, and a paper plan to work from.

The bathroom was bright, high windows on two sides letting in natural light from the south and east; there were also electrical fixtures that had been specially made for the room—a central bronze flush-mounted cluster of water lily leaves with three open globes of bloom in creamy glass as well as two wall sconces, also bronze, the leaves curving upward, and two sunlit flowers glowing with their light.

"I don't think the men need our overseeing them, Miss Oakden. I have taken the liberty of arranging coffee in our bare conservatory if you will do me the honour of joining me."

"How lovely, Mr. Graham. I would rather return here from time to time than watch the whole process. I confess it makes me nervous." She didn't tell him about the replacement tiles should anything happen during the installation of these.

When they had finished their coffee, they returned to the bathroom, where almost all the tiles were now affixed to the wall. If Flora nearly closed her eyes and squinted, she could imagine them with the thin line of grout between each tile and the overall effect of the water lilies in the light-filled room. She was very pleased. As was the client. She returned in two days, after the mortar had set, to watch the careful application of the grout, and then several days later to see the finished panel, the tiles cleaned of the excess grout and glowing in their colours. It was even more beautiful than she had imagined it might be. The border worked perfectly, the knotted joints of bamboo entering the field of water at intervals, in a naturalistic way, the water lilies floating in their cobalt and emerald pools, light both contained and reflected in the glazes. The dragonfly on its leaf as though startled by the viewer, the blackbird among the rushes poised and alert. In the far distance, the fields of a lost childhood glimmered and shone.

This time the client had celebratory champagne so that a toast could be drunk to Flora, the work crew, and Tom Lamb, the architect, who had been so prescient as to recommend the work of a tile painter unknown to most of Victoria.

"I think we must also drink to Mr. Nagy, who was uncommonly patient with my constant demands for more blue, or less green, or might we begin again because I really am not quite happy with the pink."

"Hear, hear."

TWENTY-ONE
1962

On Saturday mornings, Tessa's father gave a weekly allowance of a dime to each of his children. With permission, they walked over to Miss Leeming's store on the corner of May Street and Moss Street. "Stay together," their mother insisted. Along May Street, past the Moss Rocks with its forts and hide-outs and the old peoples' home that was good for spying on, along past the modern houses clinging to the hill, and then across Moss Street to enter the store. Once inside, there was the dilemma: how to spend a precious dime and make it last the longest? For a nickel, you could get an ice cream cone, delicious in warm weather but gone so quickly! Miss Leeming always had a good selection of penny candy in her glass showcase and was patient with a child making the difficult decisions. Jawbreakers were the best value: five of them could be had for a penny. And if you could resist the temptation to bite into one and waited for it to dissolve in your mouth, it would last for ages until finally a small seed was revealed at its heart. Licorice whips that you could use as shoelaces (pinching off a tiny bit to eat); marsh-mallow bananas, sugary strawberries, mint leaves, jujubes, sour balls, red hots, even realistic packages of candy cigarettes with flaming tips of red sparkling sugar. The trick was to get the most candy of the kind you liked best—Tessa thought the mint leaves a waste because the flavour was nasty, nothing like the green taste of wild mint in her mouth as she lay on her stomach in damp grass—and then to take the small paper bag out to the sidewalk to compare its contents with the others.

But the others, her brothers and several neighbourhood kids who'd walked with them to Miss Leeming's store, had disappeared by the time Tessa had made her choice and so she had to walk home alone along May Street. At the house where the Hungarians lived, a house that opened directly onto the sidewalk without the buffer of a front lawn, only a brief step between door and street, she walked very quickly by, hoping the curtains wouldn't part, a hand wouldn't wave from the end of a worn sleeve. The sons of that household played with her brothers and they were okay, but the women were scary. There wasn't a father, just a mother, and a grandmother who couldn't really speak English. At a birthday party to which Tessa and her brothers had been invited, they'd sat around an oval table in a kitchen smelling of cabbage and strange spices.

The table was set with tablewear unlike any she'd ever seen. Jugs and plates in rich deep colours—dark blue, burnt orange, brilliant yellows. They drank their Freshie from goblets—this is what was Mrs. Gurack called them: "Can I fill your goblet, Tessa?" But they'd eaten birthday cake almost silently off the splendid plates, the grandmother saying things occasionally and the Gurack boys answering with only one or two words. In Hungarian. There had been comments about Tessa. She knew from the way she was looked at, her hair stroked with a hand that looked like a claw. And then the grandmother said something that seemed like an order, said something in terrible English that sounded like, "And now we eat the candles," so Tessa took the two candles from her slice of cake and began to eat them from the ends which had been stuck in the cake so that they at least tasted a little of icing. She was too frightened not to obey. She had read the fairy tales in which children had disobeyed simple orders given by old women like this one, old women with hair growing from their chins, and who had been punished for their actions. Banished or burned or turned into animals.

But then the boys, all of them, her brothers, the two sons of the household, and one more, a neighbour, all began to laugh uproariously, while the grandmother smiled and Mrs. Gurack gently removed what remained of the candles from Tessa's fingers. Tommy Gurack then told Tessa that his grandmother had been joking, of course no one was expected to eat the candles. But by then she had bitten off quite a portion of one of her candles and didn't want to spit it out in front of everyone; she swallowed it quickly and then took a drink of Freshie to wash it down. She couldn't wait to leave that house. For days afterwards, the boys had teased her about her appetite for candle wax. She'd expected to suffer bad effects from the wax but nothing happened.

Progress on the map was slow. It was one thing to decide to map one's neighbourhood, but another to make it work on paper. Luckily the paper was thick and sturdy because it sometimes seemed that every line Tessa made with her pencil had to be erased at least once. After she had worked out north, using her brother's compass, and plotted out the general shape of the cemetery, then she took her bike and rode around the streets to determine what should be included and what didn't matter. Quite a lot mattered. The tall thin houses on the upper part of Memorial Crescent inhabited by the old couple who never washed and the family whose father didn't work, and the turreted house on the corner. Clover Point because that was where Tessa's family collected bark for their wood burner and where they were taken to watch the Queen being driven around in an open car and where she waved to Teddy, her gloved hand inclined towards him clear as anything. The little tidal islands just where Clover Point began, where the children played pirates and were stranded once when the tide came in without them noticing. Luckily there were big driftwood logs on the islands, so they could ride a log into shore, but their mothers were cross that their clothing was so wet. And Ross Bay was notorious for sewage—that's what Tessa's father said. Moss Rocks went on the map, with its hollows and special hidden cliffs. The house on Dallas Road where the missionary lived—the Brownie pack had been invited there to see cases of enormous preserved spiders with hairy legs and beautiful butterflies from Africa, and spears and blowpipes from tribes who had been converted to God and who didn't need to hunt any longer but who gathered in smiling groups in clothing sent by the church.

Bushby Park, of course, and Tessa intended to colour in the mint bed with a dark green pencil crayon. And then there would be the problem of how exactly to show the buried streams.

Where did they begin, for instance? Tessa decided to ask her father. He was reading in the living room and looked at her with surprise.

"Why do you want to know that, sweetie?"

"I'm making a map, Dad, and I know where they end up, but I have to show them coming from somewhere."

"A map? For school?"

"No, it's just something I want to do. Remember when we talked about Atlas? That started me thinking. I asked Mrs. Barrett for a big piece of chart paper so I could make my own map."

"I'll make some phone calls and see what I can find out. How would that be?"

He went away and returned an hour or so later. He had a map in his hand.

"This is just a regular street map of Victoria, but I think I can use it to show you more or less where the streams come from."

He took a pencil and drew a little rectangle around an area bordered by Cook Street to the west and Moss Street to the east, with Oxford Street to the north and May Street to the south.

"Okay, so this area used to be a swamp and probably still is, just below the ground. One of the creeks drains this whole area, the stream called South Fairfield Stream. I'm guessing it's the one that runs under our street and the park before it's joined by this creek, West Creek" —and he drew a squiggly line coming down the map— "which comes from a swampy area just below Government House. The other creek, East Creek, also drains that area, so maybe it runs down something like this. You know

167

Government House, Tessa. Your Brownie group went there for a garden party, if I recall?"

Tessa nodded vigorously. That had been a wonderful time. She reminded her father that they'd met the Lieutenant-Governor himself, a kind man with a grey moustache who shook the hand of each small girl and asked each one a question. What badges are you working on now? had been Tessa's question. And in a shy voice she had told him, Knots.

"That would have been General Pearkes. He was a hero in both wars. A very fine man. You were lucky to meet him. Anyway, you can keep this map. You'll have the basic idea now of where the water comes from and how to draw on the creeks. Oh, and another thing—I found out from one guy I called, someone I know from work, and whose son is an archaeologist, that when this area belonged to the Indians, they used the creeks as pathways to take them over to the Inner Harbour. Of course it wasn't called that then, but it was where there was a big Indian village, where the Songhees lived. Later on they moved over to Esquimalt."

"Dad, why would the creeks go underground?" This was something Tessa had thought about a lot. She knew about pipes bringing water to houses from the reservoir; she knew about drains and sewers. Sometimes, when the tide was very low, you could stand by the outflow by Ross Bay and see murky stuff come out the pipe. Her brothers swore they saw poo itself gushing out. And there were the things like balloons that her mother had told them never to touch; they came from people's toilets, though why a person would need a balloon in their bathroom was a mystery.

Her father thought for a minute or two before answering. Then: "Hmmm. Lots of reasons, I suppose. Running them through culverts and then using the land over top would give builders more scope for their projects. It's not always convenient to have creeks running through areas where people live."

"But our teacher said that Victoria was just a little fort when it began."

"Oh, yes, true enough. This would have been wilderness. And you can imagine those Indians making their way through the bush by using the creeks. Later, when the city began to expand, this was farmland and it would have been helpful to have a water supply. As the city grew larger, more houses were needed for the people moving here. And you know, the cemetery has been here for a long time, maybe about a hundred years. I'm sure no one gave the creeks a second thought in the early days—there would have been more than enough ground for burying people and who knows, the creeks were probably a nice feature. But then every bit of land became more precious. I remember my father telling me about storms in the early part of this century that washed some of the graveyard out into Ross Bay. I bet the creeks had something to do with that, overflowing their banks, perhaps, and flooding parts of the cemetery."

Tessa was quiet, listening to her father talk. Then, "Did some of the bodies go into Ross Bay too?"

"Oh, yes, I think so. Not very nice to think about, eh? Can I see this map you're making?"

She thought for a moment, then shook her head. "Not yet. Maybe never. I don't know if I can get it the way I want it so I'd rather not show it to you right now. Is that okay?"

Her father ruffled her hair and went back to his reading. And Tessa took her street map down into the basement so she could trace and plot some more.

The children either walked to school or rode their bikes, depending on weather. (Weather was a concern mostly just for Tessa, who wore skirts and didn't like the trail of water and mud splashing up the backs of her legs when she rode her bike in the rain.) It was a matter of seven or eight blocks, along May Street to Moss Street, and then up Moss to the five corners where Sir James Douglas Elementary School stood opposite a church, a pharmacy, a small store, and a gas station. On some fine mornings, walking, they might take the trail over the Moss Rocks and make their way down the little cul-de-sac that ran down the other side of the Rocks onto Fairfield Road. Every morning before they left, their mother would hand them their lunch kits and tell them to be careful.

What this meant, Tessa wasn't exactly certain. Of course you would not want to ride your bike so recklessly that you might fall off, or lean so precariously over the edge of the Moss Rocks that you might tumble down. *Be careful*, they'd be told as they left the house to play in the cemetery, but what could harm them on the narrow lanes leading to the graves and tombs? At dusk, there were owls. Once, Tessa had seen one swoop down over the grass and then rise again with something in its claws. And as often as her brothers told her to watch when passing the mausoleums where Helmckens and Rithets slept for eternity, to watch out for a hand grabbing from within the little houses of the dead, Tessa was never frightened in those still places. *Be careful*, as they played on the shore near Clover Point, building bakeshops of driftwood with tall cakes created of wet sand and decorated with strands of seaweed and clamshells, a sprinkling of dry sand sparkling in the sun like sugar. There was a rumour of a girl who'd been chased on the beach by a man with his pants open; for a week or two Tessa and the other girls in the neighbourhood had to do everything in groups with at least one dog with them. But Tessa's family dog, a fat old Labrador, needed much coaxing from her place by the wood heater in the kitchen, and anyway she couldn't keep up and had to be left, panting, by the breakwater. And eventually the incident was forgotten. *Be careful, careful*—and yet what dangers might be contained in a neighbourhood of tidy houses, of men leaving each morning in their station wagons for jobs, coming home each evening to eat meals at tables with obedient children, wives in twin sets or pedal pushers, of those wives tidying their houses, taking the bus downtown on $1.49 Day to buy underwear at Woodward's, nesting bowls for their kitchens, aprons and tea towels and a copy of *McCall's* to read with a cup of coffee in the afternoon while waiting for their children to return from Sir James Douglas Elementary School at its five corners, its Annex on the rock hill of oaks.

A woman went from house to house measuring women for foundation garments. She was once welcomed into homes to show her samples of elastic girdles with small clasps of flesh-coloured rubber to hold the tops of stockings, her brassieres made of oyster satin, a little rose centred between the bosoms. Tessa had seen her come up their own sidewalk with her suitcase, her straight back, the hat with a little veil covering the top part of her face. She spoke softly, with an accent. But now when she was in the neighbourhood, women would phone to let the others know. There had been an incident. Word of it spread like a disease. She had touched a woman inappropriately while fitting her for a brassiere or girdle; this was how Tessa heard her own mother describe to one neighbour what she'd been told by another. They used low voices, so the children wouldn't know, but they heard. So when the *tap, tap, tap* of her shoes on the wooden steps of the porch announced her arrival, the children were sent to the back of the house and Tessa's mother set her mouth in a very thin grim line and went to the door to send the woman away.

What kind of touching? Tessa wondered. Did she hold on to a hand too long, was there kissing or hugging, did she put her hand in the area all children were warned not to touch? What would happen if you touched a person, or yourself, there, maybe while bathing or while lying in your bed at night? One of Tessa's brothers had been given a book in Health class that suggested disease or imbecility (Tessa looked up this word in the big dictionary) if too much touching—the book called it "self-abuse"—took place. This made the washing of your private parts a very risky business, she decided, and would just splash water in that general direction when she was having a bath, hoping it would do. The man with his pants open had showed his private parts to anyone who would look. Was that what made him dangerous? Or was it the parts themselves? Tessa had been bathing with her brothers for years and they changed into swimsuits in the same room. Their private parts were as innocent as shoulders. Or so it seemed.

"Well, that got rid of her," said Tessa's mother with some satisfaction. The tap, tap, tap could be heard as the veiled woman crossed their cement path to the street. "And now I want you to come with me, Tessa. I'm taking my winter coat to the invisible mender on Cook Street for a small repair. You can help me carry a few groceries back."

She could not breathe under the weight of the sand. Outside the men were grinding stone and her brothers had vanished. Could not breathe, her neck flattened by cold sand, unable to lift her hands to push the weight off her chest, her throat. She began to gasp and panic, tried to call out but no sound came, no words, no scream. She tried to rise up from the sand, hearing the frantic pulse of her blood in her ears, when suddenly she woke up, finding herself curled in a warm hollow on the Moss Rocks, utterly alone. Shooting stars in a small cluster bloomed beside where she'd fallen asleep in the sunshine. She breathed deeply, smelling moss and something earthy and dark, something like snakes. (Her brothers had put them down her back in the past and she'd had to wriggle them free, smelling them on her T-shirt afterwards.) Quickly she checked to make certain none were around and found instead of snakes a tiny rubbery case, like a soft egg. Whatever had been inside the egg was no longer there, a tear at one end indicating exit. Snakes, she thought she'd been told, were born alive. Parting the ferns growing right against the rock, she found several more of the little cases. She put one in her pocket. Her father usually knew the answer to any question.

"A lizard, Tessa, like the ones your brothers occasionally bring home. From the Moss Rocks, was it? Yes, I think certainly a lizard. Probably the western alligator lizard. They like the warm rocks and places where they can hide away for winter."

But then he came to her a day later with a puzzled look on his face.

"It's not quite true, what I told you about the lizard, Tessa. Farther south, they do lay eggs. Or least a related species does. But here—" and he showed her the field guide he was looking in . . . "—here, it says that this far north, they produce young by means of ovoviviparity. The female carries the eggs in her body but rather than lay the eggs externally, the young come out of the shell while still inside their mother's body. It seems that they're born live, but in fact it's a slightly different process. So I've no idea what might have laid the egg that you found on the Rocks."

Another mystery to set upon her windowsill, along with a green feather, a tiny rib cage found at the high-tide line, a black arrowhead from a family camping trip to the Nicola Valley, a tooth that had fallen out of her kitten's mouth into her palm when she was tickling its tummy. These objects charmed and perplexed her. Most days she would touch them reverently, wanting to know more. Why a kitten tooth curved, how an arrowhead ended up in a little graveyard by a wooden church, how something as fragile as a rib cage could ride in on the tide, miraculously whole. And as for the egg case, she would never forget waking from a nightmare to that smell, dark and warm, like the very earth itself was alive and breathing under the moss.

Ann stopped singing in mid-phrase. It was the opening aria of a Bach cantata, "Ich habe genug," and she was pouring the day's irritations and joy into it. "'Ich habe genug, Ich habe den Heiland . . .'" She had begun her day with her usual disciplined scales and exercises, but this was opening her throat for the pleasure of singing. "'Ich hab' inh erblickt, Mein Glaube hat Jesum ans Herze ge . . .'" And now she stopped.

"Flora, whatever is wrong?"

For Flora had come through the door in tears. Grace was in bed, and the house was still, a few chords from the stopped piano almost audible.

"Didn't the meeting go well? I thought the client was very happy with your work?"

Flora brushed her eyes hastily with one glove. "Yes, I think he is. In fact I'm certain of it. Ann, I didn't mean to interrupt your singing. I love that cantata. Please continue?"

"How can I when you stand here in tears, Flora? My dear, I can't imagine anyone not wanting that lovely panel on their wall, though I said from the beginning it deserved a grander placement than a bathroom wall, however luxurious the chamber . . . So is that it, then—have they decided against it?"

"No, no, it's nothing like that, Ann." She turned her head so her friend wouldn't see that she was still weeping.

"Oh, whatever is it? Have you had bad news of some sort? Did someone shun you on the street? You know how I feel about that—you must simply smile and lift your chin a little higher.

But what, what?" She held Flora by the elbows and looked seriously into her eyes.

Flora gently removed Ann's hands. She wrung her own hands in consternation. "It's just . . . ah, I realized on the way home that what I have done is set into tile my childhood, of all things. Its passing. My loss of it. My father's water lilies. My old life. I have buried myself in the making of this work and now it's over and my father has given up on his love for his flowers. He has given up on any hope he had for the future. And my future . . . well, I haven't given up on it, but it won't be what I so dreamed of all those months ago, years now, when I lay with Gus in our little box canyon and thought he would come home to me. To us, although I didn't know then that there would be Grace. All these lilies floating in their pools of water . . . I've put them down the only way I could, and now it's over. Oh, dear, am I making any sense at all?"

She wept as she took off her coat and hung it on its hook and put her pocketbook down on the table in the hall. Then she went into the sitting room and stood by the window, looking out at the trees of the cemetery, their boughs dark in the falling light.

"I don't think I will ever see Watermeadows again. Nor my parents. My brothers are dead. My love is dead. And there are only momentary glimpses of Gus in Grace's face. There's nowhere to go to mourn him."

"Well, there is your heart, of course. You have the notebooks, the letters. I think that with time you will realize that we make our memorials out of such things. They keep the person intact in ways that I doubt any stone cross or obelisk could."

"I know that, Ann, I do. But so many have died over the past few years. Too many. I am resigned, I suppose, to never being able to visit the graves of my brothers. But I feel so lonely sometimes, as though there will never be anyone who knew me as a child or a young girl to tell me little stories of that time. I feel so far from my roots and so far from being the woman who was loved by Gus and who expected to have a life with him. And then

I feel ungrateful for thinking this because you have been so kind to me, and to Grace."

Ann ran her fingers along the keyboard, finding a consoling chord. "But I do understand what you're saying, I think. And it is still early days. It would be unusual for you to have put all this behind you, though I think you are doing admirably. The tile work, your new-found success as a designer—the architects will beat a path to your door now, mark my words—the obvious health and happiness of Grace . . ."

Flora refused to take solace. In a very small voice, she said, "I think I would be grateful for even a stone in one of the leafy places across the road. Maybe one of the little areas where I always imagine I can hear water. A place to sit and breathe in the sense of who it is I am mourning. A place to contain his memory in a solid and formal way. A stone with his name on it to say finally that he is dead."

"Then why not have one made? I think Robert Alexander might well be grateful too for such a thing. Mrs. Alexander too, if she would only put her pride aside."

Flora sniffed and wiped her eyes with a handkerchief she took from the pocket of her skirt. "Do you think so, Ann?"

"I do."

"All this unrestrained emotion: you must wonder at me sometimes. I watch the processions of people through the cemetery with their wreathes, their sorrow, watch them stand before a grave and focus the whole of their love and anguish on that small plot of earth with its precious content, and I wish for such a place. To think of him unburied, uncommemorated, oh, it's too much sometimes. But what a good idea. Thank you, Ann. And now will you finish that aria?"

"Well, you'll have to hear the whole thing because I can't just pick up where I left off. I love this piece."

"I'd love to hear it from the beginning. Is there a reason why you are singing in the afternoon, and why this cantata in particular?"

Ann smiled. "Oh, I had a little time and I thought I'd rather sing than simply drink tea by the window and gaze dreamily out. And why this piece? There needs never be a reason to sing Bach! But this cantata was composed for Candlemas, which is today of course, February 2, the time of year when wolves and bears are waking from their dens. And the Mother of Jesus goes to be purified in the midst of it all."

With that, she laughed at her uncharacteristic show of pedantry, took up her music, cleared her throat, took a deep breath, expanding her rib cage to hold the air necessary for the long controlled passages, to give platform for the rich high notes; she sang the beautiful phrases again, sung first in the eighteenth century to welcome light back to earth, the sacred cry of a woman cleansed after giving birth to a saviour, a blessing of ground and fields, of candles to serve as talisman against the passing of the long winter.

When Flora approached Robert Alexander with the possibility of a permanent memorial to Gus, he insisted on assuming the cost if she, Flora, would decide on what the stone would say.

"He knew this cemetery, you know. Walked in it any number of times as a boy. You must talk to your Mr. Stewart and order stone that you think most suitable. Choose the lettering, fine and strong as he was. And some words to fix him forever in time. I might be inclined to something from Homer, those lines at the conclusion of the *Iliad*—'Such was their burial of Hector, breaker of horses. But I leave it to you.'"

"Those are very suitable words indeed, Robert. Truly beautiful. But if you really don't mind, I have something else, a few lines, also poetry, which I think Gus would have wanted too."

And then there was never any question in her mind what those words should be. There would be his name. His dates. She kept in her box of special tokens a piece of paper, written in his hand in a tiny box canyon near the Deadman River, while hawks made lazy circles in a still sky, a code they would use so she would know he had gone to the battlefields of France. *Sed nos inmensum spatiis confecium aequor / et iam tempus equum fumantia solvere colla.* That would be his inscription.

Flora's father died in the fall of 1919. It seemed that he simply lost his will to live—the letters from her mother revealed that the doctors believed he had given up. *He sits in the wheeled chair with a blanket over his legs and looks out towards the river. Mrs. Sloan makes all manner of milk puddings and invalid foods but nothing tempts him,* her mother wrote in a letter that arrived just days before the envelope with the black border. He was to be buried in the Winsley churchyard. Mrs. Oakden would sell Watermeadows as soon as she could in order to move into a flat in London to be closer to her sister.

Is there anything you would like? her mother wrote. *Papers, books, any of the photographs?*

Why don't you decide on a few personal papers and photographs, Flora wrote back. *I'd like Grace to know something about my side of her family. Her grandfather Alexander tells her all about her Scottish ancestors and her father. She is enchanted to believe that a father she never knew, except in photographs, was once a boy in this very neighbourhood.* And Flora knew that no mention would ever be made of Grace, or the lost father. No curiosity shown towards a Scottish grandfather or the life that Flora now lived.

She wept for her father, but it was a mild grief, her sorrow at the real loss of her family and home having been wrung from her during the creation and completion of her panel of tiles. The man who had written to her such dispirited letters about selling his horses, letting the gardens go wild, having no interest in anything much any longer, was not the father she remembered from her girlhood, the proud though remote man who let her accompany him to breeders of water lilies or to Stourhead or the glass houses at Kew. She did not know that man in the wheeled chair looking out to the river, had no place in her memory for him.

A box arrived some months later. Among the photographs and a volume of her grandfather's sermons, a series of water-colours of birds done by an aunt, was a journal and a package of letters. Some of the letters, she could see, were in the hand of Henry, an ornate copperplate. The journal was bound in a marbled paper, quite beautifully, though it was soiled. When she opened it, Flora realized it had been with her older brother during his time in Gallipoli. There were notes on weather, birds, meals, descriptions of stomach troubles, and then a kind of code in which he seemed to talking about meetings away from the camp, the beauty of P., lines of verse about marble limbs. Then a direct cry, *I am nothing without you, my dearest Peter, and if we must die, let us die in one another's arms.*

Peter? she wondered. Peter?

There was more, and it broke her heart to read it. Her brother had had a lover, a young man, someone he'd known for years, although it was clear there was a class separation. Family was mentioned, and how his own might feel about a relationship with this young man. Henry wondered how their special friend-ship might continue back in England; an entire entry mused about the future, as though it was just around the corner from the landing beach at Cape Helles. And then entries about the horrors of seeing men shot as they tried to move to the sand from the sea. Her brother had been terribly afraid, she read, afraid of so many things—blood, loud noise, the Turks coming over the dunes with their weapons, the sight of bodies turning black within a day in the fierce sun. Then joy: a brief unexpected rhapsody on the beauty of the Australian soldiers, tanned and muscular as they tried to wash themselves of dust and sweat at the end of a day. Fear again—of his encounters with Peter being discovered. And of one of them dying without the other nearby.

When she finished reading Henry's journal, she felt as though she'd been through a whirlwind. He had so clearly been in love with the young soldier in his company. They had sworn to be true to each other, he confessed to the pages of his journal, and there was a photograph tucked into its pages, a young man smiling, a forelock of unruly hair falling over his brow. *With all my love, Peter*, was written on the back. He looked familiar but for the moment Flora did not think about that.

Had her father read the journal? Of course he must have. Her father, for whom the term *manly* was a high compliment. Her father's heart was so proud that two of his sons had gone to serve their King and country, full in the bloom of English manhood. And her mother, who had never told Flora the least thing about her physical body, not the bleeding, not the expectation of breasts. And now there was this knowledge of Henry passed along to her, an uneasy legacy. Who was Peter, and had he survived the war?

And like a small sharp arrow, a sudden memory of the housekeeper, Mrs. Sloan, and her son Peter entered Flora's mind; the two of them lived in what had once been the dower cottage on the Watermeadows property. Mr. Sloan, who had also worked for them, had been killed by a falling tree. She looked at the photograph again. That forelock. That smile. She almost recalled—did she, or was it the anxiety of not knowing? Of wanting to put a face to a name, to give shape to the lover in her brother's heart?— that Henry and Peter had rambled the local woods together, in search of flints and remnants of the Roman road. They'd returned to Watermeadows with their eyes shining, full of ancient stockades and tracks worn deep into the valleys from the weight of quarried rock. They'd seemed so proud and electric somehow to the young Flora, their bodies alive with the landscape they'd explored. And now she realized they had been alive with the knowledge of each other.

She thought about Henry, what she remembered of him. They had never been close. He had been born seven years before Flora and had been away at school for most of her childhood. Summers he had a tutor, sometimes the same one as George but often a special one to concentrate on Greek or Latin exclusively, whereas George's tutors needed to also help him with his maths and history, and remedial languages. Unlike George, he didn't try to amuse a younger sister; he occasionally ruffled her hair as he passed her on the terrace on his way to birdwatch or to walk the old Roman roads in search of antiquities. She thought at first her mother was being cruel in sending her Henry's journal but realized after thinking about it at length that her mother would have had no other way to share what she knew about her son. No language for what Henry was and whom he loved. Flora barely had a vocabulary for Henry, but in her own love affair, she had walked off the path and into a landscape where she had become her true self. In a box canyon, she had made love among the tracks of a rattlesnake. On the porch of a log cabin by a remote lake fringed with reeds, she had let her blanket fall to the floor and stood naked before a man who would give her Grace. What she had done and what had come of it needed new words; she had found them, taken them in, tried to take the sting away with love and hard work. Henry had paid a very high price for loving whom he loved, and she wanted to find a place for him and his Peter in her heart.

To settle that heart and to accommodate this new knowledge, she went for a walk to the cemetery, taking Grace with her. They crossed the road, and Grace slipped her hand from Flora's in order to take her own way into the quiet grounds.

"I like to go between the hedges," she explained as she came out on the other side of the privet. "I like the smell. And it's the right way to come in."

"Whatever do you mean by that, Grace?"

"I can't hear them talking when I go through the gate," was the strange reply. And she would say no more.

They walked to Gus's stone and Flora tidied the area around it a little, brushing away leaf litter and needles from the exotic plantings of pine trees from various parts of the world that provided beautiful shade in summer and restful dark in winter. When the stone had first been laid into the ground, Flora had regularly removed any moss that began to accumulate between the letters and numbers of the inscription. But now she left it. She liked the way the plushy green softened the edges of the words—*Sed nos inmensum spatiis confecium aequor / et iam tempus equum fumantia solvere colla*. Their hard clarity smoothed, the way the pain of Gus's death had been eased somehow over the years as Flora was absorbed by the daily work of raising her child, making a living for them, running the house with Ann. She bent to the stone and ran her thumb along the soft edge of *equum*, remembering as she did so the lovely eyes of Agate, the flared nostrils of Flight. In the meantime, Grace wandered in the grass, her face dreamy. Flora watched her extend her hands, as though to touch something but there was nothing but air. She could hear Grace talking softly while the crows preened and muttered.

There was less work for Flora now that the war was over and men were reclaiming jobs they had left behind. Fewer men returned than had left in a wild patriotic rush; that was certain. The speculative balloon, so elevated and promising at the beginning of the war, had burst, and buildings stood empty all over Victoria. Architects were more conservative, and although the occasional commission for tiles still materialized, many weeks went by without a call from James McGregor to ask that Flora come in for a consultation.

One architect Flora met on a walk along the Ross Bay waterfront— "Miss Oakden, surely?" "Yes, and you are Mr. Restholme! How do you do, sir?" "I have wanted so much for a client to ask for tiles so that I could commission a group from you—your water lilies are famous, you know—but it seems that the war has left people uneasy about spending money on something of beauty" —told her he would actively promote her work but nothing came of it.

Flora had been permitted to keep the extra tiles she'd made for Tom Lamb's client as insurance against cracking or breaking. With Ann's blessing, she arranged to have someone come to the house to affix a panel of them onto the bathroom wall in the Memorial Crescent house. The effect was not as grand as the room in the beautiful Rockland house, but it gave both women great pleasure.

"Little would anyone know, passing this house on the street, that its bathroom contained such a work of art!" Ann exclaimed as they toasted the installation with measures of the Islay malt they had taken to drinking on special occasions.

A sum of money had been settled on Flora once the sale of Watermeadows had been finalized, so she was not in financial difficulty, but she missed the work, the challenge of filling a space with an image that would both please and enlighten. Her life was full of Grace, but she waited for something else, a sense of purpose. When she returned to Hollyhock Cottage from a walk along the waterfront or among the graves, she'd hear Ann practising scales, and she yearned to enter into something deeply—she'd had a glimpse of what this must be like when she'd worked with Nagy to develop the colours for her tiles: the formulae, the chemical relationships. And yet at night when her child slept and she took something from her work basket to mend, she was content enough for the time being. She had begun to say a little prayer to herself as she darned stockings, a few lines from Isaiah: "'And they shall beat their swords into ploughshares, and their spears into pruning hooks.'"

TWENTY-THREE
1962

Summer arrived almost before Tessa knew it. School ended. The long two months stretched before her with promises of picnics, swimming in Gonzales Bay, go-cart races on the Eberts Street hill, endless games of hide-and-seek in the hours before bed. This was the summer she was allowed to go downtown on the bus to get her own library books once a week, her bus fare wrapped in a piece of tissue and tucked into her shorts pocket along with her library card.

Miss Oakden asked Tessa's mother whether the girl might be allowed to help with simple garden chores for a small allowance. Did Tessa want to do this? Oh, she was thrilled. To spend more time in that magical garden with the frogs and roses and then to have lemonade on the cool porch—the mornings she went to Miss Oakden's, she was always awake early with an excited feeling in her stomach. Miss Oakden was like the mysterious objects on her windowsill. She wanted to know more, wanted to be around her in order to learn how the woman fit into the neighbourhood. The world, even.

"I thought you could help me rake the grass, Tessa. I pushed the mower around very early because I couldn't sleep. Here is the basket I use to take clippings to the compost bin, which is there by the back fence."

The raking took almost no time at all. After cleaning the bamboo tines of the last bits of sweet-smelling grass, Tessa wondered what she might do next.

"Would you mind going up on the stepladder to help train

the new shoots of honeysuckle around the pergola? I feel a little too shaky to climb it these days, but I will hold it while you go up."

Tessa didn't mind at all. With Miss Oakden's direction, she coaxed strands of honeysuckle in and around the lathe. The flowers were wonderfully scented, almost like cloves, the spice her mother put in apple pie. She had to avoid the bees with their heavy pollen sacs as they moved from blossom to blossom. And was delighted to find another of the small green frogs perched on a leaf like a tiny jewel. She was almost at eye level with it. Its throat pulsed, pale pink, and its tiny feet were splayed against the leaf like tiny hands, exactly the same brilliant green as the vine.

When they'd finished the chores, they had lemonade on the porch. Tessa wondered whether it would be all right to ask Miss Oakden questions about her daughter. There was a feeling in the house, Tessa couldn't have articulated what exactly it was, but she felt the presence of a girl when she went in to help the woman carry out a tray. There was no other way to say it. The silence after a footfall. The slight movement of curtains as though someone standing at a window had moved away. Almost the sound after laughter dies away.

"Did your daughter go to my school, Miss Oakden?"

"For several years, yes, she did, Tessa. She had classes in the Annex. And then her grandfather asked that he be allowed to pay for her to attend St. Ann's Academy—you know where that is, I believe, because one of the girls on your street is a student there?"

Tessa did know. Eva Den Boer, four doors down, went every morning on the bus in her tunic and knee socks, white shirt and tie. It took her outside the neighbourhood in more ways than one, and Tessa had never really known her very well at all, though they were the same age.

"Did your daughter have a grandmother too?" asked Tessa, thinking of her own, who lived in New Brunswick—the Victoria grandparents had died before she was even born—and who had come to spend a few weeks with her family after Tessa's grandfather died.

"Well, yes, she did, although her grandmother only came around to the idea of knowing her when Grace was an older girl, no longer even a teenager, really. Families have odd ideas about things, my dear, and Grace's grandmother was stubborn. But I believe she was glad to have changed her mind, even if it meant some regret for the years having passed without contact with Grace. As for my own parents, also her grandparents, they never knew Grace. My father died just after the Great War, the one in which Grace's father was killed, and my mother never enjoyed good health, never contemplated a trip to Canada. In those years, I could not have afforded to take my daughter to England, which was where my mother lived. And when I could have managed a trip for us, it was too late. I tried to give Grace some sense of my family home there, my childhood. It was all I could do, though it seemed so little at the time."

"Did she want to know about it?" Tessa asked, knowing how she pestered her mother constantly for stories of a childhood in New Brunswick, during which she would watch her mother for any little glimmer of the child she had been. It was a very strange business to try to imagine one's parents as children, yet there were moments when those children could be found. In photographs sometimes. Or in the tone of a laugh, or at the beach when a mother might plunge into the waves like a girl, or a father helping to build a go-cart and then taking it from the top of the rise down the road, shouting with excitement like any kid.

"Yes, I think she did. I used maps so I could show her where we lived in relation to places like Stonehenge, for example, and Bath—she loved reading Jane Austen when she was a teenager. And I have some photographs of my family home, which was called Watermeadows. Grace liked the horses and the views of the river."

"I'm making a map, Miss Oakden."

"You are? What an interesting idea, Tessa. I see you in the

cemetery fairly often, with your notebook, so am I correct in thinking that is part of your map?"

"Oh, yes. The entire neighbourhood. What I'm trying to do is make it all to scale with the important places and things on it. I'm using a legend. Did you know about the buried streams? Well, you do, because we talked about them a little, ages ago. But my dad found out where they come from, and I'm trying to get them right. People think they are storm drains, but they're not. My dad told me that Indians used them as trails in the old days."

Miss Oakden was taken aback for a moment. This child was full of surprises! She gathered her thoughts and then said, "Grace's father knew about those streams, but they weren't buried then. His father told me he used to ramble all over what is now this neighbourhood, but it used to be quite wild. There were marshes and swamps, the Chinese had their market gardens where Cook Street is now—the shops and the newer buildings towards Beacon Hill Park—and there were farms and orchards all around this area. And yes, many streams for a boy to explore. The Indian people used Ross Bay for bird hunting and they had camas digging areas all over. That was a root they collected and ate. Beautiful blue flowers, like the sky. The streams would have been like roads, I suspect."

"There weren't roads?" Tessa could not imagine the area without May Street, Fairfield Road, and even the narrow lanes in the cemetery.

"Oh, no, my dear. This would have been dense bush. Much of it was when I came here to live in 1914! Lots of the wild spirea and thimbleberry, ferns, the hawthorns with their shaggy bark and sweet blossoms. And the streams running, all of them, to Ross Bay or Foul Bay or Rock Bay, or over to the Inner Harbour. I think it wasn't until much later that they were filled in or directed through culverts to the sea. For instance, in this area, no one would want to think of a cemetery with water running through it, I suppose."

"That's what my dad said too. Miss Oakden, there's a loose

board on your back fence. I discovered it when I was listening for the stream in Bushby Park. If you don't mind, I can use it as a gateway when I come here. I can just fit through it. Shall I show you where?"

"No need to show me, Tessa. You may consider it your own private entrance to my garden." And saying that, the woman had a faint and distant memory of a gap in a hedge, a small girl finding her way through it as her brother called her to come.

Later, working on her map, Tessa tried to draw in a boy in the upper waters of East Creek, at the very top of the map. She used her pencil as lightly as she could.

One day, after leaving Miss Oakden's house—she had watered that day and had been given secateurs ("Though I think of them as pruning hooks, from Isaiah, another broken promise of the Lord's.") to take the finished roses off their canes: "Find a leaf node, my dear, here, just like this, and cut a little above it, at an angle. That will encourage the plant to flower again"— Tessa made her way to the beach to spend a little time looking out to sea. She found this compelling. Sometimes there were ships in the distance and always there were gulls to watch wheeling and turning in the heat. They'd glide low over the water and rise with a little silver fish, pursued by others as they flew to shore to eat. She was sitting on a warm log when she saw the skeleton wedged in behind the pile of logs nearest the breakwater. It was stretched out on its back, chest open, head turned to one side, arms by its side and short legs hanging down. She counted the fingers. Yes, there were five. It must be one of the bodies her father said had washed down from the cemetery in that storm his own father had told him about. It was too small to be an adult. It must be one of the children who died of the diseases before there was vaccine.

What should she do about it? It looked so peaceful there in its hidden shelter behind the logs. A few strands of seaweed were caught on the skull.

She did nothing. She walked through the cemetery, thinking if she saw a caretaker, she would tell him. But what if he thought she was to blame somehow. Her brothers told ghost stories about people who dug up bodies and fished out their livers and suppose she was accused of having done this very thing? Her parents would be so angry. She couldn't imagine the punishment if they believed she had done such a thing. Returning to the beach, she collected some large pieces of bark and arranged them over the skeleton like blankets.

For a week she told no one. She had trouble sleeping. Every time she closed her eyes, she saw the skeleton. She dreamed one night that it called to her, saying it wanted its liver back, just like the story her brothers told in the dark. But there had been no insides when she found it, she knew that; just the perfect arch of its rib cage and the helpless hands hanging from the arms. She visited it in its hidden place, lifting aside some of the bark so she could make sure it was still there. In a moment of bravery, she reached down and touched the fingers. They were smooth and cool. She liked the feel of them in her own fingers. She touched the ribs. Once they had cradled a heart, two lungs, all the business of digesting. A child who had died before it had even gone to school—she was convinced of this because when she scrambled down into the hollow where it was and lay next to it in the sand, she was taller than it would have been when alive.

"Dad, I found a skeleton on the beach. I'm kind of worried about what to do about it. I think it might be one of the bodies that washed out to sea."

Tessa's father looked up, startled, from the magazine he was reading in a lawn chair in the backyard. A bottle of cold beer stood on an overturned bucket beside him. "A skeleton, Tessa? Are you sure? And what do you mean, the bodies that washed out to sea?"

"Don't you remember telling me about a storm? Your dad told you about it? When the creeks flooded out part of the cemetery and some of the graves washed out to Ross Bay?"

189

She was anxiously wringing her hands. Her father saw dark hollows under his daughter's eyes and wondered why he hadn't noticed them before. He rose from his chair and found his sandals from where he'd let them drop from his feet in a moment of uncharacteristic summer abandon.

"Yes, but that was a long time ago, Tessa. 1909, I believe. You'd better show me this skeleton."

They walked in silence down to the beach at Ross Bay just below the cemetery. Tessa removed the little cairn of bark she had placed over the skeleton. Her father looked at it briefly and then hugged her.

"Have you been worried about this for long, sweetie?"

She confessed that she'd found the skeleton a week earlier and hadn't known what to do about it. She told him she'd looked for a caretaker but worried she might be accused of digging up a body.

"You did the right thing to tell me, but you needn't have worried about this being something from the cemetery. Because, well, it's a seal."

"A seal, Dad? A *seal*?"

"I can see why you might have thought it was a human body. It's a very good skeleton—all the parts are intact. See the long bones here that end in what look like hands? Those are the flippers, but there are even fingers, aren't there? Think of the shape of the mammal sort of hidden in the outer trappings of a fish. And look how beautiful the rib cage is, like a boat. It's a neat thing to have found, Tessa, and I'm quite relieved it's not a human skeleton. I had visions of us calling the police and there being an investigation and . . . well, let's just say I'm relieved."

"I think we should bury it, Dad. I don't want it to break up in the tide and that's what would happen, wouldn't it?"

"Probably. The sea takes care of all that very well, I think. Other animals feed on a dead one and the water and salt scour the bones. But yeah, we can bury it. The sand is a good final resting place for it, I suppose. You wait here and I'll go home for a shovel."

Tessa sat in the sunshine, beside the seal, waiting for her father to return. Now that she knew it was not a body from the cemetery, she felt free to touch it and to examine the way the joints were held together, to wiggle a tooth in the skull, to hold the strange hand in her own. When her father came down the stairs from the breakwater with the garden shovel, she had picked out a place as far from the low-tide mark as possible. She had laced two pieces of driftwood together with seaweed to make a cross, ready to plant when they had dug the hole, laid the skeleton in carefully, then covered it with fine dry sand.

"We should say something, Dad. What do they say at funerals? Are there proper words?"

Tessa's father looked at her tenderly. "You have a good heart, Tess. Yes, there are proper words. I remember some of them from my father's funeral. Let me think for a moment. Well, it's probably not right to use something like this for a seal, but it does seem fitting:

Therefore will we not fear, though the earth be moved,
and though the hills be carried into the midst of the sea;
Though the waters thereof rage and swell,
and though the mountains shake at the tempest of the same.

And there, we can say goodbye and go home for something cold to drink, as is usual after a funeral, Tessa."

And so they did. Her father promised her he would say nothing about the skeleton to her brothers. She knew they would make fun of her, laughing about her conviction that she had found the remains of a child on the beach, and they would tell all the neighbourhood kids. She wanted it to be private, something between her father and herself.

PART THREE
Hecuba

TWENTY-FOUR
1962

Using a plant book of her father's, Tessa drew the Atlas cedar onto her map, then the pines, with a little gathering of crows in the high branches. A cork elm in the southwestern corner. The stones themselves were more difficult. But she resolved this to some degree by taking a little notepad to the cemetery and sketching the stones from life (if it could be put that way). Then she carefully cut out around the drawings and pasted the images into their approximate locations on the map. Some of them were difficult to draw. The angel at Charles Edward Pooley's grave, for instance. It was so elegant that she worked for a long time to get it as right as she could—which was not good enough. Several with doves were easier. And the Rithet mausoleum was fun. Mick, a good artist, taught her to use perspective; two lines coming to a point could show a road heading towards the horizon and angled lines could make a building appear less flat. So she drew the mausoleum's arch and stonework, shading and erasing until it was as real as she could manage. She wished she could have indicated every grave, but there wouldn't have been enough room on her paper so she selected the ones she felt closest to. Baby Campbell's chair and booties. Mr. Spencer's tall grey obelisk where she could hear the water and which also gave her the opportunity to sketch in part of the West Creek flowing underground, something she did by drawing wavy blue lines that, her legend explained, represented hidden water.

She worked for some time to make faint shadowy figures, those whose graves had washed away in the storm of 1909. Some of them she lightly sketched under the sea, as though swimming. And she paid attention to another grave Miss Oakden visited, with a woman's name on it, and a long inscription:

I lay myself on these wounds
As though upon a true rock;
They shall be my resting place.
Upon them will I soar in faith
And therefore contented and happily sing.

She wrote the passage into her notebook, and wondered at it. It sounded like music, maybe a hymn that would be sung in church. Tessa hated church. Mostly her family didn't go, but sometimes they had to and it was hard not to laugh when the old people sang in their shaky voices. This inscription was on a tall stone of the deep red granite, polished like glass, with little flecks of silver in it. Bluebells grew around it, the same colour as the sky. She supposed if you lived long enough, as many people you'd known all your life would be buried as not. And she knew what good company the dead could be. She sat and made a daisy wreath for her hair, right by the grave of Baby Green. But instead of putting it onto her head, she left it draped over the small footplate commemorating that baby who had no first name.

The cemetery was a cool place to while away summer afternoons when she was not needed by Miss Oakden or her mother was unable to walk with the children over to Gonzales beach. The grass, kept clipped and raked, was lovely to stretch out on, under a favourite tree—maybe the cork-bark elm down near where Memorial Crescent met Dallas Road. She could hear the sea just a few yards away. The crows were busy in the canopy, squabbling and muttering. Smaller birds nested in the hedging, and she watched them dart in and out with worms or insects to unseen young. She had taken to carrying a little notebook everywhere in order to record details that might be needed on her map. The nest sites, for example. The location of the perfect snakeskin she found shed on some rocks near the Helmcken mausoleum, its eye sockets intact. She had not wanted to touch it but sketched it so she could remember it exactly as it lay draped over the rocks like an empty ghost. And she sketched the seal skeleton too, from memory—its hands open to the sky.

On the evenings when there wasn't Little League, most of the neighbourhood children gathered at Bushby Park for a game of scrub. Teams were chosen by the two captains, usually Mick and David Grey, a boy from Joseph Street; positions were assigned—Tessa was almost always a fielder. It was exciting at first to hover in the outfield with her glove, one Teddy had outgrown, and wait for someone to hit a ball in her direction. Once she surprised herself and everyone else by catching a fly. Mostly she chased balls like the other fielders, to the end of the park, across Bushby Street, into yards, fishing among flowers and shrubs while the runner loped around the bases and her own team groaned at her slowness. The one time she played shortstop, someone hit a line drive directly into her face. Her lip immediately swelled up to about four times its size; her mother was called and came running with ice. There was quite a lot of blood from both her nose and her mouth where her inner lip had been cut by her teeth, but luckily that was the extent of the damage. The swelling took five days to go down, and she kept to herself during that period, working on her map and resisting the call of the children in the park in the evening, their voices dreamlike in the falling light.

She drew in the monumental works, on stilts at the back, with stones leaning on one another in the yard. She had been looking at other maps, several she'd brought home from the library, and liked how some of the mapmakers worked in the details of cities and buildings. The librarian spread out a map showing a bird's-eye view of Victoria, seen from the water. There were boats and lots of open areas that she knew had been covered with houses by now (the map was created in 1889). She loved how it made the city seem so real; it inspired her to make the important buildings on her map as close to real as she could. After working hard to get a house just right, she would put a face in a window, a door slightly open with a bloom leaning against it. And after thinking about it for a day or two, she drew Miss Oakden kneeling before the stone with the Latin word for horse, a basket of rosebuds beside her.

One day Miss Oakden asked her to help weed a border. At first the woman stayed close to show her which were weeds and which were garden plants, either mature ones or seedlings self-sown from the robust perennials. Tessa caught on quickly and soon worked on her own. It was satisfying to clear out the buttercup runners and dandelions and see the clumps of columbine, asters, and delphiniums with the clear dark soil between them. The earth was full of worms, which Miss Oakden told her were necessary for soil health. Their tunnels aerated the soil and their castings (a nice word for poo) fertilized it. Tessa was fascinated to think of all this activity right underfoot where you couldn't tell it was going on. It reminded her of the streams passing under May Street and under the cemetery, anxious for the sea, no one knowing they were even there. Except for her. And a handful of others, she conceded.

That day, after weeding, when she was drinking her lemonade, she mentioned a ball game and something Tommy Gurack had said. Miss Oakden looked interested.

"I knew his great-grandfather," the woman commented. "He was a very nice man who helped me a lot in the job I had during the war. The Great War, Tessa, not the one that came after."

"What kind of job, Miss Oakden?"

"I designed tiles, the kind you see around fireplaces in old houses, or even in bathrooms—if you go into mine, you will see a panel that is my work. And Tommy Gurack's great-grandfather was a master at glazes. He knew how to make such rich beautiful colours. And he was a brave man, Tessa. He came to Canada alone, sending money back to Hungary for his family. He went back to Hungary for a time but then returned, with his wife. His daughter—she is Tommy's grandmother—came later, after losing her husband in the 1956 uprising, to live with her married daughter, already in Canada."

"She was at his birthday party, the one who lost her husband. She told us to eat the candles, and I didn't know it was a joke so I did. The boys all thought it was hilarious; my brothers still tease me. But the Guracks have no father. Did he die too?"

"I believe he simply left, Tessa. And as for the candles—these misunderstandings happen. She never would have intended to embarrass you. She made wonderful pastries, I remember, with poppy seeds and sweet butter. Mr. Nagy—that was his name—died, possibly from accumulating poisons from the glazes, though no one knew of the dangers then. It's a household that has seen its share of hardship. Mr. Nagy was an artist, though. He made beautiful pottery himself as well as working in a commercial enterprise."

And Tessa remembered the beautiful plates, the goblets that held the party Freshie, all highly coloured and shining.

The family went for their annual August camping trip to St. Mary's Lake on Saltspring Island, the blue tent aired in the yard and then repacked into its canvas bag, the old black skillet cleaned and oiled in readiness to fry the fillets of bass that Tessa's father would catch on his early morning ventures onto the lake in the little wooden boat he had made himself. They spent a week camping, all of them sleeping in rows in the tent with their sleeping bags and the air mattresses that never held air for a whole night through. The dog came too and slept on an old towel just inside the tent beside the pink plastic pot that one could pee in at night if it was raining too hard to head to the outhouse.

Tessa loved Saltspring Island. There were old houses and fields of sheep and long wharves tilting out into the sea. Herons waded in the shallow bays. There were oysters, which her parents loved, but which she couldn't imagine actually eating. They looked like snot. Her brother Mick said this, and the three children all laughed until their parents told them to stop or risk not being allowed to swim that day. But then Teddy would snort and that would set them off again. She saw her father go quite red; her mother smiled at him and touched his shoulder.

They swam every day, almost all day. Sometimes they drove to ocean beaches and stopped at Mouat's Store for ice cream. The children were allowed to row across St. Mary's Lake to an abandoned homestead where they feasted on green apples from trees draped in Spanish moss. Many of the trees were broken by bears. You could tell because there were mounds of bear scat, black as tar but filled with apple pulp and seeds, at the foot of the trees. Branches were torn away, stripped of apples, and left to lie in the golden grass, little scales of lichen on them. The house was covered in weathered grey clapboards; its generous windows faced the lake. It was sad to peer in through broken windows and see remnants of the lives lived within: a cupboard with dishes on its spiderwebby shelves; a blue coffee pot still on the rusted old range; mattresses covered in blue and white ticking torn apart by mice or larger animals for the stuffing that lay on the floor. Tobacco tins full of nails and bolts. A bedstead once white but now corroded by rust, left in a field. It was as though a family had awoken one morning and decided to leave. Tessa wondered if they'd dreamed of the place for years afterwards, in all its magic. She tried to draw it; the place ended up looking shabby and old in her little sketchbook, so she burned the page in the campfire that evening. Some things were best stored in the imagination, where the rust and the weathered boards were beautiful and not derelict.

And leaving Saltspring that summer was sad too. There had been four rainy days during their week of camping, but on the last day, as with the day before, the sun rose hot and yellow. Fish were surfacing on the lake, the smell of the morning campfire was sweet with fir sap, and the pancakes were exactly the way Tessa liked them best—a little black around the edges but puffy inside with bubbles to catch the melted butter and syrup. They took down the tent, rolled up their sleeping bags, helped the dog into the back of the station wagon. Before they knew it, they were on the ferry out of Fulford Harbour, waving goodbye to the herons. It wasn't until they were back home that Tessa realized they all smelled of woodsmoke, their T-shirts and shorts permeated with it. She loved the smell and held her kangaroo shirt back from the laundry, tucking it into her closet so she could bury her face in it and remember the snap of the fire as they roasted marshmallows and wieners on sticks Mick had sharpened with his special Swiss Army knife.

"Will we ever go back?" she asked her mother as she helped with the laundry the day after their return.

"What a question! Of course we'll go back. We've always gone to St. Mary's Lake! Why do you ask?"

"I don't know. It felt so final, leaving this time."

"Watch your fingers, Tessa. And please hand me my basket; you're closer to it than I am. I'm going to take this load up to hang out."

She tried to think of a way to add Saltspring to her map, but there wasn't room. When she finished this one, maybe she would make another map. But somehow it felt that everything belonged on the same map. The cemetery, the old houses, the curve of Ross Bay, and even the lights of Port Angeles across the Strait of Juan de Fuca, and now when she thought of it St. Mary's Lake and the homestead in its ruined orchard. She was sorry she had burned her sketch, but she hoped she could draw another from memory.

It had all come about so smoothly. School teachers, reading circles, gatherings of watercolour painters: word had gone out that women were required for a staged reading of a Greek play. And on the appointed day, the doorbell at Hollyhock Cottage kept ringing as one by one the women found a place to sit by the fire after leaving their wraps and hats on the hall stand. Chairs had been moved from the dining room and bedrooms to accommodate the numbers. Flora had allowed Grace to postpone her nap a little while in order to see the women arriving, each with a bag or satchel, faces red with the bitter wind blowing off Ross Bay.

"What a lovely child! Which lady does she belong to?" A woman reached down, little foxes dangling from her neck, to stroke Grace's cheek.

Flora and Ann looked at each other and laughed. Both spoke at once: "Oh, she is Flora's daughter!" "She belongs to both of us, of course!"

It was the year following the peace talks in Paris. A treaty had been forged and signed. The newspapers had been full of the Fourteen Points, the hope for an organization that would somehow prevent another war from taking place. In Paris, in homes around the world, people endlessly consulted maps as those nations wanting sovereignty spoke out in a chorus of emancipation. The world looked upon a beaten Germany, bowed under payments and blame, expecting shame and contrition. Men still arrived home from overseas, horribly disfigured by gas burns and shells. Hospitals had special wards for those who had not regained their mental functions after the horrors of the Somme, of Passchendaele.

The session of the council of the League of Nations had met in Paris earlier in January. Newspaper headlines predicted a future of peace. Such an optimistic view did not convince Ann Ogilvie, who remembered her own husband's death at Paardeberg Drift in 1900, the death of her housemate's lover at Festubert fifteen years later, and, by extension, the deaths of hundreds of thousands of men in conditions that were now understood to be beyond appalling. For Ann, there must be pressure and demonstrations on the part of those who wished passionately for peace to remind the politicians, now in Paris but eventually to return to their own countries, how important it was to the people themselves.

Ann's correspondence with friends and family in England had alerted her to the efforts of her brother's former professor of Greek at Glasgow, Gilbert Murray, to support the League of Nations, an organization that would help the broken nations of Europe to negotiate their differences. Mr. Murray's celebrated translation of The Trojan Women was being performed in various locations—Cowley Road cinema in Oxford in concert with the conference in that city to acknowledge the peace talks in Paris; a matinee performance at the Alhambra Theatre in London to raise funds for the League of Nations Union, chaired by Gilbert Murray. Ann's sister-in-law in London had attended the latter performance and said that Sybil Thorndike's Hecuba was astonishing. When the crowds called "Author, Author!" at the conclusion of the play, Mr. Murray rose from his seat and said, "The author is not here, he has been dead many centuries, but I am sure he will be gratified by your reception of his great tragedy."

The women in the warm sitting room sat expectantly as Ann rustled through the papers she had in her hands.

"Ah, here's my folder. I have been collecting some reviews of this play, which I hope we will offer as a staged reading to the citizens of Victoria. I want to begin by reading you some comments on The Trojan Women—that is the play I mean for us to read.

I should have begun with that!—so you will understand that we are not alone in this activity, that other people, women and men who believe that there must be alternatives to the butchery and barbarism we are only too familiar with, are attempting to do what I hope we can do and that is to draw attention to the plight of the women and children in war."

There was some uneasy shuffling between two women in Ann's sitting room. Both of them had lost sons in France. Ann knew this and waited for them to speak. One of the women— they were sisters—asked, "Mrs. Ogilvie, are you saying that the Germans should have been left to take over Europe and then perhaps the world?"

"It is not my intention to offend anyone here," Ann replied gently. "Let me say that quite clearly. And I think I am fully with our Mr. Murray in that I don't believe the world should tolerate such aggression at any cost, Mrs. Styles. But I do think that there must be ways of settling our differences that don't involve the slaughter of millions. Mr. Murray's League of Nations Union is one way that civilians can support diplomacy. I am hopeful that we, too, can help, even at this distance."

There was more discussion about this, animated and spirited, though most women agreed with Ann. She had been developing a reputation in Victoria for her outspoken views on war and the emancipation of women, so those responding to her call for players were aware of her opinions. Women would not have come to her door had they not at least known what to expect. And she was a listener; that was something everyone agreed on. She would carefully listen to what people had to say and she showed every sign of considering their point of view. She was the first to say that she had not formed her views on war and suffrage until the Boer War ended and she was left without a husband and without an income—although she had enjoyed both before that war began.

Ann read them extracts from the reviews she'd accumulated, ones that mentioned The Trojan Women's tragic dramatic centre—

the distribution of the women of Troy to the victorious Greek princes and kings—and drew parallels between the recent war and the old story of victors and their spoils. The women were silent when she finished.

After a moment or two, she said, "I have copies here of the script for the play and wonder if we might think about roles. Essentially these are the parts: the play opens with Poseidon and Pallas Athena. These are important characters, a god and goddess respectively, but they make a fairly brief appearance so the parts might interest someone who would like to play another part as well."

A woman murmured softly that for herself at least, playing a goddess would be enough to last a lifetime. Those around her chuckled in agreement.

Ann smiled too, then ran her finger down the cast list. "So perhaps two of you who might want to be part of the Chorus can also consider those roles? Then we'll have a Hecuba. She's queen of Troy and widow of Priam, mother of Hector and Paris, both who've been killed, and of Cassandra who also appears in the play. Cassandra is . . . well, she is a prophetess. A bit mad, but I believe that's understandable when one thinks of what she has gone through. Yes, Agnes?"

A middle-aged woman had raised her hand. "Will those in the Chorus sing, Ann? Is that the intention?"

"Ah, well, that's something to decide. The usual thing is for them to chant, but I've read of productions where they do in fact sing. It is Mr. Murray's belief, however, that the actual words are the important aspect of the Chorus and that music detracts from their power. Or can, at least, though that is not inevitable. Some performances have used melodies that are very simple and, I suppose one could say almost primitive. But I don't think we have the resources to investigate such possibilities at the moment. However, the Chorus is important and powerful. We will want strong voices for it, whether it be sung or recited. Does that answer your question?"

Agnes Hunter nodded. She smoothed her skirt, a dark blue gabardine, and touched her hair thoughtfully. It was her brother who'd gone to France and come home shell-shocked, a sad presence in the family home as he rocked and rocked in a chair by a window in a dark room and ducked with a shriek when the lights came on.

Ann continued, "So, Hecuba, then, and her daughter, and her daughter-in-law, who is the widow of the Trojan hero Hector. That's Andromache. I hope I'm pronouncing these names correctly. She has an important part too, because she must endure the murder of her young son Astyanax. And Helen, she's here too—the reason for the war in the first place. Her husband, Menelaus, who must decide whether to take her back (she left him for Paris) or have her killed. There's also a Greek herald, Talthybius, and some other soldiers and attendants. You remember that in Shakespeare's day, female parts were always performed by men? Well, we will do one better and have women performing the male and the female parts!"

Amid the laughter and commentary, one woman said that during the war years all the women she knew were accustomed to being both mother and father, housewife and handyman, so this would not be a hardship at all.

"How many in the Chorus, Ann?" asked Flora, looking up from her copy of the script.

"Well, that depends. It's a representative body, I gather—women who've lost their husbands, been captured, and are about to be assigned to Greeks as war spoils. I don't think numbers are as important as quality, if that doesn't sound simple-minded. I mean, it will depend on how many of us will want to try that role, but we don't need too many, I wouldn't think. I've been reading about the function of the Chorus and will have some ideas to share with you once we've decided our roles."

A woman who had said nothing all this time but sat, wrapped in a dark shawl with a cloche pulled down over her eyes, suddenly said, "If no one objects, I would like the part of Cassandra."

The others looked at her with interest. Her face was intense, dark eyes aglow beneath her cloche. Her hands were clasped in front of her as though in supplication. Ann smiled at her, then replied, "Well, that gets the ball rolling, doesn't it? Miss Leach, isn't it?"

"Yes, Caroline Leach," the woman responded. "I am quite new to Victoria. I'm a companion to an aunt who has managed on her own until now. I came here today because I was lucky enough to see Lillah McCarthy in *The Trojan Women* at Princeton on the tour in 1915. It was the most moving event of my life. In the open air, those words . . . Oh, I can't tell you . . ."

She shook her head, as though in disbelief. "In any case, I would love the part. I will give it everything I have."

Ann reached for her hand and held it between her own. "I'm so pleased you came. And how lucky for us that you've seen a production and will have some knowledge to share with us. You will have to tell us more about the Chorus because I think that music was composed just for that tour. But before we talk about that, are there others who think they might like to try a role?"

A tall, stout woman in her later middle years said, "I don't think there's any doubt that you will be our Hecuba, Ann. You have the voice, the knowledge of the play, and I think you are a natural for the role. Like Miss Leach, I, too, have seen this play, in Chicago a few years ago. The Woman's Peace Party—my sister is a member—organized a tour. And I, too, will never forget it. I would like to be part of the Chorus, please, as I don't really think I am bold enough for a part of my own. But do the others agree that Ann should play Hecuba?"

There was instant assent. Many of those present had heard Ann sing at one time or another and were aware of her confidence in front of an audience, the strength of her voice, her projection.

"I would honoured to play Hecuba if you are quite sure no one else wants the part?"

No one did. In the next few minutes, other women chose

parts, a few of the younger ones gleefully asking for the male roles and the youngest of all, a girl in her late teens who had arrived with her mother, asked to be Helen. The part of Andromache went unclaimed until Ann suggested Flora.

"Oh, Ann, I was thinking I'd paint sets, if we decide to have sets for a simple staged reading. Painted curtains, perhaps. I have some ideas . . ."

"Flora, nothing would make me happier than to have you opposite me as my daughter-in-law. We have the perfect domestic situation for our rehearsals, don't you think? We can practise as we do the sheets on Monday mornings! And there is no reason why you cannot also think about sets. A little team can help with that."

That was it, then. The play was cast. Ann and Flora had baked a special cake for the occasion, rich with sultanas and Madeira wine. The lovely Aynsley tea service had been set out on the dining-room table; two pots were quickly warmed for India and China. The cake was sliced and served on plates so delicate one could almost see through them. The room was filled with the sound of laughter and talk as the women discussed the play, theatre in general, the state of world politics, their own domestic circumstances. Some of them were friends; others were unfamiliar, but, before long, they were forming bonds as they discovered that a brother or sweetheart had served in the same battalion in Europe.

Before they departed, Agnes Hunter, gathering her wrap and gloves, asked, "Is there a reason why you've suggested a staged reading, Ann? I would like to say that I, for one, think we could make this into a proper production. Flora, for instance, said something about painting sets. Surely if we go to those lengths, we can think larger? My cousin's daughter has been working with Carroll Aikins in Naramata . . ."

"Naramata?" someone exclaimed. "Surely you don't mean there's a theatre in Naramata, of all places?"

"Indeed there is. Or soon will be." Agnes Hunter replied. "Mr. Aikins is building a theatre over his fruit-packing shed, very professional, with proper lighting and everything. He has people come in to help with lessons in movement and so forth. A few young people from UBC have gone up to study with him, my cousin Amelia Carr's daughter Anne among them. I know she would give us advice if we wanted it. If we are going to the work of getting together and reading the play, I think we ought to aim to be a little more ambitious."

"Oh, yes," said Caroline Leach, holding her hands up imploringly. "Let's do the thing properly! I would do any amount of work to have this happen!"

And everyone agreed.

A tentative schedule for rehearsals was set. Ann would find a rehearsal space suggested. When the women left, pulling down hats against the bitter wind off the sea, they were eager for their next meeting.

Evening. The lamps were lit. A log fire snapped in the grate. Ann and Flora sat in the warm room with The Trojan Women, each reading and making notes in the margins of their scripts.

"These women! Well, they're not strangers to us, are they? What strikes me at once is, they're so familiar, somehow."

Ann looked up from her pages. "Absolutely, Flora! When I read something like, oh, so much of it really, but this speech, for example: 'And I the aged, where go I, / A winter-frozen bee, a slave / Death-shapen, as the stones that lie / Hewn on a dead man's grave ...' —well, it is completely taken into one's heart, isn't it?" She clutched hers in emphasis. "How many women, widowed by this war, or the last, or now faced with the loss of their sons, their brothers, might read this also and weep?"

Flora took a handkerchief from her pocket and wiped her eyes, hearing Ann read those words. "I have been reading the part where Andromache learns that her son is to be killed. To lose her husband, and now her child! How will she bear it? I've not come to the end yet so don't tell me but this play seems like a dirge, beautiful and yet so heartbreakingly shocking."

Ann got up from her chair and went to the window. Pulling the curtains aside for a moment, she looked out into the darkness, her hands small fists against her thighs. "Who would have thought when we were girls, you in Wiltshire and I in Scotland, that men we loved would die in combat so far from home. That we would go on without them. And to read this play, to realize that it was happening in the five centuries before Christ, well, it brings out the need to do *something*, if one only can."

The practical details took some time to work out: what would be a reasonable time frame for rehearsals; where might a performance take place. And the most immediate problems of direction. Ann would take on that role as much as she was able to do. The women who had seen productions would offer information, insights. There were a few scholars in Victoria who might be consulted about the conventions of Greek drama. Ann knew some basic but important points—that a tragedy contained two key structural elements, the choral song (with or without musical accompaniment) and the dramatic exchanges between characters. But it seemed that this play by Euripides was unusual in that it did not adhere to those traditional conventions. It had very little plot, no straight narrative. It did not focus on heroes or kings but on the anguish of women who, having lost everything, are in the tragic position of being divided up among the conquerors as spoils of war.

"Gilbert Murray says in his introductory notes that this play—and I will quote—'is something more than art. It is also prophesy, a bearing of witness.'"

She paused to let the words take effect.

"All of us have done it, one way or another. Witnessed the wounds, the terrible sorrows of others, tended those we love, or stood in a room with a letter in hand, wondering how we could possibly go on after learning of the death of a husband, a brother. And knowing that we have no real power to do anything about it."

"But, Ann," said Priscilla Foley, "we have the vote now. Surely this means something."

Other women nodded and agreed.

Ann paused, smiled a small smile, then continued. "I think it will take a long time before we can make any difference with our vote. At present, though, and at risk of repeating what some of you have heard me say so many times, I have no voice they'll hear to protest the treatment of innocent citizens. But maybe they'll hear Hecuba, Andromache, Cassandra . . ."

They were gathered at the Women's Christian Temperance Union Hall to begin the process of blocking out the action, learning their lines, their cues, learning how to project their voices to the audience. Not one of them was an actress. Indeed, only two had done any theatre work at all. Although Ann had performed many recitals as a singer, she was quick to acknowledge that the experience of singing to an audience as a solo performer was as different to theatre as chalk to cheese.

"But I'm not shy," she smiled, "and I know how to make my voice reach the far corners of an auditorium—or my singing voice at least, if not my political one. Hecuba's wild lament will reach a few ears. I think we should begin by simply giving this play a read-through, all of us taking our parts, the chorus perhaps standing together and trying to read more or less in unison. I don't expect any of us will be very satisfied with the results of this, but it will at least give us a sense of how it might shape up."

With much confusion, and some laughter, Ann gave directions for the opening prologue. Agnes Hunter and Alice Ramsay took their places self-consciously on the stage. Ann arranged herself on the floor, tucking her clothing under her neatly, and pretended to be asleep. The room was cold and most women kept their coats on. So Poseidon stood in her long grey wool coat, fox collar around her neck, one tail casually tossed over one shoulder, with a small felt hat close on a head of bobbed chestnut-coloured hair. Her bright eyes twinkled as she declaimed the opening lines:

Up from the Aegean caverns, pool by pool
Of blue salt sea, where feet most beautiful
Of Nereid maidens weave beneath the foam
Their long sea-dances, I, their lord, am come,
Poseidon of the Sea.

Everyone laughed, Alice most of all. Despite her fifty years, she had the sweet voice of a young girl. Hecuba raised her head from the sleeping position and said, "I hadn't realized how funny that would sound, coming from a woman! Never mind. We'll work on making you sound stentorian, Alice. And for now, we'll just keep reading, I think, in order to see how the whole thing sounds."

Agnes Hunter's Athena was something to hear, speaking firmly and clearly, the voice of a woman accustomed to being heard:

Is it the will
Of God's high Brother, to whose hand is given
Great power of old, and worship of all Heaven
To suffer speech from one whose enmities
This day are cast aside?

Agnes was a Presbyterian minister's daughter, middle-aged and unmarried, an intelligent woman who had spent her life doing good works. It was her mother who'd suggested she participate in Ann Ogilvie's project, revealing a side that Agnes never knew existed. Her mother, who'd watched her son sit by the window, catatonic, or else moaning in his bed with the covers over his head, said, "There must be another way, Agnes, for nations to settle their differences. This is simply too high a price for anyone to pay." So Agnes put down her work basket, took up a script, and was now attempting to be the voice of Pallas Athena in an ancient play.

The reading progressed, awkwardly, hesitantly, ill timed and at times faintly, but each woman stood in place on the bare stage and read her part, or in the case of the Chorus, read in unison (more or less) with others, until the final lines:

Farewell from parting lips,
Farewell!—Come, I and thou,
Whatso may wait us now,
Forth to the long Greek ships
And the sea's foaming.

And then there was silence in the cold hall as the women waited for what Ann might say. She stood with head bowed, in silence, as though allowing the play's words to settle into her before she might speak. And when she did, it was with emphatic pride.

"Oh, brava!" she exclaimed, clapping her hands. "It is even better than I hoped, this play, in our voices."

"But, Ann," said Mary Morrison, "I know I'm a little disappointed at our awkward reading. Are you saying you're not?"

Ann smiled at Mary, a lovely willowy girl of eighteen or nineteen, not long out of school. "I didn't expect us to be perfect, Mary, not by a long shot, not on our first reading. But I was very moved, both by the language of the play and by the way each of us took it so seriously. We will get better. I know this. There are things I know I can help you with, having given voice lessons for some years. I have some ideas about comportment that I'll share with you too, as we progress. And you are all here so now we can set the next rehearsal date. And perhaps make a cup of tea for ourselves in the kitchen . . . Oh, Flora, how good of you! You've anticipated my hope!"

For Flora had already slipped away to set the kettle on the gas flame to boil. She and Ann had packed a basket with a packet of tea leaves, a flask of milk, some sugar, and a tin of Ann's shortbread, crunchy with brown sugar. Soon each woman held a cup of tea and a shortbread biscuit as they chatted, clearly excited about the play.

"It is so different to hear a thing aloud rather than just reading it on the page, do you agree?" asked Frances Gibbs, who had taken the part of Menelaus. "Like poetry, the way the lines sing out and rhyme. And it asks something of the voice, I think."

And Alice Ramsay, whose Poseidon opened the play, laughed. "Asks of the voice what might well be impossible, I say! But I am really thrilled to be part of this and hope to be . . . what was your word, Ann? Stentorian?"

"I wanted to cry many times throughout," said Elizabeth Washburn, who was a member of the Chorus and one of the sisters who had first expressed concern about the thrust of the project (her sister, Mary Styles, was playing a soldier). "Every time Hecuba spoke, it tugged at my heart. The words felt so timely and so personal. And of course your Andromache, Flora—I can tell you've been working on your part already. You read the lines as though they came from somewhere deep inside you, with such a clear and steady voice. Your performance is something to aspire to, my dear."

Flora blushed. "Well, yes, Ann and I have practised a little. I needed convincing that it wasn't beyond me."

Ann told the group that she had some ideas for blocking that she would try to work out before the next time they met. And could they arrange, if possible, to get together in small groups to work on the script together? Poseidon and Pallas Athena? Menelaus and Helen? She and Flora would rehearse together in the evenings and would welcome others—Cassandra, for instance—to drop by as was convenient. She told them again how pleased she was with their work thus far.

Robert Alexander was waiting for Flora and Ann in his car. He had taken Grace on an outing for the afternoon. The child was animated, having had the attention of a doting grandfather as well as a sumptuous tea with cream wafers, a current favourite treat.

"The thespians return! How did it go, ladies?" asked Robert as he helped them into their seats.

"It was excellent, Robert," Ann replied. "For a first reading, I think we did very well indeed. They are keen, the women, and I think we might be able to do this old play a kind of modern justice."

TWENTY-SIX
1962

When school started again, it seemed too soon. The days in Miss Oakden's garden had been lovely. Tessa hadn't wanted to take the money that the woman pressed into her hands each week, but Miss Oakden insisted.

"Oh, yes, my dear! You've worked hard. I could never have trained the honeysuckle so well myself and you've been a godsend when it comes to the fruit. And see how tidy the borders are! My knees no longer like to bend, Tessa, the way they used to, so weeding has become a trial, I'm afraid. You have been a willing and cheerful helper and you deserve this."

Tessa had never heard the term *godsend* before and she cherished it. To think of herself as special to someone, to have helped someone's knees—it felt like an honour.

She was no longer in the Annex. Grade threes went to the big building. At first Tessa worried that she might not be able to find her classroom—there were so many doors!—but after a week, she was confident. In any case, when the bell rang each morning, her class lined up outside like all the other classes. They were led to their classroom by Miss Anstey. Tessa didn't like her as much as she had liked Mrs. Barrett. She was very brisk and efficient, giving directions or instructions once, expressing impatience with those children who didn't catch on the first time. Luckily Tessa was a quick learner, but she felt a little pang of anxiety when she realized that someone else needed more help and Miss Anstey got the look on her face that indicated she was not happy to have to say things twice. Or three times, even.

Mrs. Barrett had encouraged Tessa to pursue her own reading interests after discovering that she was a fluent reader of novels and other books, saying, "You must participate when we do things as a class but for the quiet reading, I see no point in you having to work on the Readers. Dick and Jane are perhaps not quite as interesting as Nancy Drew!"

"Oh, and Cherry Ames!"

Mrs. Barrett had given her the paper for the map and allowed her time in the school library to look up information on mapmakers. Even though Tessa was no longer in her class, she sought her out to find out how the map was progressing.

"You may keep that atlas as long as you like, Tessa. We have plenty in the classroom and I'm glad to know that you find it so useful."

But Miss Anstey said she did not want a student who was not a part of every classroom activity, so Tessa was required to do all the assignments on *Streets and Roads*. When the class went to the library on Thursday afternoons, she had to choose her book for the week from the stack the librarian had put on a table for the grade threes. Most of them she had already read; the ones she hadn't seemed very dull. There were several Bobbsey Twins stories, for example. Tessa tried one, involving a trip to the beach; but the two sets of twins were boring and their ideas of fun too lame. The book was a lot like those previous Readers in which Dick, Jane, their little sister Sally, the dog Spot, and the cat Puff had adventured confined to things that might happen in one or two syllables. When the class read the chapters aloud in the earlier grades, Tessa had felt she would burst with impatience as some of her classmates sounded out each word, each sentence, one syllable at a time. Not that she was cross with the kids themselves, but she wanted to be reading something herself, something that grabbed her attention the way a good Nancy Drew could do, taking her away with the girl detective as she drove her smart car off on adventures involving mistaken identity, kidnapping, sinister dealings on ranches and golf courses.

She dawdled on her way home those September days, her lunch box swinging in one hand, her tartan schoolbag in the other. She didn't feel like riding her bike with the others. Walking, she could think her own thoughts. She could look closely at houses and the store at the corner of May and Moss, figuring out which ones she needed to include on her map. If she walked over the Moss Rocks on the trail, she could pause and look behind her to Juan de Fuca Strait shimmering in the morning sunlight, a few freighters far out in the blue water. And it was an easy thing to stop and make a quick note in her little book, fishing it out of the pouch on the front of her schoolbag when she had a thought she wanted to record or a view of the cemetery from the high point on the rocks.

One night, when she was lying in her bed, waiting for sleep, Tessa heard her parents talking in the living room. They were discussing Miss Oakden.

"There is some connection, I think, with the Alexander family. Someone mentioned a son who died and was the father of her child. A hard thing for her, to have been an unwed mother in those years. Even now it would be difficult." This was Tessa's mother.

Her father's voice: "She has dignity, though, in spades. She told me once that she worked during the first war at a brick works, making tiles. And that she had been left the house by a friend who died just after the war. All those years in that house. What changes she'll have seen."

"She was something of a suffragette, I've heard. A group of them performed a play that had the city talking! When you think of it, though, there must be many of these old-timers with stories to tell. Old men working in their gardens who probably fought in the Great War. The old Hungarian woman, Eva Gurack's mother . . . her husband was executed in the revolt, I understand. And yet we all live these domestic lives, raising our children, paying our taxes. I suppose what I really should be doing is sewing patches on the boys' jeans. I've never known children so hard on their clothes."

Her father must've switched on the television then because Tessa couldn't hear their voices, just Jackie Gleason yelling at his friend Art and anyone else who got in his way.

Classroom activities centred on seasonal events. Bright turkeys were crowned with wattles made by tracing your hand onto brown construction paper and the straw cornucopia was filled with offerings from home—Tessa brought four bright apples from Miss Oakden's tree and some walnuts she found on her way to school. Then it was time to start thinking about Halloween. This involved long-term planning for costumes. Most children knew what they would wear a month ahead of the actual day. Most worked out a route well in advance that would include the houses known to be most generous. Word of these spread. There was one legendary address to which trick-or-treaters flocked each year for the ten-cent chocolate bars given to each child along with a bag containing a popcorn ball and a lollipop ghost, made by tying a Kleenex over the top part of the sucker and drawing on a scary face.

It was not as though her brother Mick had never had firecrackers. But this was the first year they were sold legally to minors, and he had spent his own savings on fifty firecrackers and a punkstick to light them. He'd been told to save them for Halloween night itself but couldn't resist lighting just one or two for the loud blast and the smell. He found it intoxicating!

Arriving home from school that day, excited about trick-or-treating that evening in her pirate costume (Teddy's striped T-shirt, an eyepatch of old black sock, a front tooth blacked out with special wax, and a big dotted handkerchief of her father's tied over her hair, one of her mother's hoop earring fastened to it), Tessa was idly walking up the path to the front porch when she heard Mick call out, "Watch this!" as he threw a lit firecracker up into the air. It exploded, causing Tessa's heart to catch briefly—she didn't like the noise or the smell. But then her brother suddenly shrieked, a horrifying sound, and he was down, he was screaming and rolling on the porch as the sound of many firecrackers exploding at once filled Tessa's ears. And her mother's too, for there she was at the front door, in a panic, shouting, "What's wrong, Mick? Oh, dear God, what's wrong?" Teddy was behind her and the two of them rushed to Mick, who was still bellowing and moaning. This was not Mick's voice, not the boy who shouted and yelled and only sometimes cried. This was guttural, like the sound animals made on the nature shows they sometimes watched on television. The smell was terrible— firecracker powder and something else, a burning meaty smell. Mick's trousers were smouldering, smoke rising from his legs as he moved in anguish, trying to stop the firecrackers that were still popping and flashing from his pockets.

"Run and ask the Godwins to call an ambulance. Quick, Tessa! Run!"

And she did, knocking wildly on the neighbours' door, gasping out her mother's request that they call for an ambulance. Mrs. Godwin ran to do that as Mr. Godwin rushed to her house to see if he might help.

"Roll him in the doormat!" he cried as he took the stairs two at a time. "Roll him in the mat and then bundle him tight. It will starve the fire."

Mr. Godwin gently but quickly moved her brother's body onto the mat that her mother pulled from the doorway. Between the two of them, they managed to roll Mick up and then they embraced the bundle to extinguish the smouldering. Mick had stopped screaming and was lying white-faced inside his wrapping, small moans coming from his throat.

"He's in shock," said Mrs. Godwin, who had come immediately after calling the ambulance. (She had been a nurse in her younger years, had nursed during the First World War; she had told the family this when they'd introduced themselves over the fence on the day they'd moved to Eberts Street.) "I hear the ambulance now, though. It won't be long. Can you hear me, Mick?" She was leaning down to the boy, trying to catch his eyes, which were full of darkness, staring off. He was far away. Tessa worried he'd gone too far away to ever come home to them.

"Do you have a drop of brandy, Katherine? I think he could do with a little."

The elderly woman gently spooned a tiny bit of brandy into Mick's mouth. Most of it dribbled down his chin. But Tessa saw his throat gulp a little.

The sirens were close, closer, and then the ambulance men were bringing a stretcher to the porch and they were carefully lifting Mick from the mat. His trousers were in ashy shreds. They spoke to him quietly. One man began to take his blood pressure while the others removed his shoes and arranged his blackened legs on the white stretcher. The smell was awful, burned meat and sulphur. He was draped with a clean white sheet and a strap was fastened over his chest. A small crowd of neighbourhood children stood on the sidewalk, watching.

"Go with him, Katherine," Mrs. Godwin was saying to Tessa's mother. "We will care for Tessa and Teddy. Don't worry about them. Your place is with Mick."

Tessa and her brother went to the Godwins, where they sat at the kitchen table while Mrs. Godwin made them a drink of hot chocolate and put shortbread fingers on a plate for them. Then, remembering, she went to a cupboard and brought out small bags of chocolate-covered raisins, bought for trick-or-treaters. But they couldn't eat, couldn't take more than a sip or two of the chocolate.

"Will he die?" Tessa was finally asking the question that clutched at her heart like a claw.

Mrs. Godwin came to her and gave her shoulders a little squeeze. "No, my dear. I think he will be fine. From what I could see, the injury is to his legs. He will be in pain, yes, and probably there will be scarring, but I am quite sure he will be home in no time. It was a terrible thing, though. For him, and for the two of you who saw it."

The phone rang and Mr. Godwin answered it. "Yes," he said.

Then, "Oh, good. That's good to know. Thank you, Katherine. We'll expect him when we see him then."

It was the worst Halloween ever. Tessa's father came home from work, shaken by the phone call he had received from the hospital. He knocked on the Godwin door and gathered his children in his arms, patting their backs as they sobbed. He thanked his neighbours and assured them that yes, he would certainly call on them if he needed their help in the next little while. Then he helped his younger children into their costumes, insisting they go trick-or-treating, for Mick's sake as much as theirs.

"He will be disappointed, you know, if no one in this family gets a pillowcase of candy! And you can take him a share to the hospital. He'll be glad to get it in a few days."

Trudging from door to door, a pirate and a skeleton, Tessa and her brother collected their bags of candy. The night was punctuated by the snap of firecrackers. Tessa thought she might be sick at the smell of them. She could not eat a single piece of her candy, not even the ten-cent Dairy Milk from the special house. When she went to bed, she lay awake for hours, thinking of Mick. Every time she tried to close her eyes, she heard his terrible screaming. The phone rang several times. Very late, she heard a car door slam and then footfall on the porch steps. She recognized her mother's voice, low and urgent, and she went out to the kitchen.

"Oh, Tessa, you should be asleep by now. It's very late, sweetie. And a school night too!"

"I can't sleep, Mum. Will Mick die?"

Her mother hugged her close. "Absolutely not. But he is badly burned and will need to be in hospital for some time yet. We'll talk about it in the morning. "

Lying in her bed, hearing the murmur of her parents' talk in the warm kitchen, Tessa tried to bring happy images into her head: the tiny frog in Miss Oakden's pool; the pleasure of Saturday afternoon at the library when the children would be set loose and told to meet back at the entrance in one hour; walking with her mother to Gonzales Bay along Hollywood Crescent with the anticipation of a swim in cool water followed by a Popsicle for the long walk home; finding the mysterious egg cases on the Moss Rocks. She tried to dream her way into the long golden grass on the other side of St. Mary's Lake, eating green apples in the sunlight. But the smell, she could not get the smell of burning leg and sulphur out of her nose. It filled her, made her want to throw up. She rushed to the bathroom just in time.

TWENTY-SEVEN
1920

Elizabeth Washburn had been a teacher in a public school in England before marrying and coming to Canada with her school-master husband. Ann asked her if she would act as the play's dramaturge, the person who would do some background research on the history and geography of *The Trojan Women* and then share her research with the cast.

"I think," said Ann, "that it would help us immensely if we could all have more information on the background of the Trojan War, for example, so that we know exactly who these women are and what their circumstances were before they ended up being the spoils of the Greeks."

Elizabeth was happy to find out what she could. She came to a rehearsal with a carton of materials to share with the other women. First she put a map of the Mediterranean Sea and surrounding lands on the wall and used her knitting needle as a pointer to indicate the locations—Greece, the various areas where the Greek princes and kings had come from.

"Here is Sparta," she pointed. "Sparta, where Menelaus was king, and Mycenae, where Agamemnon ruled. Odysseus, to whom Hecuba was given, came from way over here . . ." (knitting needle tapping) ". . . a little island called Ithaka."

"And Troy itself?" asked Flora. "Was it a real place?"

"Oh, yes," replied Elizabeth. "In fact, archaeologists have uncovered many layers of cities upon the site where Ilium, the other name for Troy, stood, right here, in Turkey, just across the Dardanelles from the Gallipoli Peninsula where so many of our army perished in those middle years of the war." Her pointer was tracing a line on the map from a little dot marked Troy to a long finger of land immediately above it.

At the sound of that place name, Flora caught her breath sharply and looked more closely. There it was. Near Troy. Gallipoli, where Henry had been killed and where he now lay in a cemetery called Twelve Tree Copse. He left no wife to mourn him, though two parents sat in an empty house for months with the loss of him hanging in the air like dust. And no child to take his name forward into the future, though he'd been loved by a young man with a forelock of dark hair and a sweet smile.

Others saw the terrible irony too. Caroline was first to comment on it. "For Heaven's sake, Elizabeth! The naval attempt on the Dardanelles—it was the same area!"

Elizabeth showed them Cape Helles and where the ANZACS landed beyond Suvla. What had happened all those centuries ago had happened again in the recent past, and would happen again, in the future, near or far: was this the lesson that history was teaching? Flora hadn't paid enough attention to history. Walking the Roman roads, she had listened to poetry and collected a few flints, never realizing that both had been products of conflict. The elephant umbrella stand at Watermeadows was an invitation to high-minded discussions about the white man's burden and the treachery of the Boers; it had been easy to ignore as she went from dress fitting to dress fitting or else rode Seraphim down leafy lanes. Now she found herself listening and reading with a voracious hunger that surprised her. Ann's family in England sent copies of The New Age and Flora read them cover to cover. The writing on credit power and democracy was hard going, but Flora followed the lively arguments on art and women's suffrage with great interest. There was not a single opinion promulgated by the journal but rather many views, all eloquently and often provocatively presented.

And she took to visiting the library regularly to seek out books that attempted to come to terms with what had happened during the 1914–1918 conflict. A book called *The New Elizabethans* offered short memoirs of various poets, scholars, and athletes who had died on the battlefields of Europe. There were pictorial histories of Mons and the Somme, which broke Flora's heart over and over again. And a long strange essay caught her attention: *Aristodemocracy* by Sir Charles Waldstein looked at the ethics of conflict, taking the reader on an archaeological tour of history from Moses to Christ to Plato and the modern autocrats.

"Ann, I am reading this, well, it is called a 'sketch,' but it is rather more than that, by Hillaire Belloc. It was clearly written near the beginning of the war and he's talking about the nature of aggression, German of course, and Prussian, Austro-Hungarian . . ."

"Ah, portray them as demons and the rest will be taken care of?"

"Something like that, I suppose. What is shocking to me is how ready we were—and I count myself among those! At least in 1914—to believe this. Most still are. Belloc was a man my parents greatly admired, I believe. But listen to this: 'Germany must, in fulfilment of a duty to herself, obtain colonial possessions at the expense of France, obtain both colonial possessions and sea-power at the expense of England, and put an end, by campaigns perhaps defensive, but at any rate vigorous, to the menace of Slav barbarism upon the East. She was potentially, by her strength and her culture, the mistress of the modern world, the chief influence in it, and the rightful determinant of its destinies. She must by war pass from a potential position of this kind to an actual position of domination.'"

Flora paused and tried to find a way to articulate her thoughts. "He is characterizing the German position as this. But surely the other nations might say the same of themselves? Mistress of the modern world—surely that is England's goal? And what of the Belgian colonies in Africa? The Dutch?"

Ann was quiet for a moment. "It is always sobering to read this sort of thing, Flora. It determines me all the more to find a route that is mindful of the similarities of nations rather than the differences. My grandmother was a Quaker. Her notion of loving kindness towards aggressors rather than punishment, which seemed so naive when I was a girl, has much to commend it now, I think."

"Yet there is this other kind of pacifism too, Ann, which I read about in *The New Age* and other places. One that suggests that force is occasionally necessary as a defensive measure but never in an offensive context. What do you think of that?"

It surprised Ann a little to hear Flora asking such questions. She remembered the young woman who had come to Hollyhock Cottage and who had been taken aback when Ann spoke of the war as unnecessary, the machinations of its leaders vile. But she approved of Flora's attempts to understand the dimensions of pacifism. "Oh, I think that might be Gilbert Murray's own position. That peace-loving nations might band together in a collectively secure way against violators of peace. And maybe this is where the League of Nations will take us. We can hope, can't we?"

Ann clutched her copy of the *Iliad* to her chest and crossed her ankles. The women were sitting in a circle. They took time before their rehearsals to hear what Ann had to say about their progress, or to listen to tidbits from Elizabeth about the play, or simply to catch up on their lives. It was cold in the hall and all of them wore layers of woollen clothing topped by shawls. A few knitted while they sat. Ann opened the book.

"This is the *Iliad*, ladies, the poem that details one period in the ten-year duration of the Trojan War, part of the tenth and final year, to be precise. I would say that it really encapsulates the war as a whole. And its awful concluding event, the death of the Trojan prince, Hector, who is of course a child of Hecuba, sets a whole other cycle of events into motion—Odysseus heads home and the *Iliad*'s companion poem, the *Odyssey*, follows him on that journey. Another hero, Aeneas, heads off and ends up founding Rome. Now, let me see . . ."

Ann found the place she wanted in the book. "This translation is by Samuel Butler. It's prose, really. Not poetry. But it does have a kind of music, I think. So there's the appeal to the Muses, which is usual in epic poetry, and then the narrator says, 'I will tell the leaders of the ships and all the fleet together.'"

She read to them, her rich voice giving them the names of the places, Hyria, Aulis, the fair city of Mykalessos, where the poet itemized the haunts of doves, the pastures, the fortresses, the vineyards, the young men filling the fifty ships of the Boeotians. Then the chieftains of the Phocaeans, with their forty ships, and Ajax—not the great Ajax son of Telemon but a little man, with a breastplate of linen—and his forty ships. More magnificent men with fifty ships and then the great Ajax of Salamis with his twelve ships. Agamemnon himself, 'all glorious in his armour of gleaming bronze, foremost among the heroes,' with a hundred ships, and his brother, Menelaus, with sixty ships, going 'to avenge the toil and sorrow he had suffered for the sake of Helen.' And on it went . . . Yes, Caroline?"

"It's those ships, Ann. The naval fleets of the Gallipoli campaign, the British and the French. Remember their names? The Lord Nelson, the Charlemagne, even the Agamemnon!" Her face was alive with this knowledge and the others watched her, uncertain how to respond. Her intensity rubbed some women the wrong way. A couple of them were irritated and wanted to listen to Ann; one dreamy member of the Chorus was forming a map in her own mind, one punctuated by abandoned kit bags and graves, and wanted to keep that intact while Ann read the ancient story.

Elizabeth, who had taught nervy young women, moved to sit by Caroline and linked her arm through the other's, saying softly, "Extraordinary, isn't it, how there are such echoes in these histories? Plus ça change, plus c'est la même chose."

Mary Morrison, who had never heard of the Iliad and was enthralled with Ann's reading, particularly as it mentioned her own character Helen, said, quite sharply, "Hush and let her continue."

Priscilla Foley clicked her tongue and reminded Mary that she was the youngest there. It was her opinion that entirely too much attention was paid to the girl's beauty. Let her have a houseful of children and she'd learn quickly enough that flowers faded with no one to remember their brief season.

For a few minutes, the air was tense in the Women's Christian Temperance Union Hall. Ann waited for quiet and then continued: "'All the soldiers and farmers, the young men, the fierce men with long hair flowing behind them, leaving their groves and vineyards, their women and children, their elderly parents, their flocks of well-bred sheep, but taking their horses, their armour, their spears and their chariots.'"

Just as Ann finished reading, Agnes Hunter broke in. "No different this time around," she spat, suddenly angry. "My brother went off with his hunting rifle, which of course was of no use whatsoever. Once he got to Quebec, they were all given those horrid Ross rifles, which we know now were hopeless once things got hot. They'd jam. How many wounded or dead because they couldn't get their own rifles to fire? My poor brother went off on the train, a boy who'd never even travelled past Vancouver, and then by boat to England, then to France and the battlefield of the Somme. Now he's a shadow and I doubt he'll ever be well again."

Elizabeth Washburn spoke next. "What I heard in that, Ann, was how those young men left settled lives, farms, orchards, families, to rally behind a man whose wife had gone off with another man. Willingly or unwillingly—does it matter? All that manpower, all those lives lost, because one man's pride was injured and he needed to take revenge. My son didn't know where Germany was, never mind Bosnia, yet he was off to enlist before the ink on the newspaper headline on August 5, 1914, was dry. He was killed at Ypres, him and too many thousands of others."

Ann looked thoughtful and then replied, "Yes, all the young men. The best. The strongest. All of them fired up to follow their kings and their chieftains. And whole worlds left behind to function without them. Each household an empire . . . That little portrait of Protesilaos with his flowery meadows and sheep, dead before he even arrived on Trojan soil, killed while leaping from his ship."

With difficulty, she found her place in the *Iliad* again. "'He had left a wife behind him in Phylake to tear her cheeks in sorrow, and his house was half-finished . . .' I think that passage is so poignant." Ann sighed and took a deep breath. "But so many echoes in that too—of our men and the Australians and New Zealanders being mowed down by Turkish gunfire as they tried to come ashore at Gallipoli."

"He might have been my brother." Flora hadn't realized she'd spoken aloud until she looked up to see that every eye was upon her. She tucked her hands into her sleeves—it was really very cold in the hall—and said again, "He might have been my brother, that man. I've recently been sent my brother's journals from home. He was killed at Gallipoli. He was frightened most of the time, I think, and was only thirty years old."

"Oh, Flora," said Mary Styles, who had lost a son herself. "And did he leave a wife and house?"

"I can't draw that particular parallel, Mary, but Henry would have inherited my family's home in Wiltshire, I can say that, and everything within it. But his life was certainly half-finished. He should not have died."

She wrung her hands together, violently. "Who knows what he would have done, would have been, in the fullness of time? He knew about birds and the old Roman ruins. He was loved. We hear numbers, so many numbers, in this poem, and in the newspapers, and in every speech about nobility and sacrifice but the numbers were lives, weren't they? Individual lives. My brother, oh, both my brothers. Your sons. Caroline's cousin, Agnes's brother, my dear Grace's father who was so splendid."

And she began to weep into her cold hands. Mary Styles, seated beside her, gathered Flora into her arms and let her cry against her woollen shoulder.

There was silence for a minute or two, broken only by Flora's quiet sniffling.

Then Alice Ramsay said, in a very quiet voice, "For each of those men, there was a woman. More than one, likely. And as spoils, well, the women aren't exactly divided up among the victors, because surely that was related to position and accomplishment on the part of the men. But they must do as Andromache does, as Hecuba does: carry on in a world made meaningless without the loved one nearby."

She looked around the circle of solemn faces. "As we've rehearsed this play, I've felt Hecuba's sorrow, her helplessness. I didn't expect to. I was lucky, I know, because my son returned pretty much intact, though his nightmares are something to behold, but a nephew was lost, every part of his body it seems, at Gallipoli, a boy I haven't seen since he was an infant when I cradled him in my arms before we left England. That we are reading these lines and offering the story of these lives—I think it's as important as a church service to honour the dead or another memorial service by a cold tombstone."

"Luck?" Everyone looked to see who had shouted that word. "Luck?" It was Caroline Leach. "For you, maybe. For him, though? What will his life be, from what you've said? Will he ever sleep without dreaming of carnage again?"

"Don't speak of something you know nothing about," retorted Agnes, her face livid.

And Alice, who could have been offended, crossed the room to sit by Caroline and to say something to her that resulted in the two of them embracing.

Ann judged that it was time to take up the scripts, so she asked women to turn to the lengthy section of the Chorus, beginning, "O Muse, be near me now, and make / A strange song for Ilion's sake . . ." She had some ideas for choreographing the Chorus as they chanted this, the strophe and the antistrophe, and she wanted the women to consider a very simple dance as they moved.

It had been decided they would not have music. Ann corresponded with groups in England who were also working on productions of the play, including an acquaintance who spoke to Sybil Thorndike—Miss Thorndike had performed in both *Hecuba* and *The Trojan Women* and had made the role of Hecuba in each play her own. She told the mutual acquaintance to relay to Ann that the twelve chords struck by eight trumpets that had opened the performance at the Alhambra in London had thrilled her to the very core. But that said, she agreed with Gilbert Murray that her preference was for a spoken chorus, not a singing one, and that however moving the use of Hebridean folk melodies or the simple notes of a psaltery, she wondered if the stark power of the language might somehow be undermined. This correspondence helped to confirm Ann's own inclination to simplicity.

But then Elizabeth Washburn brought the information that she had overheard two Indian women from Songhees—well, not the old Songhees any longer, not since the area at Mud Bay had been sold for cash ten years earlier and its residents moved over to Esquimalt Harbour—who were hanging out her family's laundry chanting a most strange and powerful song in the back garden where the clotheslines were. When she asked them about it, they told her it was a cleansing song, owned by their family, and that they were practising for a ceremonial to honour cousins who'd been killed in France and whose personal belongings had recently been returned to the family.

"It was so unexpected and moving to hear these two women, usually so quiet when they come to do our laundry and heavy cleaning, singing in my back garden. It was such a dignified sound and yet otherworldly, because of course they sang in their own language and not in ours. For some reason it reminded me of what the Chorus does, though I can't explain why exactly. And so I wondered then how it might work for us. They told me they usually sing with a rattle made of sheep horn—wild big-horned sheep, that is. And that the song is generally performed with dancers who wear masks. I gather, though, that the dancers are young men so that perhaps is not appropriate for us. In any case, it was the rhythm, its evocative sound, and the fact that it was used to heal, or cleanse, that caught my ear."

She looked to Ann and then to the other women. What might they think of such an idea? On the edge of the Empire, where allegiances were to England and the King, most people thought of Indians, if they thought of them at all, as colourful but savage. One might hire them to clean, wondered one member of the Chorus, but was it really on to have them mix with this group of women?

"One hears of disease and squalor," said Mary Morrison, wrinkling her pretty nose. "My fiancé's family has a summer home on the peninsula where the Indians cure their fish. It reeks! Some of them won't even speak English. The children never wear shoes!"

"And yet there is that artist, Miss Carr, who travels up the coast and paints their houses and boats and the mysterious totem poles," Frances Gibbs remembered. "Very powerful paintings."

Priscilla Foley was inclined to dismiss the idea. "Whatever do Indians have to do with this play written by a Greek?"

Ann thought for a moment and replied, "Well, one might also ask, What does a play written by a Greek two thousand years ago have to do with some women in Victoria in the twentieth century? Or what did Hebridean music have to do with the play performed in London? Or . . . ?" She left the idea open.

Flora, wanting to help Ann make her point, suggested inviting the Indian women to come to a rehearsal if Elizabeth thought they'd agree. Would the others agree that this would be a good idea? She was remembering Mary at Walhachin, who cleaned Flora's house with polish and whose biscuits were light as any. Whose cabin on the Deadman River was swept and smelled of sage.

Most did, and the ones who didn't were willing to give the Indian women a chance. And so it was decided that they would be invited to attend the next rehearsal in four days' time.

"This is Nancy Cooper and this is Sara Richard." Elizabeth introduced her two companions to the assembled cast of *The Trojan Women*. The two Indian women smiled shyly. Both were attired in cotton dresses with woollen shawls wrapped around them for warmth. They wore bandanas of brightly flowered calico over their heads. Each carried a basket.

Ann explained to them that the women would like to hear the song they had been singing in Elizabeth's back garden. They reached into their baskets and took out objects that proved to be the anticipated rattles. Nancy's was shaped like a duck, carved of wood and polished, whose long tail functioned as a handle. Sara's was a curly horn, a sheep horn, and had tassels of wool hanging from it.

"How fascinating," commented Ann, her eyes shining. "May we hear them?"

And the gathering of women was treated to the song that had so entranced Elizabeth. She had been right to call it otherworldly. The rattles were used along with the voice, but neither sounded as one would expect it to. One could hear wind in the rattle, could hear tides washing up on a stony shore, rain falling. And the voices of the women were low, centred in the throat and chest. It was as though the earth itself was telling what was lost, not with words but with the essence of sound articulating grief in all its registers.

The room was completely still when Nancy and Sara stopped singing. The song had spun a web of sorrow, an elemental dirge for what needed mourning.

Priscilla was the first to speak. "Let me take back my petty reservations about what might be appropriate and what might not be. To my mind, this is exactly what we should have in our play, if Nancy and Sara are willing to join us."

Ann thanked the two women and offered them a cup of tea. It was clear to her from the faces in the room that others felt as Priscilla did.

"Would you be willing to play your song for our performance?" she asked the two women as they drank their tea. They nodded.

"Our cousins," began Nancy, "they joined the fight for the King, same as the white men. They were lost to their wives. Instead of them coming home, ready to fish and gather clams, or to do farm work or pick hops, only a box with their extra shirts and papers came back. There was a pipe. A little bit of French money, which won't help their families at all. We can share our song if it will help. It's owned by our family and we have permission."

Elizabeth asked them to wait for a few minutes and she would take them back in her car. And then she worked out some details with Ann regarding rehearsal times and when they would need the Indian women to be present.

The new dimension to the production gave the women a sense of urgency, a sense that they must make this whole effort meaningful not just to themselves but to the larger community. There had been talk in Victoria about the silliness that some women would go to in order to draw attention to themselves. It was felt that women on the stage were akin to dance-hall entertainment. Or worse. Frivolous, and not a little unseemly.

Agnes Hunter observed tartly that it had also been thought frivolous for women to be given the vote, though men had been happy enough to be nursed by them in field hospitals overseas. And those men who returned were happy enough to find that households had been kept running, businesses kept in good shape, factories kept producing, and who deserved thanks in large part for it?

"What is that terrible remark that Dr. Johnson once made?" asked Agnes. "Something to the effect that he was fond of ladies, he liked their beauty and delicacy, but he liked best their silence. I think that is not an uncommon sentiment among many men, even the ones we love. It is most distressing in the ones we love, perhaps. But this is an opportunity for us to speak not just with our words—or Euripides' words, to be precise—but also with the action we are taking by working so hard on this play."

"Well said, Agnes." Caroline Leach peered up from her sewing—she was working on Cassandra's robe—to give Agnes one of her infrequent but glorious smiles.

TWENTY-EIGHT
1962

Mick did not die. He had operations to patch his burned skin with skin from other parts of his body. His teacher visited him at the hospital so that he would not get behind in his school work. Tessa and Teddy were allowed to visit after a week. They brought a bag of their best Halloween candy and three Superman comics. And Mick was happy to get these things although he seemed like a quieter boy than the one who had been their brother before Halloween.

Some evenings the Godwins came so that Tessa's parents could go to the hospital together. The children would have their instructions—any homework had be done before they could watch one show on television; bedtime at eight would be observed although they could read quietly in their beds if they couldn't sleep. Mr. Godwin had been a headmaster at a school just outside Victoria and he was very helpful if there was a question about arithmetic or phonics.

On one of these occasions, when Tessa was crying in her bed— she did this most nights because the terrible events of Halloween would not go away, no matter how hard she tried to think of other things— Mrs. Godwin came quietly into her room.

"It's the smell," Tessa gasped through her tears. "It was so awful and I keep smelling it."

"I know just what you mean, my dear."

"You do?"

Mrs. Godwin stroked Tessa's hair with her old wrinkled hands. "I was a nurse, you see, during the Great War—you will know it as World War One, but for me it was a baptism on every front—and I was sent to a hospital near Étables in France. So many of the patients had been burned, either by gas that blistered their faces and ruined their lungs or in explosions. That smell, oh, of burned flesh and gunpowder and worse, if you can imagine worse, stayed with me for a very long time. But it will go, you'll see. Mick was very lucky not to have been blinded or to have lost his fingers or a foot. He will be himself again, I do believe this, and you will gradually forget that smell."

"Did the patients die, the ones in France?"

"Many of them did, yes. But others got well and were sent back to battle or else home. That is where I met my husband. He was injured at Vimy Ridge, the third battle of Arras in 1917, and brought to us. Luckily he was not burned but suffered shrapnel wounds, some pieces lodged in his knee, which is why he limps a little . . ."

"He took the stairs two at a time when he came to help Mick," Tessa remembered. And she also remembered her father walking her to school one day, she must have been in grade one, and passing the street called Vimy that met Moss Street just a few blocks before the school. He spoke then of that war and its battles, but mostly she had been thinking of the day ahead, whether her pencils were sharp enough. And yet it had something to do with the Godwins, with this moment, although she could not have known it at the time. Some days it seemed that everything was connected, that little trails led from one moment to the next, across the years as though across a map. Mrs. Godwin as a young woman nursing a man who was not yet her husband. A place called Vimy. The Cross of Sacrifice in memory of those who were killed in that war. And the other one too.

Mrs. Godwin was reassuring. "Oh, yes, he certainly recovered well and he has never thought of himself as lame. But I tell you this so you will understand that this terrible event will fade away as the weeks and months pass. I expect we'll see Mick playing catch across the road this spring just as he always has. And racing off on his bike to ball practice. Right now you think that the world is a very frightening place and it can be, no doubt, but happy things will come to you. So please try to snuggle down under your covers and sleep."

What Tessa remembered most in later years about Mick's accident and the kindness of the Godwins was how she learned that people were full of surprises. An elderly woman, previously only seen in her garden and occasionally shaking a rug out the back door, had taken care of men who were burned worse than Mick; her equally old husband had not only been a teacher but a soldier as well. In books, soldiers were young and handsome, and Mr. Godwin was ancient with almost no hair and brown spots on his hands and arms. But once he had been one of those young gallant men and then he had been hurt and that was what led him to Mrs. Godwin. And to the house next door to Tessa's family home in Fairfield. She decided to draw that house onto her map and made faint drawings of two people standing on the porch, holding hands.

TWENTY-NINE
1920

They were all extremely nervous, except Mary Morrison, who was of course Helen. She stood in the dressing room in her simple blue gown, a crown of airy wildflowers (fashioned by Frances Gibbs from silk and bits of ribbon and gauze) in her long hair, which was braided into a loose cord to fall over one shoulder.

"I should be nervous, but I'm not. I can't wait to take the stage! My parents say I have always been theatrical and perhaps they're right." She twirled across the dressing room and her ribbons rose in the draft. "And I do have to say that it is not often one gets to portray a character of whom it has been said, *'Was this the face that launch'd a thousand ships. / And burnt the topless towers of Ilium?'* That is courtesy of Theodore, who of course reads far more than I."

"And does he mind that you are Helen?" asked Alice Ramsay.

"Oh, I can't say. Nor will he. He has reservations about the arts in general, I think, so no doubt dramatic presentations will possess a whiff of dubious utility in his world of getting and spending. But he'll be here tonight, with his parents, and with mine. I told him I wouldn't marry him if he didn't come."

Ticket sales had been brisk. The *Colonist* ran an article about the women and their production that was slightly derisive but that at least alerted the city's citizenry to the opportunity to see the play. Their anonymous patron, known only to Ann, had paid for the rental of the theatre, and the women had collected enough money among themselves to produce a simple handbill that they distributed to likely venues. That, and the newspaper article, was their only sources of advertising. Word of mouth provided the rest.

Costumes had been kept simple—robes for the female roles and tunics of coarse burlap (potato sacks begged from a grocer) for Talthybius and Menelaus and the attendant soldiers. Helmets for the soldiers had been discussed and then voted against as silly. "Let us suggest rather than insist," was the sentiment. Sara and Nancy had been asked what they thought they should wear, and after conferring, they suggested their cedar capes, which they would wear in cleansing ceremonials. It was agreed that the two of them would sit together, to one side of the stage. A few pillars, stored at the theatre for the various operas performed there, were brought on to the stage and strung with ivy to give the set a pagan look. One of them was artfully broken at the top, which added to the suggestion of destruction. The backdrop curtains had been painted by Flora with help from most of the cast at one point or another. The first featured Troy in ruins and the second, which would come down over the first during the final scenes of the play, was the same view but with an overcast sky and wisps of smoke rising from the ruins that were now on fire.

Programs had also been kept simple although Ann wrote an introductory paragraph for the play that made oblique reference to Troy's position opposite Gallipoli across the Dardanelles, to suggest how the characters in the play would have been held within the same landscape as the men in 1915–1916 as their drama unfolded.

"This is it, ladies," Ann told her cast of women as they stood in the wings, listening to the sound of their audience settling in. "I am so proud of how hard you've all worked. I think we have something fine to show this city. What's more, I feel we are part of a larger movement. There are people in England who are waiting to know how our production is received. Are you excited?"

Of course they were. Frances Gibbs was trembling, and her robe kept sliding down her shoulders. Priscilla Foley spoke softly to her and hugged her. Caroline Leach closed her eyes and took deep breaths to calm herself. But if they were not ready now, not after the two months of rehearsal and days spent painting backdrops, designing and sewing costumes, organizing and distributing handbills, pleading with friends and family to buy tickets, then they would never be ready. Or this was how the practical Agnes Hunter expressed it to the group.

The voice of Poseidon, through Alice Ramsay (who had developed extraordinary projection since her first timid and tentative attempt), intoned to the audience an immortal and timeless observation:

The groves are empty and the sanctuaries
Run red with blood. Unburied Priam lies
By his own hearth, on God's high altar-stair,
And Phrygian gold goes forth and raiment rare
To the Argive ships; and weary soldiers roam
Waiting the wind that blows at last for home,
For wives and children, left long years away,
Beyond the seed's tenth fullness and decay,
To work this land's undoing.

The audience settled themselves in. The theatre was cold; puffs of grey air could be seen as Poseidon spoke. It gave the stage a strange atmosphere, unworldly and severe.

As the two divine beings discussed their various dissatisfactions with the victorious Greeks and how they might be punished for their desecration of Athena's temple, the heat of the assembled audience gradually warmed the theatre. By the time Poseidon and Athena exited and the heap of rags on the stage rose to reveal itself to be a woman, there was no more grey breath to suggest anything other than a mortal woman waking to grief.

O ships, O crowding faces
Of ships, O hurrying beat
Of oars as of crawling feet,
How found ye our holy places?

Threading the narrows through,
Our from the gulfs of the Greek,
Out of the clear dark blue,
With hate ye came and with joy,
And the noise of your music flew,
Clarion and pipe did shriek,
As the coiled cords ye threw,
Held in the heart of Troy.

The audience sat riveted as Ann recited the ancient words of Euripides, words giving voice to Hecuba, alone outside the walls of her ruined city, the curtain of broken pillars and the background of fallen walls behind her. Ann's training as a singer allowed her to offer each phrase as a discrete dramatic unit, with power and clarity, and she delivered Hecuba's speech to the far ends of the theatre easily and immediately. Those in the farthest seats heard her as though they were sitting in the front row.

Who am I that I sit
Here at a Greek king's door,
Yea, in the dust of it?

Slowly the other women of Troy gathered around her on the stage, wondering at their fates.

How have they cast me? asked one Trojan woman, played by a shy dark-haired person called Celia Munro who had barely said a word all through rehearsals apart from her lines and who now stood with complete confidence, asking with a strong voice, How have they cast me? and to whom / A handmaid?

As the Chorus turned to begin their second strophe, Hecuba's mournful lament rang out:

And I the aged, where go I,
A winter-frozen bee, a slave
Death-shaped, as the stones that lie
Hewn on a dead man's grave . . .

Those in the audience shivered as they heard these words. And Flora, listening in the wings, remembered how those lines had given her a window into the play as she and Ann had read the script in their own warm sitting room. She took deep breaths as she stood waiting for her own entrance, while Cassandra uttered her mad speeches containing within them the tragedy of that war's terrible violations—her own body, the temple of Athena, the unburied bodies of fallen men—and her bloody prophecies.

But part I must let be,
And speak not. Not the axe that craveth me,
And more than me; not the dark wanderings
Of mother-murder that my bridal brings,
And all the House of Atreus down, down, down . . .

It was going remarkably well, Flora thought, still in the wings. She was anticipating the great choric moment, between the strophe, O Muse, be near me now, and make / A strange song for Ilion's sake . . . and antistrophe, O, and swift were all in Troy that day, / And girt them to the portal-way . . . It described arrival of the large wooden horse; the Indian women were to accompany the chanted verses, the slow and dignified rattles making an eerie rhythm for their voices to enter, to portent the warriors and all that fell with Troy.

The audience craned their necks to see where the sound was coming from. The Indian women were just within sight, seated on cedar mats they'd brought with them, wrapped in cedar capes. The sound they produced was as elemental as wind in coastal forests. When the passage ended, the single maiden from the Chorus sadly calling, Weep, weep for Ilion, Sara and Nancy began their own chant, a song to honour the dead of their own families, to cleanse their possessions of sorrow, to quiet their souls and give them rest. It was so moving that Flora had to remind herself that her own entrance was imminent.

The stage went briefly dark. The light cutout of a chariot was quickly moved into place and Flora positioned herself in front of it, cradling Astyanax on her lap. Forth to the Greek I go, she intoned, Driven as a beast is driven.

(In her arms she carried a large cloth doll. The idea of using Grace had been considered and abandoned, not simply because she was a girl and Astyanax a male child, but because Flora thought it might trouble her daughter to be put in the role of an infant whose fate was to be cast from the stone walls of a ruined city.)

I and my babe are driven among the droves
Of plundered cattle. Oh, when fortune moves
So swift, the high heart like a slave beats low.

So sang Andromache, who was Flora. Then Hecuba answered, who was Ann:

'Tis fearful to be helpless. Men but now
Have taken Cassandra, and I strove in vain.

And then the exchange, whereby Andromache tells her mother-in-law that another daughter, Polyxena, has been slaughtered on the tomb of Achilleus (and Andromache given to his son, Neoptolemus). Then Andromache rues the lot of women given to victors, forced to share the beds of the men who have killed their husbands.

O shame, shame!
What woman's lips can so forswear her dead,
And give strange kisses in another's bed?
Why, not a dumb beast, not a colt will run
In the yoke untroubled, when her mate is gone . . .

And worse, if worse could be imagined, to come, for Astyanax, condemned to die as a future prince of Troy.

Go, die, my best beloved, wept Andromache, my cherished son:
In fierce men's hands, leaving me here alone.
Thy father was too valiant; that is why
They slay thee! Other children, like to die,
Might have been spared for that. But on thy head
His good is turned to evil.

In the beautiful poetry of Euripides lay all the grief and sorrow of the ages, the slaughter of innocents, the loss of husbands, of fathers, of lovers; victors distributing the spoils as prizes, burning the sacred sites, forbidding the simple rituals of honour and remembrance.

When the moment arrived when Menelaus first sees Helen, the ostensible reason for the conflict between the Achaians and the allies of Troy, the audience let out a collective hiss. Hecuba's urgent plea to Menelaus to let Helen speak but also to allow her, Hecuba, to answer gave Helen her moment to absolve herself of responsibility. It was, after all, Hecuba who gave birth to Paris, and Priam who exposed him to the elements as an infant that he might die and not fulfill the portent of his mother's dream that he would bring destruction to the city of his birth; and Paris's judgment, that Aphrodite might be given the golden apple of discord in return for her gift to him of the loveliest woman on earth. No, she was bedazzled, she insisted, and not herself: *My wrong done / Hath its own pardon.*

Enough of that, snapped Hecuba—

It was by force my son
Took you, thou sayest, and striving . . . Yet not one
In Sparta knew? No cry, no sudden prayer
Rang from thy rooms that night . . . Castor was there
To hear these, and his brother: both true men,
Not yet among the stars!

And the Chorus backed her up, telling Menelaus, *Be strong, O King . . . not weak, / But iron against the wrong!*"

Yet the scene ended with the suggestion that Menelaus would take his wife back, into his arms, his heart. (Hecuba remarked, *A lover once, will always love again.*)

It was exhilarating for those in the wings to know they had the audience's complete attention. There was no rustling of programs, no unnecessary murmuring, and only a little coughing. During the burial scene of the infant Astyanax, put into earth on his father's shield, his grandmother Hecuba performed the rituals of purification, her words clear in the chilly air of the theatre.

All is gone.
How should a poet carve the funeral stone
To tell thy story true? 'There lieth here

> *A babe whom the Greeks feared, and in their fear*
> *Slew him.' Aye, Greece will bless the tale it tells.*
> *Child, they have left thee beggared of all else*
> *In Hector's house; but one thing shalt thou keep,*
> *This war-shield bronzen-barred, wherein to sleep.*

As the remnants of Troy were set ablaze (the second painted curtain quickly lowered in front of the first) and the Chorus chanted the final *Farewell* ... *Forth to the Greek ships / And the sea's foaming*, the Indian women again performed their eerie song while the Trojan women left the stage to be distributed to their masters.

After the last notes of the rattles sounded, Nancy and Sara rose quietly and left the stage. The curtain fell. And the audience began a long and loud applause.

Backstage there was delighted and relieved laughing. Then, "Ann, they are calling for you!" and Agnes was leading Ann to the stage again to receive the applause and a sheaf of lilies the women had arranged to have delivered to the theatre. The cast joined her, and they stood for a brief period in the glow of lights and acclamation.

And still: "They are calling for you, Ann." Seemingly without any kind of preparation, Ann stood with her sheaf of lilies, her simple gown hanging around her, and drew her shoulders back, her chest filling with air. Was Ann to sing then? And she opened her mouth. It was a song Flora recognized from Ann's repertoire, Dido's lament:

> *When I am laid, am laid in earth,*
> *May my wrongs create no trouble, no trouble in thy breast;*
> *When I am laid, am laid in earth,*
> *May my wrongs create no trouble, no trouble in thy breast;*
> *Remember me, remember me;*
> *But ah! Forget my fate.*
> *Remember me, but ah! Forget my fate.*

Dido's words shimmered in the theatre, offered by Ann as a gift to the audience, a gift and a reminder.

"There is a message for you, Flora, as well as this big bouquet of roses." Alice Ramsay put the flowers into Flora's arms and tucked a little envelope into her hand. Everyone was gathered in the largest of the dressing rooms, excitedly discussing the performance. Outside the door, family members waited, messages were passed back and forth between sisters and husbands and children, and someone had brought champagne to toast the cast.

"How lovely," murmured Flora, burrowing her nose into the roses. "Who would be sending flowers to me? Robert Alexander, I suppose."

She allowed Ann to take the roses from her so she could open her message. She read it, made a small cry, putting her hands to her cheeks, and then got up suddenly to run from the room.

"I wonder what that's all about?" asked Mary Morrison, as she began removing the heavy stage makeup that had already begun to run. "Perhaps Flora has an admirer!"

Flora ran to the side door of the theatre and looked into the crowd making its way along the sidewalk, scanning faces with such urgency. Yes, yes, there they were! They saw her at the same moment she located them in the crowd.

"Jane! Allan! Oh, how wonderful to see you!"

The two women embraced, tears running down their faces. Allan waited and then took his turn to embrace Flora. He held her for a long moment, patting her back, then releasing her to Jane again.

"We were very impressed with the play, Flora," he told her. "Who would have known you were an actress as well as a ceramics artist?"

The McIntyres were staying at the Empress Hotel and had left their Thomas with a cousin of Allan's for the evening.

"May we take you back for a late supper?" asked Jane. "Then we can arrange to have the little ones meet, perhaps tomorrow. I'm dying to see Grace."

Flora took Jane and Allan into the theatre by the side door

and introduced them to Ann and the others. Ann insisted that she would return home to relieve Grace's minder and that Flora should go with her friends and have a meal with them. Quickly Flora put herself together, making certain that the cast did not mind her leaving them to clean up the dressing room she had shared with Ann and several members of the Chorus. She looked at the woman in the mirror, a little older than the girl who had first known Jane and shared stories of her coming out, her white dress and beaded slippers; Jane, the first person she had told about Gus: she saw the older Flora in the mirror, shadowed by the knowledge of Gus's death, her brothers' deaths, her father's death, Andromache hovering behind her like a ghost. She took up her coat and pocketbook and left the room.

O v e r a l a t e supper of roast chicken and a bottle of hock, the two women filled each other in on the years of their separation while Allan sat quietly, adding a mild sentence from time to time.

"And will you come to us over the summer? We could sew again under the spreading cottonwood—I still have my bodice, you know, although it would not fit me now—and the children could play or ride with Allan. After Grace has found her seat of course. And think of the picnics we could have down on Oregon Jack Creek!"

"We'd love to, Jane, if you're certain. I know that my situation is . . . well, irregular and might cause you some embarrassment."

"I hope you're not serious? Of course we're certain! Why on earth would you think otherwise?"

"My mother never refers to Grace in her letters and so I know that she, for one, is sensitive about my unmarried state of motherhood. Gus's mother won't see us, though his father has been a tower of strength and love. I know that some in Walhachin would not be pleased to see me. And I would understand your reluctance to have us come when you know the train would stop in Ashcroft where you are so well known and thought of."

Jane and Allan both laughed. They began to speak at the same time: "Flora, do not even consider . . ." "Nonsense, Flora . . ."

Allan let Jane continue. "You are a beautiful and accomplished woman, Flora, and you have a daughter with a proud name. Your mother has cut off her nose to spite her face, it seems to me. And I know that Grace's father would delight in every inch of her."

"Bless you both," said Flora quietly. "I don't feel the stigma here any longer because Ann has been so supportive that many other women simply wouldn't dare to shun me."

At this point, Allan mildly interrupted. "I know they have a most delicious apple charlotte if I can interest the two of you?"

As they nodded, he said to the waiter, "Three portions of apple charlotte, please. And I think three glasses of your finest port to go with it."

"T h e r e i s a review in today's *Colonist*," said Ann as Flora came in from tea with Jane and Allan, two days after the performance.

"And . . . ?" Flora was removing Grace's coat and hanging it, putting her hat on its hook, and smoothing her child's hair with one hand while she unfastened the buttons of her own coat with the other. She looked expectantly to Ann, who was holding the newspaper open as she greeted them.

Ann reached down to give Grace a kiss. "First, will you tell me about your tea, Grace? Did you like Thomas?"

"He has a pony, Ann. And he says I might ride it if we go to visit. I'm going to draw a pony now." Grace ran to her room where paper and pencil waited to receive this new dream.

"So—do tell, Ann! Have we been praised or condemned?"

"It's quite positive, on the whole. You are cited as dignity personified for the way you portrayed Andromache. He didn't quite see the point of Sara and Nancy, but we knew that would probably be the case. He does see the point of Greek tragedy, though, and that's something for which we can be grateful. Let me read you that part. 'A Greek tragedy was a religious experience in the form of a ceremonial, a ceremonial, moreover, which was not the affair of the actors merely, but of everyone who was present at it. There was in it, accordingly, what will be found in no modern tragedy, even the greatest: the rhythm of a high experience, rising with the natural inevitability of rhythm from the beginning, reaching the summit of exaltation, and ending at the last in calm. The form here perfectly expresses the inspiration.'"

"Well, that's something, isn't it? Anything about the staging? The others?"

"He is quite kind. He has good words for Mary and her beauty and her presence. And he admires my Hecuba, saying that her laments are uttered not by her precisely but by humanity through her. I thought that very perceptive and of course I wonder how this person has been allowed to say these things in print, in a newspaper not known for its pacifist views. But we can be grateful for this in any case."

"And who is he?"

"I don't know. He signs himself Didascalia, which is perhaps a little coy—I believe that was the process of teaching drama to the Chorus by the playwright? But he is obviously familiar with this play and with its tradition as well as the other performances. For instance, he seems to have attended at least one of the Granville-Barker productions with the marvellous Lillah McCarthy, though he doesn't say which one. Anyway, we haven't been drawn and quartered, not yet, and judging from the cards that have arrived in today's post—you'll see them on the mantel, Flora, just there—there are some in this city who feel as we do. Though I fear they are almost all, to a writer, women."

They continued to talk about the play. It had taken up so much of their time, it was hard to believe it was over. There had been several unpleasant phone calls to say that women had no right to question the patriotic requirement of men to serve their King and country or that the CEF were hardly a pillaging army, taking women as their slaves. As Ann observed, subtlety was lost on some. They waited for what they hoped would be a ground-swell of support for their message, but Ann reminded Flora that this might take longer than they hoped.

Flora told Ann about her second visit with Jane and Allan, how warmly they treated Grace, and how charming was their young Thomas.

"They've asked that Grace and I visit them this summer and you know, Ann, I think we will. I don't imagine I would care to return to Walhachin, having left in a cloud of disgrace! That won't be forgotten, or forgiven. But it would be lovely to spend a week or two at the McIntyre Ranch. You won't feel we've abandoned you?"

"Of course not, Flora! Not as long as you both return!"

THIRTY
1962

"Your dad has some news, kids." The three children looked up from their pork chops and Minute Rice, a favourite weekday supper. Their father was smiling from his place at the head of the table, his napkin tucked into the neck of his shirt (he was notoriously messy with his food).

"Well, it's good news, kids. At least I think it's good news. I've been given a new job, one which I applied for and never thought I'd get! Doing research in field corn and peas, at the Morden Research Centre in Manitoba. It's a chance to really dig into the diseases that affect our food crops and I'm awfully happy to have this opportunity."

"Manitoba, Dad? Are you serious?"

"Yeah, completely serious, Teddy."

"That's pretty cool. When are we going?"

"Well, they want me in the new year. So the plan is, we'll have Christmas here and then head away just after. It's a long drive—your mother and I figure it will take us about five days, depending on weather. But an adventure, I think, and a change for us all."

Tessa was completely quiet. *Manitoba?* She knew it from the maps she'd been looking at. One over from Saskatchewan. *Three* over from British Columbia. Which was where they *lived*, where their home was. How could her parents think of moving? And was it forever? What would happen to their house?

She slipped away from the table and went into her room to think about it. She couldn't think with everyone else talking and

Mick and Teddy giving each other high-fives. She lay on her bed in the dark and closed her eyes. She saw the cemetery, the trees all covered in spring growth, ground dotted with daisies. Little birds entering the dark centres of trees where their nests were concealed from the crows who patrolled in groups, loud and energetic as boys in a schoolyard.

And what about school? She couldn't say she'd miss her teacher. Some of the kids, yes. She'd made one close friend this year, Melody Sangster, who lived on the other side of the Moss Rocks. When Tessa visited her after school one day, she discovered that Melody's mum had a job and her father stayed home. He had a condition, Tessa wasn't sure what it was, but it made him too nervous to work. It was odd but not unpleasant to be served milk and cookies by a father for a change, and he let them fasten wax paper to their feet with strips of soft cloth so they could skate up and down the wooden floors of the long hall. So she'd have to leave Melody. And the Godwins. And Miss Oakden and her tree frogs. When she thought of this, she got a hard lump in her throat. She swallowed. A few tears trickled down her cheeks. And then she realized her father had come into her room.

"Is it upsetting for you to think of us moving?" he asked.

She couldn't speak at first. She swallowed again and the hard lump moved a bit. "No. Yes. Well, you know. Exciting but sad. This is where we live. If we don't live here, I'm afraid I'll forget everything I know about it. Will we come back?"

"I can't answer that, sweetie. Maybe. Maybe not. We'll see how it goes. We might end liking Morden so much we'll never want to leave. We won't sell our house, though. Or at least not right away, not until we know how we feel about everything."

It seemed her mother was always too busy. There were lists to make, movers to consult—they came with stacks of paper for wrapping things and big wooden boxes they called "tea chests," and padded blankets to put around wooden furniture and other objects before fitting them into the back of the huge moving van. The family had Christmas in a house bereft of half its furniture, but the tree was lovely in the window as usual, decorated with lots of candy canes and tinsel and one string of lights (most of the ornaments had already been packed). Santa Claus came, bringing oranges for their stockings, and little whistles shaped like birds that you filled with water and that gurgled like red-winged blackbirds, a Chinese fan for Tessa, and the wrapped parcels under the tree held wonderful surprises: a camera for each child with two rolls of film; knapsacks with canteens and first-aid kits; heavy parkas and snowboots for the Morden winter they'd be driving into.

Although the basement was cold, Tessa worked daily on her map. She didn't want to forget anything, not a building or a tree or a particular gathering of birds. She drew a dead dogfish on the beach below the cemetery, a group of three children around it, one with a stick. The school at its five corners and the Annex perched on its rocks. She added the Guracks' house, with the shape of the grandmother beyond the big window.

In later years, Flora would be grateful for the play, for the intense relationship with Ann as they rehearsed while folding sheets, doing dishes, or walking the quiet lanes through the cemetery. (Hecuba: *Death cannot be what Life is, Child; the cup / Of Death is empty, and Life hath always hope.* Andromache: *O Mother, having ears, hear thou this word / Fear-conquering, till thy heart as mine by stirred with joy.*)

How bitter it was for her to return from Jane and Allan's ranch to discover that Ann was suffering from an invasive cancer ("I had been feeling slow, even before the play, though it was easier to put any concerns aside during that time! And I had no appetite. Robert advised a consultation with my doctor. I'd not expected such bad news, I'm afraid, and was rather sharp when the doctor gave me my death sentence. 'You will not see another summer,' he said, which was not a pleasant way to put things.") and would be dead within three months. How could such a robust and vital woman die, with so many projects planned, so many years anticipated for seeing them through? It was almost too much for Flora, and for Grace too. The child had bloomed in Ann's care while Flora had found work with James McGregor. When Flora would return from work, weary from the long ride home, it was reassuring to walk into a warm home with a bathed child waiting in sweet-scented flannel to be kissed and cuddled and put to bed.

"Let's do what we can, Flora—put in some bulbs, walk by the sea, and I'll sing while I can. What about this? My cousin in

England sent me sheet music for some Robert Burns songs. They are very sentimental, I'm afraid, but the melodies are pure gold. Do you know this one?"

She was rustling some music at the piano and then playing the opening bars of something Flora thought was familiar. It wasn't until Ann began to sing that Flora knew it was "Ae Fond Kiss," a song she had first heard at a Scottish aunt's home when her family had gone up for the grouse season. But she had not heard it as Ann sang it, a melody of abiding sweetness, and lyrics to break the human heart. 'Had we ne'er loved sae kindly, / Had we ne'er loved so blindly, / Never met, not never parted, / We had ne'er been broken hearted.'

Flora listened and thought of her own love, her "first and fairest," the way her life had changed as a result. What would have happened if I'd answered otherwise when he asked if I minded when he kissed me? she wondered. And she could not imagine.

In Ann's last weeks, she was permitted to come home to Hollyhock Cottage with Robert Alexander's promise that he would be available at any time to come to ease her suffering with whatever means were available to him. ("My own doctor felt my place was in the ward with the nuns tightening my sheets and bringing me dreadful puddings. I do not have his blessing for this, but Robert was persuasive.") Flora filled Ann's bedroom with late asters and roses and brought her cups of beef broth or plain soups. She'd walk around the block to the grocery store on Eberts Street and ask Mrs. Sturgeon for a block of special chocolate or a wedge of nougat to place on a tiny porcelain dish to accompany Ann's tea. She sat up many nights while Ann weakened, holding her friend's hand, reading poetry to her. The beautiful sonnets of William Shakespeare, the glorious odes of John Keats.

"I am leaving the house to you, Flora," whispered Ann one night as Flora bathed her face during a particularly sleepless spell. "I made the arrangement when I first knew about the cancer. So you will always have a home. It has given me so much pleasure to have you here, to have had a child to love and share responsibility for, and to have watched you make a real life for yourself after losing your lover and your family. I have been so proud of you."

"How could I have done any of it without you? Lie still and I will change your nightdress. Oh, smell this, Ann! This fresh one still has the smell of the outdoors in it. You taught me to love that. We have done a lot of laundry together."

Mornings were best. Ann had lucid hours when she sat up in her chair and laughed. She was very thin, but there was still beauty in her long fingers, her spirit. She quietly gave up singing because she could no longer gather enough breath.

"Shall I play for you, Ann?" asked Grace.

"I'd love that, my dear."

Ann had been teaching Grace piano before the summer, simple songs, which filled the house, never again to ring with Ann's voice practising arpeggios, scales, the full-blown beauty of a Bach cantata, or the sweet sadness of a Robert Burns poem. Though Grace said later, "I hear her every morning," and would add no more to that.

The Trojan Women visited and brought food—cold hams, poached fish with parsley sauce, dishes of small minted potatoes, all designed to tempt Ann, who loved the sight of such pretty dishes but who couldn't eat much at all. And who finally couldn't see anyone but Flora, who knew to expect the sudden gasps, the odours, the grinding of teeth that made her suspect that Ann was dreaming of something terrible. Calls to Robert Alexander became more frequent. He would arrive with his medical bag containing the precious vials of morphine that allowed Ann to relax into a state of painless oblivion.

One morning Flora woke to silence. She had been so exhausted that she had slept deeply and wondered whether she had missed Ann's call in the night. Fearfully she pulled on her wrapper and ran to Ann's bedroom. The bed was empty. The bathroom? Empty. Rapidly Flora determined that Ann was not in the house and not in the garden—or not that she could see. Checking the bedroom again, Flora could see that Ann's shoes were not there and checking further, she discovered her coat was missing from the coat rack near the door.

I will not panic, she thought as she put on her clothes and drew on her warm coat for the day was drizzly and grey. She is so weak that even if she was able to get herself up and out, she could not have gone far. But thinking she would not panic, and stilling her racing heart, were two different things.

She went into the garden and searched carefully, thinking that perhaps Ann had wanted air in the night and a last look at the trees she and Phillip had planted more than two decades earlier. Perhaps she'd fallen and Flora, sleeping deeply, had not heard her call for help. Nothing. She tried to think as Ann might—a favourite neighbourhood location, a . . . well, what? Where?

Ann loved the ocean. She kept the windows open to hear the waves at Ross Bay crash to the shore during windstorms and she loved the iodine smell of the sea. Checking first to make sure that Grace was still asleep, Flora quickly ran the scant block from Hollyhock Cottage to the shore. The water was calm under the soft rain, swells coming in to the sand and rock regular and precise as a human pulse. And then she saw the scarf.

It was Ann's paisley cashmere scarf, a gift from her one sister still in Scotland. She always wore it with her winter coat, the one that was missing from the rack. It was draped over some rocks by a little sandy area. Flora's heart beat rapidly, fluttering in her chest so that she bent double to catch her breath, and her blood chilled as she saw the footprints in the sand, leading from the rocks to the water. They disappeared as the wet sand showed the progress of the tide's recession. Flora put her own foot into one of the prints—she and Ann had the same size feet—and sure enough, the fit was exact.

Returning to the house, Flora tried to calm herself, tried to determine what she needed to do next. She closed Ann's bedroom door so that when her child awoke, she would think that

Ann was sleeping. Then she made porridge for Grace's breakfast. She telephoned Robert Alexander for advice.

"I will make some calls, Flora, and then if what we both believe has happened has truly come to pass, I think we will simply have to wait."

Flora walked the beach for hours each day, watching the waves as though they might bring Ann to shore like a rich gift, a Venus in a wet camel-hair coat. Gulls cried out and the wind tossed them through the sky while skeins of geese passed overhead on their long journey south. And then, after four days, Ann's body washed to shore in secluded Gonzales Bay, just south of Ross Bay, where it was found by a man collecting firewood from the beach. Her face had been partially eaten by seals, but she was still wearing her winter coat. In the generous pockets, confined with sturdy hat pins, were two large stones—the gypsum containing the ammonite and the chunk of smooth limestone with the little bones and scales.

"She would have wanted to sink," Robert told Flora. "She was so emaciated that her body would have remained buoyant, and I don't think she would have had the strength to swim out very far. She'd thought about this, it is clear. Were the stones meaningful to her?"

"She and her late husband collected them on their honeymoon at Blue Anchor, in Somerset. They were two of a quartet that she kept on the hearth. You will have seen them a hundred times, Robert."

Saying that, Flora imagined Ann standing by the fireplace and choosing the stones. In her mind's eye, she saw Ann holding each stone in her hand to determine its weight, selecting two, and then carrying them to the shore wrapped in her paisley scarf, cradled in her arms like a child. What would it have felt like to tuck them into her coat pockets and then walk purposefully into the tide? The Ann Flora was imagining was the fearless woman who had staged a play full of women lamenting the losses of war to a city perhaps not ready to be told such a tale. Flora imagined her smiling the ghost of her radiant smile as the water lapped at the hem of her coat, then her waist, and then pushing herself forward into the waves as the stones did the work of taking her down. A few gulls watched impassively from the breakwater.

"You are very quiet, Flora."

She looked up, breaking her eerie reverie. "I cannot be angry that she ended her life this way, but I am worried that we might not be allowed to bury her in the usual way."

"Because she took her own life, do you mean?" He took note of Flora's nod of assent and thought for a moment. "I don't think Ann was guilty of despair, which of course the Church considers a sin against God. She was certainly not mad. But she was clearly at the end of her life and this only hastened her death by days, or a week or two at the most. I think she simply tired of the pain and the sheer difficulty of staying alive and wanted an end on her own terms. I don't believe this will present difficulty in arranging a burial, Flora. In the old days, yes, but not now. I may well be asked to sign something testifying to her mental state."

"Robert, how did she have the strength to walk to the shore with the weight of those two stones? She could barely move from her bed to the chair by the window. I don't understand it."

"People often find reservoirs of strength they never knew they had, Flora. I have seen dying people possessed of extraordinary strength, as though everything depended upon this last moment of courage. And courage it surely was that helped Ann to rise from her bed, her deathbed, really, to make that last journey towards peace."

"How will I tell Grace?"

But that did not prove to be difficult. When Flora sat with Grace and gently began to tell her that Ann had died, the child stroked her mother's hands and said, "Don't cry, Mummy. Ann has gone home. I heard her leave and she was singing."

"Do you mean the other morning, Grace?"

"She has been leaving since we came home from Thomas's ranch. I could hear her singing every day. She sang the whole story."

Ann had bought a plot in Ross Bay Cemetery almost as soon as she'd known her cancer was not curable. It was near the sea, with little glimpses of water between the hedges, and away from the dense shade of the yews and pines. Open air, grass carpeted with English daisies for at least nine months of the year: Flora felt it was as perfect a resting place for her friend as might be found anywhere. She imagined Ann walking slowly around the various available plots of earth, wondering, and wished she'd been there to help, to take Ann's arm, point out gulls, a clump of trilliums in the lea of the hedge.

And had she been prescient, on stage at the end of the performance, when she had spontaneously sung Dido's lament, *"When I am laid in earth,"* with its haunting final refrain: *"Remember me, Remember me; but ah! Forget my fate ... ?"*

The burial ceremony was simple, as had been directed by Ann in her last weeks. Her friends gathered by the grave after the church service (though one or two were censorious enough to absent themselves) and heard the familiar "ashes to ashes, dust to dust;" they sang the Twenty-third Psalm together before returning to Hollyhock Cottage for sherry and a slice of Ann's good fruitcake. "She was always prepared for visitors," commented Flora, cutting cake that had been baked while Flora and Grace were in the Upper Hat Creek Valley, when Ann must have only just learned of her illness. Baked and wrapped in brandy-soaked cloth to wait for this very day. Flora poured out little thimbles of sweet golden sherry from the glass decanter that had belonged to Ann's mother. After the guests left, Flora and Robert shared a dram of the fine malt whisky that Ann had loved, and sent her soul on its way to reunion with her beloved Phillip. The two remaining stones from Blue Anchor looked lonely on the hearth, but Flora had insisted that the other two remain with Ann in death; her choice of them as final companions determined this decision. When Ann's body had been prepared for her burial, Flora had wrapped the stones in the paisley scarf and placed them at her feet.

Soon afterwards, Flora spent an afternoon with Mr. Stewart at the monumental works. "Me again, I'm afraid, Mr. Stewart, looking again for a perfect piece of stone."

"I am sorry for your loss, Miss Oakden. But I believe Mrs. Ogilvie would love this red granite from Aberdeen."

"I have five lines of verse and of course the other details. Perhaps you could read the verse and recommend a style of lettering."

He read the text carefully, the lines from the final aria of Bach's Cantata 199:

I lay myself on these wounds
As though upon a true rock;
They shall be my resting place.
Upon them will I soar in faith
And therefore contented and happily sing.

"Strong and beautiful words, Miss Oakden. I think nothing would suit them better than a Roman face. Let me show this one, similar to that used on the Trajan column. See how handsome it is! The serifs are bold and give the face a timeless quality."

After the stone was completed and placed, Flora lifted clumps of bluebells from Ann's garden and planted them around the granite, along with a few snowdrops, already showing their green.

Leaving Pennies that cold December day on the train, I could never have dreamed what lay in wait for me in Victoria, a city I had never even seen, thought Flora. How much of it would have been possible without Ann? And what happens now with the rest of my life?

Without Ann, the world felt less sheltered, less loving. Flora had to learn her own company, the absence of Ann's capable hands on laundry day, the shape of a room with only one cup on its table, one coat on its rack. On a cashmere blanket Ann had kept on the settee, Flora could smell her lavender water for a time and then it was gone.

There were mornings when Flora lay in her bed, remembering

the view from her bedroom at Walhachin. She recalled hills, covered with grasses that smelled so sweet after rain—wild rye, bunchgrass, needlegrass, ricegrass. Each had its own bract, awn, panicle which caught the small rain or scattered pollen, a fine gold powder on the arms and legs. This was what it was like to know a place, a person, in all its intimacy, and then to lose its specificity. And she recalled the rasp of grasshoppers as they jumped from stem to stem, the vault of blue sky; she remembered the texture of the dust, caught in wind and dry with seeds, particles of sand. She had not come with the expectation of love and yet she had found someone who held her breasts in his hands and entered her body so completely that it made her wish that the world would stop with the two of them in its own private embrace. Ann did not replace that love but she had helped to occupy its absence. A small precious part of the absence. Flora had not expected to love the miles of grassland, the flinty smell of the river, and yet she could bring these to mind, across the miles and years, with no effort at all as she lay under her linen sheet, listening for Grace.

THIRTY-TWO

Miss Oakden invited Tessa to come for a tea party, just the two of them. She had set the table with china, white napkins with embroidered letters (two *A*s and an *F*), there was fruitcake (which Tessa didn't really like but ate anyway) and little sandwiches with the crusts removed. There was lots of tea poured from a silver pot.

"I'll miss you, my dear. I hope you'll write to me occasionally. I have a little gift for you."

She handed Tessa a small parcel wrapped in soft blue tissue. When the girl opened it, she discovered a cushion cover depicting a water lily leaf, immediately recognizable, even the sheen of a few water droplets, and on it was perched a little frog, its green colour slightly darker than the leaf. And there was an inscription too, on the other side, stitched in the most beautiful small letters: *For my young friend, Tessa, with much affection, Flora Oakden, Hollyhock Cottage, 1962.*

"I never knew your name was Flora," Tessa said as she gave the woman a hug. She ran her fingers over the stitching, the satiny feel of the leaf and frog, the rougher texture of the fabric itself. It was the first grown-up present she'd ever received.

"Sometimes I feel like Flora is someone else, a young woman I knew long ago, and just where she has gone, I'm not certain. She is the one who came to this house about this time of year nearly fifty years ago and who never really left, though her intention was temporary shelter. The house belonged to someone who became my dearest friend. My daughter was born here.

Our lives were contained here. Mine still is, I suppose, though increasingly I yearn for my childhood home or for the bungalow at Walhachin."

"Our house will be empty in a few days. I'm scared of forgetting it. I've never lived anywhere else. I finished my map and I'm taking it with me. I just hope I've put everything important on it."

The old woman smiled. "What a sensible idea, your map. And you must trust your heart to remember as well. I don't think we ever forget the things that are really important to us. I used to occasionally buy linen for my needlework, which had patterns faintly printed on in a blue ink. It came with pre-cut yarns. Kits, I suppose they were. If I didn't manage to work with that fabric right away, the pattern faded a little too much for my eyes to see it so I'd draw my own design and then stitch in my own silks and wools. But then I'd see the older pattern emerging. It was sad in a way, as though the original ink wanted to be remembered. But oh, what am I saying? Such silly observations from an old woman, Tessa."

"You told me once you'd show me some of your photographs, Miss Oakden. Of that home in the desert, those horses." Tessa was remembering the table with its arrangement of photographs, like Patience, or Solitaire, on the day she'd first seen the tree frogs in the garden.

"Yes, I'd like to show you some of that. Perhaps you could take the cups and plates to the kitchen, my dear, while I hunt out the box."

She went away and returned after a short time with a tin box, carefully setting it on the dining-room table, now cleared of its party. She opened the box and stood silent for a moment, her fingers sorting among the bound bundles of letters, some with blue ribbon, some with faded pink, and loose photographs, some newspaper clippings.

"This was our home in Walhachin," she said softly. "There was the loveliest screened porch, or balcony as I thought of it, where I slept on hot summer evenings. You could hear coyotes yipping sometimes, and once I heard wolves. Here is the little garden my brother made. See his pool? That was where my white water lily grew. And these were rose bushes he brought from England. Gloire de Dijon was this one. And this was an ancient moss. I remember a brilliant pink rambler too, though I can't see it in this photograph."

It looked sparse, not like the lush garden behind Hollyhock Cottage. But then there was a photograph of an orchard, the trees in neat rows, laden with blossom.

"These were our trees, our Rome Beauties and Wealthys and some Jonathans as well. They were just starting to produce well when the men went away to war. And we had potatoes and onions too. Some farmers grew tobacco. We didn't bother. This was Miss Flowerdew's hotel where we had parties and teas. And look, here is the Marquis of Anglesey's swimming pool. I swam there occasionally, but mostly I paddled in the river myself. Oh, it was marvellous! Clean and cold, and in late summer you'd see these muscular fish, steelhead they called them, moving past on their way to the spawning beds up the Deadman River Valley. And later in the fall, the red sockeye salmon. Such a long way they travelled, from the ocean and the Fraser River, into the Thompson River and eventually to Shuswap Lake. Sometimes I felt a little like them, having travelled so far myself."

"My dad took us to see the salmon at Goldstream Park. It was sad, but then we went back a few months later and you could see some of the tiny ones there, the new little salmon—they were still attached to their egg sacs—and so it was as though they hadn't really died at all. And we saw a bear quite far downstream, and my dad said how good it was for them to have fish to eat before they went to hibernate for winter."

"He's wise, your father. That's a very good way to look at it. And here, Tessa—you asked about the horses. Here is my brother's mare, Vespa. I rode her quite often. My brother took this photograph of me heading out to make some sketches. Can you imagine trying to ride in such a cumbersome outfit? I wonder what ever happened to that hat? And here's another one of the two horses I've already shown you, Agate and Flight."

Tessa drank it in. The old woman who was Miss Oakden sharing the life of a girl called Flora, a girl who swam in a river and rode horses over hills that went on forever in the photographs, undulating and fading until they disappeared off the edge of the paper. Such interesting details—a valley named for dead men, the apples, swimming with fish!

"This is a young Chinese woman who died of a rattlesnake bite. I took her photograph one day when I went to buy vegetables from her, not long before the tragedy. It was so sad. Her husband watched her leave in a car with a doctor who didn't know what he was doing and didn't save her." She hummed a little of the aria Ann sang all those years ago as she looked at the photograph. "'Che faro senza Euridice? How could I live without my Euridice?'" And yet Song had lived without May, she had lived without Gus, and the world kept turning on its axis as though nothing had ever happened.

Then Miss Oakden was handing her a tiny pair of booties, made of rabbit fur, the soles worn almost transparent. Tessa cradled them in her palms, imagining the feel of them on her own feet.

"These were given me by an Indian woman in Lytton. I bought this basket from her" —and there was the basket, faded but durable—" and found them tucked into it later on the train. I used this larger basket for years for my mending. And my Grace wore these little shoes as a baby. I loved how they looked, poking out from her pretty smocked nightdresses. She took her first steps in these."

"My old friend Jane McIntyre sent me this," the woman said, indicating a little package of material dated 1928. "She'd been to the opening of a hotel in Kamloops, Tessa, and wanted to share the experience with me. There'd been a banquet and then dancing on the roof, in a garden created there. Look at these photographs in the paper! Doesn't it look like a wonderful affair?"

The paper was dry and crisp, the photographs grainy and hazy, but when she got used to the blurriness of the images, Tessa could make out the dancers and the band. And yes, the roof garden looked splendid with its railings and wicker furniture, and the Japanese lanterns hung from the eaves like balloons. It was so airy and dreamy, thought Tessa, like something happening so long ago, in a library book or on television.

"Jane died not long after that, still quite a young woman. She died having a child and the child didn't survive either, though her first baby, the first to survive, that is, Thomas, was robust and bonny when I last saw him in the summer of 1921. Here, somewhere, yes, here, I have a photograph of Jane and her little family. She sent this to me once we'd found each other again after a few years of silence."

"Did they visit you here?"

"Yes, they did, Tessa. They came down from their ranch in the Upper Hat Creek Valley to see a play I helped to organize, all the way to Victoria to see it. They sent me roses to my dressing room in the Royal Theatre. Here is one that I dried."

In a thin envelope, a little cluster of red petals, fragile as paper. A drawing of a man's face, not finished. A theatre program, some photographs of women in costumes, very stern-faced, on a stage.

"Was that valley near where you lived on the desert?"

"Well, not too far away. You got to it by a beautiful road that ran along the Oregon Jack Creek. It climbed quite high and couldn't be used in winter. Oh, the wildflowers were so lush. It was like the Garden of Eden, that road and the valley it led to . . . I spent a few days there with Jane before I ever moved to Victoria. We sat under the trees and sewed. How unexciting that sounds, I expect, but it is one of my happiest memories. And I took Grace there too, the summer after our play. She loved it. She learned to ride a pony called Chatters. Here, here is a photograph of her and Thomas on their ponies helping Allan with the cattle."

And Tessa looked at that one for a long time. A laughing

Grace, younger than Tessa herself, with a little straw cowboy hat, on a shaggy pony with the boy, about the same age, on his pony, one with spots and white stockings. They were in a corral, fenced with slender poles, with a few cows standing near them.

"We went to a play at the Royal Theatre, Miss Oakden. It was *Peter Pan*, with a little light that moved around for Tinkerbell. Do you think it's changed much? From when you did your play there?"

"Oh, I don't think so, Tessa. I've been to concerts in recent years and it is much the same as it was. When we performed our play, we thought there would be more to follow. We thought we might actually change the world. But then our Hecuba died, the woman who owned this house, and we couldn't seem to organize ourselves without her. Life took up so much time that everything else had to be put aside. And then it was too late to do anything else but work in the garden and attend one funeral after another as people I loved died. Several of the women in the play, Mr. McGregor who helped me to find a way to make a living, Grace's grandparents, Jane, of course."

"Who was Hecuba?" It was an interesting name to say.

"She was the mother of the Trojan prince, Hector. Oh, it's too complicated to tell you now, my dear, but she was a very brave woman and there was a play written about her. And she said so many things that we felt, as women who had watched men we loved go off to the Great War and not return, many of them, or return to us broken and hurt."

The woman took out a small green notebook and held it to her chest. Then she returned it to the box.

"That is not to share, I'm afraid." With her hand still on the notebook, Miss Oakden was again the young woman who bore the imprint of her lover's body upon her own and carried him in effigy into the future. Unthinkable now, in this room, with her arthritic hands and white hair, where a child sipped her tea and waited.

So she smiled and said, "But what about this? A drawing my

daughter did that caught the eye of Emily Carr herself, who gave Grace a few art lessons as a result. And that led to Grace leaving for Paris, where she teaches art and English and paints and writes home far too seldom."

She handed a sketch to Tessa, who looked at it and knew immediately what and where it was. It was one corner of the cemetery, where the trees grew low over the graves. It was a place where she had sat herself many times, grateful for the cave the trees made, and for the daisies that grew so profusely each spring, enough to crown a girl daily with a wreath of plaited blossoms. And it was a place where she most often heard the murmuring sounds of the dead, a sound that might be confused with birds but that a child knew came from under the earth with its tangle of secrets, even hidden water moving among the graves. She had heard ghosts in that very place, talking quietly, and she had not been afraid. She made a little mental note to herself to draw it on her map. She would put that girl into it too, the girl she sometimes felt in this house, waiting behind a door for Tessa to discover or reflected in the pool of water lilies on the bathroom wall. She'd thought that her map was finished, but maybe she would think of things to add to it for some time yet. Maybe you wouldn't know everything that was truly important until later.

"Did you ever go to Paris, Miss Oakden?" Tessa knew from her atlas where Paris was. She had looked it up the first time she learned that Grace had gone there to live. The very sound of the name filled her with longing.

"Oh, yes, I did. It's a beautiful city, full of narrow streets and flowering chestnut trees—I was there one May, Tessa, and loved it. Grace lives in a little apartment on the Rue pot de fer, and it was lovely to shop in the markets on the street nearby and visit the museums and churches. I meant to go back but didn't and now it's really too late. I'm not able to travel comfortably any longer and now simply wait for my Grace's letters."

It was getting late. Whatever light the winter sun had held

was fading fast. Miss Oakden spoke then, but it was as though to herself. "Some days I look out and I see this entire area as it was then, when this was Lovers Lane, when I had some hope of Gus, who was my sweetheart, returning from the war to hold me and our Grace in his arms. It's as though the apartment building over there had never been built, just the original Ross Bay cluster of houses from the original Hudson's Bay Company plan. I can see right down to the sea, hear the waves tumbling over themselves in their hurry to reach the shore so that they might slide back again into deep water. The trees in the cemetery—oh, they're young and supple, as I was, able to dream and reach for the sky, not the knotted tangle over the lanes, letting in almost no light at all to reach the ground and the poor sleeping dead. And my hands, knotted with arthritis, no longer able to sew as nimbly as I was once able to."

And then, remembering her guest, she spoke directly to her: "It was a golden age, Tessa, a time of birth and new beginnings, even as the sorrow of being cast out by my family enveloped me at times."

Tessa interrupted. "Did they do that, Miss Oakden? Did your parents and your brother cast you out?" It was a biblical image, thought the girl, or maybe from a fairy tale, where a wicked stepmother sends the beautiful young woman away from her loving father to live in the woods or in this case a low cottage by a cemetery. In the fairy tales, a prince came to rescue the young woman, but somehow she did not think a prince ever came for Miss Oakden. Not after her sweetheart died so far away and before the baby Grace was born. There were frogs in the garden and a girl might dream of their kiss but not, Tessa thought, an elderly woman.

"There were two brothers, Tessa, both killed overseas. I've told you something about George, who knew about Grace and wouldn't have liked it, but not about Henry, who never knew but who might have been forgiving. My parents would never acknowledge my daughter and would have been ashamed to have me return to them with a child. But this city was young, we all thought the war would be over within weeks, and of course no one ever dreamed of that next terrible war with its death camps and atom bombs dropped on Japan."

She stopped talking for a minute and wiped her eyes with a hanky pulled from her sleeve. It was edged with the prettiest lace. She smiled at Tessa, who was listening to every word.

"When I think of those years, Tessa, that time, I think of it as an age of water lilies. I painted them so often onto tiles, some of them in grand houses, and some in much more modest ones, like this house and I stitched them onto linen. Well, you can see for yourself on the little cover I made for you! I thought I might reclaim my childhood at Watermeadows by doing so, I suppose, and perhaps my poor brother's small hope of water lilies at Walhachin as well. Now there is only the one plant in my garden pool, just enough for nostalgia to wrap me in its spell at times. Like now, I expect. And do you think, child, that your mother might want you home?"

Tessa supposed she might. She began to cry. "But I'm afraid, Miss Oakden, that I won't see you again." The woman held her and smoothed her hair.

"Go now, Tessa. Take your parcel with you. Treasure your map. And write to me? I should like that very much."

Tessa went out the back door and found the gap in the fence that let her small body through into the park where she paused to listen for the buried stream. Another few months, another year, and she would be too big to fit through the gap. She'd have to walk the long way around to Memorial Crescent and enter through the gate like anyone else.

THIRTY-THREE
Early 1963

And end now with a girl on her stomach in a basement, quietly finishing a map. It is the world contained within twelve square blocks, a cemetery at its heart, stones and obelisks telling their news of the living and the dead. Waves meet the shore on a stretch of ocean facing south. A school receives its neighbourhood of children, some of them riding bikes and some of them climbing up and over the rocky hill where clumps of shooting stars grow in an elegant seclusion, where lizards are born in a miracle of adaptation in the ferny clefts. A map of houses and days, of secrets and details noticed by a child fiercely in love with the pattern trees make with their shadows in sunlight, of the softening touch of moss on an inscription set in motion in a box canyon where lovers lay in dry grass and dreamed of a future now collapsed by violence. Off the edges of the map, the world settles its story and what can anyone do but remember the route water takes through the decades on its singular journey to the sea.

ACKNOWLEDGMENTS

I am indebted to my family for their support over the years. I wish to particularly thank my daughter, Angelica Pass, for translating the passages of Latin that occur in this novel and my son Forrest Pass for help with historical details (though of course any errors are mine). My husband, John Pass, and my son Brendan Pass have both provided love and encouragement for which I'm very grateful.

Penny Connell offered some good advice about the conventions of theatrical production. Patricia Anderson was extremely helpful at a difficult time in the manuscript's evolution. Other friends and scholars were generous with time and information. Ruth Linka and Emily Shorthouse at Brindle & Glass have been enthusiastic and responsive. Lynne Van Luven was an excellent editor, perceptive and challenging. I thank them all.

Readers interested in the community of Walhachin might enjoy Joan Weir's *Walhachin: Catastrophe or Camelot* as much as I did. A few real people make cameo appearances and I hope their ghosts will forgive me. I wish I'd known, at age fifteen, that Bertram Chase Footner, the elderly man who used to come out from his house in Saanich to tell me that my horse was a fine animal, was in fact the man who designed and built many of the Walhachin houses. There's so much I wish I'd asked him.

At a fundraiser for the Sunshine Coast Arts Council, Sechelt businessman Tom Lamb bid generously for the opportunity to have a minor character named for him in this novel. I thought I'd make him an architect. Later, reading Donald Luxton's indispensible *Building the West*, I was delighted to discover that there was in fact an architect called Thomas Lamb working in Victoria for a brief period in the 1920s. Any resemblance between the two is serendipitous.

The staff of the Sechelt Public Library was unfailingly efficient in obtaining books, microfiche, and other materials. The Canada Council for the Arts and the British Columbia Arts Council provided assistance during the writing of this book for which I am grateful.

Theresa Kishkan is an accomplished author of eleven books of poetry and prose. Her work has appeared in numerous anthologies and literary journals such as *Geist, BC Bookworld, Brick, The Canadian Forum, Fiddlehead, The Malahat Review*, and *Quill and Quire*. Her collection of essays *Phantom Limb* was nominated for the 2007 Hubert Evans Non-Fiction Prize and her novel *A Man in a Distant Field* was shortlisted for the 2008 Ethel Wilson Fiction Prize. Born in Victoria, BC, Theresa has lived on both coasts of Canada as well as in Greece, Ireland, and England. A mother of three children, she now makes her home on the Sechelt Peninsula with her husband, John Pass.